FALLING

LANDMARK MOUNTAIN
BOOK 4

WILLOW ASTER

Willow Aster
www.willowaster.com

Copyright © 2023 by Willow Aster
ISBN-13: 979-8-9880213-6-0

Cover by Emily Wittig Designs
Photo: ©Regina Wamba
Map artwork by Kira Sabin
Editing by Christine Estevez

NOTE TO READERS

A list of content warnings are on the next page, so skip that page if you'd rather not see them.

CONTENT WARNINGS

The content warnings for *Falling* are an animal death, profanity, and a surprise wedding.

CHAPTER ONE

PULLING A RUNNER

RUBY

I love my dress.

In the front, it'd almost be proper, with a high neckline, long sleeves, and a fitted A-line skirt, if it weren't for the sheer peekaboo bohemian lace and the cutout in the back that dips low. But my veil is a contender for being the showstopper. Longer than my dress, the sheer tulle is edged with lace and attaches to my low bun of artfully arranged curls, courtesy of Lydia, the stylist who's been doing my hair since I was thirteen.

Since the day I tried it on, I've imagined my veil blowing behind me as Junior and I run hand-in-hand to the old-fashioned car that will be waiting for us outside, the Wasatch Range standing proudly in the distance.

There's a knock on the door and my mom peeks her head in. She gasps when she sees me and my cousin Kess. "Oh girls, you look gorgeous."

"Thanks, Aunt June," Kess says, smiling. "So do you."

"Oh thank you, love. I've got your dad with me, sweetheart," she says to me. "Is it okay if we come in for a minute?"

"Of course, I was hoping you'd get here soon."

My mom steps in and my dad follows, stopping in front of me and carefully kissing my cheek.

"Absolutely breathtaking," he says.

"Thanks, Dad."

My mom sniffles next to me and when I reach out and squeeze her hand, her lips wobble as she smiles.

"My baby," she says.

"No tears. We promised." I laugh.

"I know. I know." She dabs her nose with a tissue and laughs too. "But it's hard not to with you looking like a dream." She straightens and exhales like she's shaking it off. "I'm sorry we got hung up." She holds up a set of keys. "You are looking at the proud owners of a Class A, 35-foot motor home! Love, light, and sunshine, baby!" She laughs again as I stare at her in shock.

Most of the time, hippie parents are cool, but...

"What?" I stand up. "But, how? Can you afford that?"

She waves me off and leans into my dad who gazes down at her like she hung the moon.

and orange Formica tabletop or the excessive use of brown... everything, but I loved all the memories we'd made in this thing. And I had a vision for what it could become.

I'd call it a vintage vehicle, except I feel vintage evokes images of silver Airstreams or those dainty red camper Christmas tree ornaments.

This is not that.

You'd never know it from the brown and orange pinstripe on the outside, but inside my petite 1979 Class C RV is a white and pale pink homey oasis. After I removed the circular burnt orange chairs and stripped the wallpaper and the brown shag carpet, I had a clean canvas to work with and a clearer perspective of how to accomplish it. The white subway tile in the kitchen area makes a huge difference, as does all the white shelving and the built-in couch with the pale pink cushions and throw pillows. A long plush runner lets the maple plank flooring show through, and the trailing plants I've hung up high add pops of green.

I'm not the only one in love with Jolene. From the beginning, I've documented my progress on TikTok and my website, and it's blown up. It's how I was able to pay for the wedding, how I've managed to keep the creditors off of my parents' backs a little longer.

I just didn't expect to be *driving* Jolene. She's been parked on our property in Utah while I've been renovating her, and I didn't have any plans to take her anywhere else. She was going to be my adorable office space near our business, not where I live full-time.

My new home was supposed to be with Junior Fitzgibbons, a little starter house we were going to take our time renovating. It was simpler than he wanted, but he relented, knowing it was the next project I was going to dive into as soon as we got home from our honeymoon.

That's all changed now.

I swallow down the lump in my throat. I cried through most of Utah. And the most surprising of all of this is that it's barely been about Junior.

Yes, I feel stupid.

I can't believe he tricked me into believing he cared about me.

And yes, I'm tempted to tell the world that he has a two-inch willy and doesn't make up for it by figuring out how to satisfy a woman in other ways either, but the joke's on me, because I almost married him despite that.

But even though my former fiancé turned out to be a hate-ful, money-grabbing maggot who didn't mind trashing me to his friends on our wedding day, I wouldn't stoop to that level.

I have a hard time wishing ill toward anyone.

I just could not let Dolly stay with him—I still see red that Mitch called her an idiot. It was hard enough to let the others go. I had to give in…but there was no way Dolly and I would survive without each other.

I was there the day she was born, helped her come into this world, and from the time she opened her eyes, we had a bond.

When I pull into Landmark Mountain city limits, I breathe a sigh of relief. I can't believe I made it. Even with all this snow, I did it.

I hope Uncle Pierre is okay with me showing up like this. I haven't been able to reach him, but he's always wanted me to come stay with him. At the end of every phone call, he says there's a place for me here. I think he's lonely for family even though he claims he's happy.

The pretty shops and all the twinkle lights make me smile, but to avoid all the traffic on the main road, I pull down a side road and keep driving, thinking the map will update to tell me a different route to Uncle Pierre's. There's more snow on this road though, and navigation takes a minute to update. As the voice says *rerouting*, I brake quickly and it's a mistake.

"Noooo," I yelp.

Losing control and veering all over the road, I plead with the universe to protect me and Dolly. After a little dip, I hear a really weird sound and we crunch to a stop in a deep snowbank.

It's way darker out here—I should've stayed on the busy road with all the lights after all, but I think I see house lights in the distance. When I try to shift into reverse, nothing happens. I turn the ignition and...nothing.

Jolene is dead.

I open my door and my eyes widen when I see how much snow there is and hurriedly close the door. It's amazing how fast the chill went to my ears with that blast of cold air.

Grabbing my phone, I jump out, cringing with each step. My white lace ankle boots with the satin ribbon ties aren't going to survive this and that's just a shame. Snow seeps through to my feet and in some places, it hits me mid-calf. It's jarring to my skin, but I don't care, I'm too laser-focused on getting to the trailer behind my RV. Fortunately, the trailer is on the road more than my RV is, and it's just barely tilted.

"I'm coming, Dolly," I yell, and I can hear her answering call. "Thank goodness," I whisper.

I hit Uncle Pierre's number on speed dial as I'm still hopping to the back of the trailer and when I unlock the door and see Dolly, I start crying.

She's huddled in the corner with all her blankets and when she sees me, she scrambles to her feet, her head bobbing as she walks up to me and lays her head on my shoulder. I shuffle to hold back all the material flying around us and wrap my arms around her, rubbing her back and speaking in my calmest voice.

"You're okay, Dolly. I've got you."

She squawks and nestles her head in my neck the way she does when she's scared.

"We're okay, pretty girl. Yeah, that's right. You're good. We're gonna be all right."

I glance at my phone again, realizing Uncle Pierre never answered and I try again. This time, he picks up.

"*Ruby*," he breathes. "Where *are* you?"

"Uh, I'm here, actually. Well, not at your place exactly. But I made it to Landmark Mountain. I just…ended up in a snowbank. Not far from the main road…"

"What do you mean, you're there? Oh, honey." His voice rises.

My heart drops when he says there…like maybe he's not *here*.

"I'm okay, I promise."

"You're in a *snowbank*?" He sounds just like my mom when he's upset.

"Yeah, I'm just a little bit stuck. I hope it's okay that I came. I had to—"

"But, honey, I'm not there," he says. "I came for your wedding…"

I slump and Dolly nestles deeper into my neck. "I didn't…ugh. I didn't think you were coming."

"I didn't think I could at first. It was going to be a surprise."

"I can't believe I had no idea. Thank you and…I'm sorry. How is it there?"

"The question is how are *you*? Everyone has been worried sick. You should call your mom, Ruby."

"I will. I'm just…I couldn't talk to anyone yet."

"Are you hurt?" His voice breaks. "Hang up and call an ambulance. I'll call a few friends to get there right away."

"No, no, it's okay. I'm not hurt, Uncle Pierre. Really." I try to inject lightness into my voice so he doesn't panic. "I'll be okay until you get back. I might just need some help getting out of this snow so I can get to your place."

"Oh dear. I didn't leave a set of keys there. Oh, honey. The thing is, I'm supposed to fly from Provo to LA on Monday for a conference, but I can come home and see about you and then fly out from there."

"*No*," I insist. "Don't change your plans for me. Do what you need to do."

"It's almost a week. I was supposed to be there until Thursday."

"Do it. I'll be okay...I'll figure this out."

He clears his throat and his voice is authoritative when he speaks again. Uncle Pierre in action is something to be seen. "Tell me exactly where you are."

I describe where I turned off and the lights I see in what seems to be a house not too far away.

"I'll call you back in two minutes," he says. "Get back in your vehicle until then."

"Okay," I say, but he's already hung up.

I don't get back in the vehicle. Dolly's too shaken up to leave her right now. And Uncle Pierre does call back in two minutes.

"Help is on the way. I was able to reach Callum Landmark. You're on his property and he'll help you. You can trust him. His sister owns a resort and they'll be able to set you up until I get back."

I start to tell him I have a little more than just myself to consider in staying somewhere overnight, but a truck pulls up behind me, lights shining bright.

Dolly's chirps turn into a drumming sound, and I pet her reassuringly. When the truck door closes, a tall man strides toward me. When he steps into the light from his truck, it's just bright enough for me to see that he might also be extremely good-looking.

At least from what I can tell, I think…maybe…oh yeah, he is. He's also wearing the biggest scowl I've ever seen.

Fierce.

Yikes. I giggle and cover my mouth.

I stand up taller and forget to hold onto my veil. It flies out in front of me and brushes across the man's face.

He dusts it off, his frown deepening, and stalks closer. I feel a rush of nerves and adrenaline.

Uncle Pierre said I can trust him, I remind myself, shuffling my feet in the freezing cold.

My mom's motto plays on repeat. It's like she's perched on my shoulder saying it: *Ruby Sunshine Jones is afraid of no one. Love, light, and sunshine, baby!*

"Ruby Jones?" His voice is husky and wraps around me like a cozy blanket.

How that's possible with his grumbly voice and deep glower is beyond me. Fascinating.

"Callum Landmark," he says a little louder. "Your uncle called."

Dolly moves quickly and steps protectively in front of me, the drumming sound intensifying from her chest. Callum shines a flashlight on us and she startles, getting louder.

"The hell?" he says under his breath.

"Uh, hi! Yes, I'm Ruby," I say, peering around Dolly. "And this is my emu, Dolly."

CHAPTER TWO

SATAN'S WHISPERS

CALLUM

"You late for a wedding?" I don't normally ask questions that aren't my business, but I want to know what kind of time-frame we're dealing with here.

And an emu?

Last thing I expected to see out here tonight is a bride and an emu.

It's a damn good thing Delphine and Irene are put up for

the night. I have a large herd of dairy cows and a few goats, but my goat Delphine and Irene the cow defy expectations.

They think they run the joint.

The way this emu keeps edging in front of Ruby, looking ready to peck me to death, I'd say she might be cut from the same cloth.

Out in the dark, it's hard to tell how old Pierre's niece is. She's tall but sounds young, and given her attire, she's not a child. I was shocked to pull up and see this rig out here. Pierre just said she was stuck on my property.

He left a helluva lot out.

I sure as hell wouldn't want my sister stuck out here at night.

"No, no wedding." Ruby holds her hand out and I shake it, eyeing the emu carefully as she straightens to her full height.

She sniffs my hand and stares at me with her beady eyes. It's only now that I realize that weird rhythmic sound is coming from the bird.

Ruby hums. "I think she likes you! Normally, she doesn't allow men to get near me."

I mutter *thanks for the warning* under my breath.

Ruby shivers while her hand is still in mine, and I frown as I look her over from head to toe.

Some sheer wedding ensemble that can't be very warm. The hell?

"What?" she asks.

I clear my throat. Didn't mean for that growl to actually come out.

"Truck's warm," I say. "Hop inside. I'll work on this."

"My RV's not starting," she says through chattering teeth. "And I'm okay. I'll just stay here with Dolly. She's scared."

I take off my coat and hand it to her and she tries to

protest, but I give her a look and she puts her arms through the sleeves as quickly as she can while fighting with a wayward veil. A deep sigh comes out as she lifts the collar as high as it'll go.

"This is such a nice coat," she says. "Thank you. Much better."

"Hmm," I mutter, turning back to look at her when she snorts.

She lifts a shoulder. "You sure are a grumbly thing."

My eyes narrow on her. "Grumbly *thing*?"

"Grumbly bear," she adds.

I huff and turn back to the task at hand. Her laugh bites through the cold and I shake my head. No damn time for this nonsense, especially if she's gonna keep freezing her ass off next to that bird.

I don't waste too much time trying to start her RV, the thing's dead like she said. Instead, I walk back to where she's huddled next to her emu and point toward my place.

"I'll drive you to a hotel. The emu will be fine in my barn. I'll work on this in the morning." I point to her RV.

It's been a long day helping my brother Wyatt get the space behind The Gnarly Vine ready for his proposal to Marlow tonight. I got Pierre's call right as everything was going down, so I'm missing the celebration. I don't love big shindigs, but I love my family. If I have to miss being with them, I at least want to get some sleep. I get up while it's still dark every morning, and I've already put in overtime with people today—I don't have the energy to say much more.

"It's just," Ruby starts, "I'm not comfortable leaving her. If you give me a blanket, I'll stay out in the barn with her."

"No."

"No?" she echoes.

I understand wanting to take care of my animals, but even

I am not gonna stay out in the barn sleeping with them. And it's a fucking stellar barn.

"Come on," I say, motioning for her to follow me.

"What? Where?"

"I'll show you the barn. But you're not staying out there. Pierre would kill me. You can stay in one of my spare rooms. You seem to have forgotten you're in a wedding dress," I add.

I glance back and even in the dark, I can tell her eyes are wide. But she doesn't argue. She grabs a few blankets and a bag of feed from the trailer. I take it from her and she teeters on heels that appear to be—shit.

Even her boots are made out of fucking lace.

What is this?

"My ID is in my phone case, but…do you think everything else in the RV is okay?" She glances back at the RV with concern.

"It's safe around here."

I motion for her to step where I've walked so her legs and feet can stay drier and she and that damn emu follow. We walk to the barn and go to the side that's the newest, the section of the barn I use for calving. Fortunately, it's empty right now and I know Dolly will be left alone in here.

When we step inside the stall, Ruby looks around and Dolly walks around the perimeter. I set the bag of food on the ground.

"This is really nice," Ruby says.

She takes the blankets from me and places them in the corner before opening the bag of feed, and then she pulls out a bowl from the bag and fills it with food.

I grab another bowl from outside the stall and fill it with fresh water, bringing it in and setting it on the floor.

"Thank you," she says.

I nod and we watch as Dolly sniffs the bowls. She takes a drink and then goes over to lie on the blankets.

"I exercised her a lot on one of the stops and I think she's a little shaken up from the change in scenery, so she should be pretty tired," she says. "I really wouldn't mind sleeping out here with her…"

She turns to look at me and gasps as she stares at me in what seems like surprise.

I'm surprised myself, seeing just how pretty she is in the light. Her big honey-brown eyes and light brown hair, and her full lips…damn. She's beautiful. I smooth my hair back, wondering if it's out of control or something. She blinks rapidly and her mouth parts before she clears her throat.

"Not happening," I rasp.

I clear my throat too, suddenly conscious of how my siblings always nag me about how little I talk, how grouchy I am, yada-yada.

"The barn…it's a no," I add. "I can drop you at my sister's place or my sister-in-law's, if you'd be more comfortable there."

She swallows hard and shakes her head slightly. "Uncle Pierre said I could trust you, and I wouldn't feel right about leaving Dolly…so I'll stay."

I nod again and she gulps. Good God, am I that terrifying? I attempt a smile. It feels more like a grimace, but it must work because she smiles tentatively back at me.

Her eyes smile as her lips lift and it's kinda nice. Without thinking, I humph. Her smile drops and I sigh.

"Come on," I mutter.

She hugs Dolly, telling her softly that she'll be back in the morning and to not be scared.

"You'll be okay out here," she says as she walks to the door. "I love you."

We walk out of the stall and I secure everything, feeling Ruby's eyes on me every step of the way. When we step outside and start walking toward the house, she exhales loudly.

"I was trying to stay silent until we got out here," she says. "It's a good sign that Dolly stayed quiet that whole time. If she'd heard me talking, she might've put up a stink." She laughs softly. "You must think I'm crazy…"

"No," I say.

"Oh, well. You'd be the first then," she says. "I, uh…I didn't exactly tell Uncle Pierre that I'd be bringing Dolly with me, so it's actually really fortunate that I came across your place first. Are you sure she's okay out there?"

"She'll be fine."

"She's trained better than most dogs," she says. "As long as she gets her exercise for the day…she's—I'll, uh…I'll stop talking about my emu now. Just…thank you. I don't know what we would've done if you hadn't shown up when you did." Her mouth drops when I open the door to my kitchen.

I motion for her to step inside and she does, looking around the kitchen with wide eyes.

"Wow, this is…*wow*," she says. "I did not expect—"

I look around my kitchen, wondering how she sees it. I worked hard on this place and it's better in the daylight when you can see out all the windows, but in my opinion, it's beautiful in here just about any time of day.

"This is gorgeous, Callum."

My chest swells with pride. I duck my head, looking down at her wet lacy boots.

"You need socks," I say abruptly. "And I've got any necessities you might need in the guest bathroom. Grinny… my grandma…and my sister Scarlett…they made sure of that." I motion toward the other room. "I'll start a fire so you can warm up." I frown. "How old are you?"

Her brow crinkles. "Twenty-three, why?"

"Wine or beer?"

She grins and giggles. "Uh no. You think I'm chatty now, you'll never get me to shut up if I have a drink."

"Hot tea, hot chocolate, or hot rum?" I list quietly.

She laughs. "I was not expecting you to be such a great host either..."

"Pierre's been good to my family."

She hums and tugs my coat off of her shoulders and turns to set it on the hook by the door. My eyes drag down her bare back, taking her in, and my mouth goes dry.

The sight of this woman in my house with that wedding dress on...well, it fucks me over a little bit. Not gonna lie.

Twenty-three, I tell myself. *Too young, and again, Pierre would kill you. Not to mention, she's in a fucking wedding dress.*

"Actually, hot chocolate sounds amazing," she says.

The devil on the other shoulder whispers, *Nine years younger isn't that bad.*

I grumble and she turns, her eyebrows lifting in question.

I move past her and get the socks and a sweater, bringing them back to the living room, where she's now walking toward the couch with bare feet, her veil trailing behind her.

"Oh, thank you," she whispers when she sees what I'm holding.

She's said *thank you* a lot since she's been here. Polite little thing.

Her hands brush against mine and we both freeze, our eyes flying to each other's. Her chest rises and falls, and I glance down, my eyes stalling on her peaked nipples under the white lace. Poor girl is cold and I need to think about warming her up in a way that doesn't involve my hands. I exhale a ragged breath and turn around, curse words flying around in my mind as I turn my focus on building a fire.

My brothers have been giving me a hard time for how long it's been since I've had a woman in my life, and they're not wrong.

But that doesn't mean I can be with this one who's practically fallen from the sky.

I'll be hospitable to Ruby Jones tonight and get her out of here as soon as I can tomorrow.

CHAPTER THREE

PROPER NAMES

RUBY

I can't get over how beautiful this place is. The ceilings are unbelievably high, arching into a point with a catwalk around the sides, as if it's a mini lodge. The beams are incredible, but the whitewashed ceiling and touches of whitewashed wood mixed with the dark wood opens it up so much more than the typical mountain lodge or log cabin. The stone fireplace is an art piece in itself, and the oversized furniture in various distressed woods has my little designer-loving heart salivating.

Don't get me started on the floor-to-ceiling windows that go up into the arch of the wall. I cannot wait to see the view in the daylight.

The floorplan is open and from the fireplace I can see Callum in the kitchen. It's like something I would've picked out, only more masculine, but he has white subway tile like Jolene, and long wood beams for shelves that I totally thought about doing. His white dishes and clear glasses are stacked neatly on the shelves, and there are closed white cabinets underneath the white granite countertop. The island is dark wood on top with a pretty green distressed wood on the bottom, and the barstools have a curved back that are perfect for the space.

I turn to tell Callum again how much I love his house, and he's got a pan out, stirring the liquid until it's smooth. It's hard to even look at him for any length of time, his muscular arms in that flannel shirt and his sexy scruff. But I also can't keep my eyes off of him for very long.

My cheeks burn with my thoughts.

I didn't know I liked longer hair on a man—it's in desperate need of a cut, almost to his shoulders, but it's *good* hair. Dark and thick and slightly wavy. That, paired with his growls and piercing eyes, gives him a feral look that is undeniably *hot*.

For someone other than me.

Obviously.

I fan my face, feeling faint.

This day. Goodness, I can't think about it too much.

"You're making hot chocolate from scratch?" My voice comes out breathy and weird. I clear my throat. "I don't think

I've ever had it like that. I've only ever had the little white packet with tiny marshmallows…"

"This tastes better."

I wait for him to say something else, but he just stirs as his eyes momentarily meet mine. He's not much of a talker, I've noticed.

Since I've been sitting for so long, I keep wandering to different areas, finally landing in front of a small nook with a cozy chair, a lamp, and two framed pictures on the bookshelves. There's a huge group of people in front of a lake, a bride and groom in the center. I find Callum right away. He looks amazing in a suit. The next photo is of a smaller group of some of the same people in front of another pretty house. Everyone looks younger in this one. Callum's wearing a beanie and his smile is bigger than I've seen on him yet. His arm is around a beautiful dark-haired girl, and there are three other guys on either side of him and an older couple in the center.

"Is this your girlfriend? She's gorgeous." I pick up the picture and study it closer.

"Sister."

I smile at the photograph, relieved that I won't be dealing with a jealous girlfriend when she finds out I'm staying here tonight. "Are these your brothers?"

"Yes."

I nod. "I can see the similarities between all of you now. Beautiful family. I always wanted a lot of brothers and sisters, but," I lift a shoulder, "it's just me. And a bunch of emus." I laugh, but it quickly fades.

I really need to call my parents and let them know I'm okay…and find out what they're doing with our emu farm. I've been too upset to talk to them yet, frustrated that they'd sell our home to Junior without talking to me about it…and without making sure I was on the deed. Knowing them, they probably assumed I was or that Junior would be sure to handle it.

It's remarkable they've kept that land as long as they did. I sigh and look up to see Callum studying me.

I set the picture down when he lifts the pan and pours the chocolate into two large mugs. When he's divided it evenly, he sets down the pan and moves toward the refrigerator, pulling out whipped cream, and then he grabs a bag of huge marshmallows from the pantry.

He holds up the two choices and I make a face.

"That's a really hard decision," I say.

"Both then."

I laugh as he drops in a marshmallow so big I'm not sure it'll fit in the oversized mug. It fits perfectly. And then he sprays a dollop of whipped cream on top of that.

"It's hot," he says, holding it out for me.

I take it carefully, trying to only touch the handle.

"Thank you," I whisper.

His head nods once and then he frowns. "Should've asked if you're hungry."

I shake my head. "I haven't had much of an appetite today."

He leans back against the counter, his mug in his massive hands. He must be at least 6'3" or 6'4" because I'm 5'9" and he towers over me. Junior hated when I wore heels because he's only 5'10" and he didn't like it when I was taller than him. He would've hated my wedding boots, now that I think about it…

"Have you lived here long?" I ask, blowing on my hot chocolate.

"About five years in this house, Landmark Mountain my whole life."

"Is that…did you say Grinny? Is that her in the picture?"

He nods. "Grinny and Granddad. My grandparents raised us."

"Oh…your parents aren't living here too?"

"They died when I was twelve…car accident."

I gasp. "That's devastating. I'm so sorry. I-that sounds trite to say, but I mean it."

He ducks his head and takes a sip of the hot chocolate. "They did their best."

"Are you and your siblings close?"

"Very."

"The wedding looked beautiful." I pointed toward the other photograph.

"My brother Theo and his wife Sofie got married recently."

I finally take a sip of the hot chocolate, anxious to try it.

It's still too hot to drink as fast as I want, but my eyes close as the flavors hit my tongue and a long moan escapes.

"This is…the best thing I've ever tasted."

When my eyes open, Callum is staring at me with the most intense expression. He swallows and sets his mug down, turning to put the pan in the sink and washing it. I'm watching him so intently that when he turns to face me again, I jump and the entire mug of hot chocolate spills down the front of me.

I gasp. It burns painfully, and I know I should move quickly, but when I look down, it's like I can't believe I'm still wearing my wedding dress. I watch, dazed, as the liquid oozes through the white lace.

Callum has jumped into action and is in front of me with a wet cloth, holding it out for me to take.

"Are you okay?" he asks. When I don't say anything, he

adds, "Here, take this cloth. It's cold. You should take your dress off, so your skin doesn't burn under there."

"I'm still in my wedding dress," I whisper.

"Yeah," he says softly. "Ruby? I'm concerned you're going to burn," he says louder. "Are you...in shock?"

"I think maybe so," I say.

"Turn around."

In a trance, I turn my back to him and he shifts my veil to the side. His finger fumbles around the top button, but he gets it undone and gently pulls my sleeves down my arms. When both sleeves are off, the top of my dress drops and the cool air against my burning skin is sweet relief.

He passes the wet towel over my shoulder and I cover my chest with it.

"That's better," I choke out.

"Are you okay?" he asks. "Maybe we should go to the hospital, get you looked at."

"No, I'll be okay," I tell him.

"It was pretty hot. How does your skin look?"

I lift the towel and wince. My wedding dress is hanging around my waist, my chest completely bare, in a kitchen with a man I don't know...and there are red, angry burns between my breasts and down my stomach.

"I'll be okay," I repeat.

"I'll call my brother. He's a doctor." He's already dialing. "Shit. He's not answering—I'll call Emma..."

"Is that your girlfriend?" I whisper.

Tears fill my eyes, but I refuse to let them fall. My skin really, *really* hurts, but I've cried enough today.

"No." He snorts. "Hey, Em. Yeah, it's Callum. No, I had to leave the party. Got a friend with a burn here, really hot liquid. Should I bring her in?"

He's quiet for a moment. "I'd think with how hot it was, it

could be second-degree, but I haven't exactly seen the burns. Uh, her chest…and stomach, maybe? Is that right, Ruby?"

I nod.

"Yeah, her chest and stomach. I tried. I suggested she come in, but she doesn't want to…yet anyway. Mm-hmm, I've got that. Yes. Okay. All right. We will. Thanks, Em."

He hangs up and I hear the faucet running behind me. He hands me another towel and takes the one I'm holding.

"She said you should rinse the burns with cold water or keep applying cold cloths in five to fifteen-minute intervals to keep the swelling down. And then antibiotic cream and wrap it in gauze. I have all of that here, but I'd feel better if you went in."

My gaze is focused on the floor where my lacy white boots are sitting. "I was gonna get married today," I say.

"Uh, I thought that might be the case."

"I would've been on my honeymoon by now. I wonder if Junior went to Bali. He probably did. I hope he gets an STD while on the honeymoon I paid for. I bet he's bragging to everyone there about how he was just marrying me for my family's property." My voice cracks. "What is he going to do with all the emus? He never liked them. That should've been my sign right there. Dolly despised Junior." I take a shaky breath. "I should've stayed to deal with our emu farm, but I had to get out of there. My parents can deal with it…they've been checked out for too long, it's time they deal with what they started." I shake my head. "This really hurts." A whimper comes out and I drop the towel, letting the cool air hit my skin.

He hands me the original towel, now freshly cold again.

"Thank you. You're a nice guy. And Callum Landmark is such a nice name. What was I thinking, almost marrying a guy named Junior Fitzgibbons?"

"Ruby?" Callum says softly. "I know it's been a day, but are you sure I can't talk you into the hospital?"

"I'm fine." I sniff as tears roll down my cheeks. "Thank you. You've been really kind."

"*Fuck*," he curses under his breath and it strikes me funny.

Bill and June Jones don't appreciate cursing or even saying the proper names for body parts…or the words moist, cellar, or jiggle, but that's neither here nor there.

"How about I lead you to the bathroom? You can rinse the burns in the tub or shower as long as you'd like, and I'll give you some ibuprofen, antibiotic cream, and gauze to put on it."

I turn toward him.

"Whoa." He holds up his hand, looking toward the ceiling.

"Oh, sorry." I lift the cloth to my chest. "Didn't mean to flash you."

His eyes stay trained on the ceiling.

"That sounds like a good plan…the bathroom and all the things you said."

He nods and starts moving toward the hall. I follow him into a bedroom with an iron bed, a white quilt, and navy and white sheets. It's tasteful and simple but beautiful. He keeps walking into a bathroom that takes my breath away. So unique. The wood in here is like thick stripes on the walls and a white freestanding tub sits in front of windows. The glass to the shower is so clean I barely see it on the left.

He gets a towel and washcloth out of the wire basket and sets it on the bench near the tub. Next, he opens a cabinet and gathers the supplies, lining them up in a row on the counter.

"You're extremely organized. I don't think I've ever owned gauze."

"I like to be prepared."

He's still avoiding looking at me even though my towel is firmly in place.

"I picked the right place to crash." My shoulders sag, and I'm suddenly exhausted. "Tomorrow will be a better day."

He's moving into the bedroom now and he brings back a large T-shirt.

"This will swim on you, but at least it won't be tight against your burn."

"Thank you."

"You don't have to keep thanking me," he grumbles, but it doesn't sound mean. It sounds like a low bass-y rumble.

"I'm really glad my name's not Ruby Fitzgibbons."

"That would've sucked," he says.

I look over my shoulder and smile at him.

I think he smiles back. At least, it's an almost smile.

"You sure you're going to be okay, Ruby Jones? Can I get you anything?"

"You've done enough."

He grimaces. "I feel terrible about the burn."

"That's not what I meant!"

"I still feel terrible about it."

"Junior's the one who should feel terrible tonight. He didn't even get to see me in this dress. I can't believe I'm still in it. It was surprisingly comfortable on the drive, kinda slipped my mind."

"Do you…need help getting out of it?" He clears his throat.

CHAPTER FOUR

INVESTED

Callum

Need help getting out of it?

I run my hand through my hair, trying not to look at her. Nothing I say is coming out right. Especially after that momentary glimpse of her exceptional tits.

"That sounded…wrong," I say.

Her laugh is quiet, but it still echoes in the bathroom. She looks at me over her shoulder and winces before quickly turning back around.

"I hate to say it, but yes, I might need help. It hurts to move. There's just the small zipper there at my—"

I stare at her beautiful back and the way the lace is barely hanging onto her perfect ass. A deep inhale and exhale.

"I don't see a zipper." My voice is husky, and I lift my eyes to the ceiling in a silent prayer for strength.

"I know, right? It's exquisite detailing. I was really impressed with the seamstress."

The girl has got to be in pain, in more ways than one if she was supposed to get married today, but she's yammering on about exquisite detailing. I shake my head slightly, needing some focus to find this zipper, not the way her hips dip in like a landing spot for my hands. Or how her perky ass curves into an upside-down heart.

I clear my throat. "Okay, I'm coming in."

Fuck *me*.

Why is everything I say the absolute worst?

I decide to not even try to make it better. The gutter my mind is dwelling in couldn't possibly help.

My fingers slide between her skin and the material, and I freeze when I hear her gasp. Another deep inhale and exhale…from both of us this time, I think. I pull the material out slightly to get a better look, nearly letting out a string of curses when I see the zipper.

I slowly lower it and when it's all the way down, the dress falls to the ground, leaving me in a world of trouble far greater than before. The sight of her in the barely-there lace, her curvy cheeks peeking beneath the edges, will be permanently burned into my memory.

I gulp and move quickly to the doorway. "Let me know if I can do anything else. I'm just across the hall."

"Thank you, Callum."

I mutter something, no idea what, because I've clearly

lost my mind. I should've insisted she go to the lodge or anywhere but here. Not because I don't trust myself around her—I'm not a fucking caveman despite the way I sometimes sound—but because something about her in my space looks a little too right.

And there's no way it could be.

She's in a wedding dress.

I wait around for a while, mostly pacing in my room or trying to read while I'm really listening for her to start the water. And later, when I'm sure she's not using the water anymore, maybe she's even gone to bed, I take a quick shower, my boner protesting angrily when I don't do anything to relieve it.

It already feels depraved how much I want her when she's in distress. I deserve to live with my situation, at least until she's out of my house.

The next morning I get up half an hour earlier than usual and check on Ruby's RV. I'm able to move it off of the street and onto my property, but the thing dies again and won't restart. I consider calling Bill to see if he can take a look, but it's too early and I should probably ask Ruby first if she's okay with that.

The whole thing took longer than I was expecting, maybe an hour. I'd hoped it'd be an easy fix, but I've gotta get started on my day. I head to the barn and watch the cows perk up as I walk through. For a dairy farm, I don't have a big production going on here compared to most—although our organic milk and cheese are used in every local restaurant and many in the surrounding region, our cheese is sold in several top-notch wineries and select boutiques, and it sells out faster than any other vendor every week at the farmer's market. It feels good to be able to say that and know I'm doing it in a way I can feel good about.

Initially, my income came primarily from being smart in the stock market from an early age, and that jumped drastically this past year when I received an inheritance from my granddad. But for as long as I can remember, I've loved animals, and when Granddad and Grinny told us as kids which parcel of land would be ours one day, I knew I wanted to raise cows in an ethical way.

My farm isn't crowded, and my cows have plenty of time to graze. They're not milked too much. Cows are highly social animals, and I give them plenty of time to socialize. Irene takes advantage of that on a frequent basis, and she's not the only one. She's so dang cute though, I have a hard time resisting. My calves are given time with their mothers, and I don't slaughter my cows when they're done producing.

I also don't eat beef.

I don't judge other people for eating it, but after I look in the eyes of my friends and they give me milk and joy each day, I just can't do it.

I've gotten hassled a bit by the other farmers in the region for all of my choices, but I just tell them in no uncertain terms that they're welcome to their opinions. I'll deal with my farm my way.

As for what I choose to do, once my cows have stopped providing milk, I want to let them enjoy the rest of their days roaming and chilling, and I'm fortunate to have plenty of land to do just that.

I start the cleaning process and then move on to the milking, the machines making it go so much faster than it used to by hand. Once that's done a couple hours later, and I've let the cows out to graze, I check in on my goats.

Delphine, as always, is the first to run up to me and nuzzle in for an ear rub and treat. She usually can't get to Irene fast enough. I swear the two besties are like Grinny and her besties—the Golden Girls—Peg and Helen. Once the goats are out, I peek in on Dolly. She lifts her head and when she sees it's me, she tucks it back in, like she's waiting to see Ruby before she'll get up. It's just as well, I don't want to interfere with the feeding schedule Ruby has her on.

It's eight thirty by the time I head into the house to get another cup of coffee and make breakfast. I leave my boots at the back door and walk toward the kitchen, my nose perking up at the smells coming from there. The sight that greets me is that lace-covered heart ass in the air as Ruby bends down to pick something up in front of the refrigerator.

"Ahh," she squeals when she turns around, my T-shirt hitting her upper thighs and my sweater falling off one of her shoulders.

Her long legs are a sight to behold in the brief millisecond I allow my eyes to take them in.

"I didn't hear you come in," she says, laughing.

If she's self-conscious about being in only my shirt, she doesn't show it, so I try not to act rocked by it either. She tosses something in the sink, and I glance over, my eyes catching on the scrambled eggs with mushrooms and cheese on the stove.

"I thought maybe I could say thank you by making you breakfast," she says.

"You've said thank you plenty."

"Oh, well. I don't think so." She smiles.

"How is—" I wave my hand toward her upper half.

She makes a face. "It's pretty painful...and kinda awful to look at."

"I should've insisted on taking you to the hospital last night."

She shakes her head. "I'll be okay. I'm a bit klutzy, but I *hate* going to the doctor. Growing up, we usually always did home remedies anyway, and I guess that stuck. I'll just keep doing the cream and making sure it's clean. Hopefully it won't scar, but if it does, I'll have a good story to tell, right?" She lifts a shoulder, grinning.

I just stare at her, unsure of what to even say.

She turns back to the stove and turns the heat off. "I hope you like mushrooms and cheese in your eggs."

I nod. "I do. Thank you."

She beams. "You're welcome. I made a fresh pot of coffee too...and boiled water for tea. I hope you don't mind that I dug into your pantry. English Breakfast is my *favorite*."

"That's fine," I mutter.

She takes two plates down and hands me one, dishing a pile of eggs on hers. "I'm going to eat quickly and get some clothes from the RV...so I can see about Dolly."

"She looked good this morning. I waited to feed her... wasn't sure when she usually eats, but she looked comfortable."

"You checked on her?" She gapes at me and I nod.

"That okay?"

"Of course. I just can't believe you...I'm not used to—" She smiles. "Thank you."

I nod again.

She glances at the clock and makes another face. She's like watching an animated movie, constant movement and dramatic expressions. I can't take my eyes off of her...but I force myself to, dishing up some eggs.

"She's normally eating in about fifteen minutes, but I

think she'll be okay if I'm a little later today. She's probably still exhausted from the drive. Thanks for checking on her."

"No problem."

She pours hot water over her tea bag, while I get my coffee.

"Can you believe I'm getting close to boiling water again so soon?" She laughs. "Gotta get back on that horse."

"How about I carry that to the island...or table," I say, motioning for her to go ahead while I pick up her mug.

"Either place is fine by me," she says. "There's a beautiful view everywhere I look...although the view out those windows is unlike anything I've ever seen."

I bite back my proud smile and move toward the table near the floor-to-ceiling windows. It's one of my favorite places in the house. The snow-capped mountains are majestic, and the snow flocking all the trees is spectacular. The green shows through the fir and spruce and pine, and the barren branches of the aspen are their own kind of beautiful in the winter. I love it through every season though.

"Is that an ice rink out there?" she asks excitedly.

"It's a little rough right now, but in a few weeks it'll be better for skating on. My nephew likes to come out here and skate every chance he gets."

"How old is he?"

"Eight."

"Is he your only nephew or do you have nieces too?"

"I have a niece now too. She's four, and my brother asked her mom to marry him last night. She said yes," I add.

I grin, thinking about the way Dakota announced to all of us that Wyatt and Marlow are having a baby.

"That's incredible. You're so lucky to have such a close family. They all live here, right?"

I nod and take a bite of my eggs. My eyebrows lift in surprise.

"Is it okay?" she asks.

"Delicious."

"Oh, good." Her expression relaxes and she leans back in her seat like she's too relieved to move, but then she sits up and takes a big bite of food.

She dusts her mouth with her napkin when I keep staring. I look down at my plate and focus on the food. When she carefully lifts her mug, I pause and barely breathe until she takes a sip and sets the mug back down. She laughs when she sees my face.

"I hope I wouldn't burn myself two days in a row. My luck's not always the best, but..." A cloud crosses her face and she swallows hard, looking down at her plate as she picks up her fork.

I find myself wanting to know what caused that look, what made her go quiet, what if she's in pain?

The sound of our forks on our plates is all that fills the air for a few minutes, and I wish that I were good at any of this. But that's just foolish. She won't be here long anyway.

A sound in the kitchen has our heads turning in that direction. Her phone. I don't miss the sag in her shoulders.

"I'm going to deal with life after I feed Dolly. Wish me luck."

She stands and takes her plate to the sink. I watch her go, at odds with this curiosity I have about her. I keep eating, forcing myself to shush all the questions warring inside.

What's her story?

Who did she leave behind?

Where did she come from and how soon is she going back?

Just how hurt is she? And I don't just mean the burns...

It's none of my business.

End of story.

And there's no way I'm going to make an effort getting to know her.

I learned my lesson about that a long time ago. Every woman I've ever been invested in leaves.

CHAPTER FIVE

GRATITUDE OVERLOAD

RUBY

Sleep was hard to come by last night. I ignored all of Junior's texts and voice messages, not in the mood to hear his ranting about how I embarrassed him. After I called Kess and explained to her exactly what happened and I texted my parents saying I'd call them today, I thought I'd collapse into a deep sleep. Being in a strange place, as comfortable as it is, my brain was on high alert despite the exhaustion. And the burns on my chest and stomach look and feel worse today than I expected them to. I'm sure they'll just take a few days to heal.

It's surprisingly easy to talk to Callum. Maybe because it seems like he's intently listening to every word. I have no idea what the man is thinking with his grunts and intense expressions. He thinks before he speaks and doesn't ramble on like I do. But I don't get the impression that he's annoyed by me, and that's saying something.

I dated Junior for nine months and my parents were so excited for me to be dating someone who had it all together. A successful real estate agent from an upper middle class family, I was surprised when he started pursuing me. When I mentioned to my mom that I wasn't sure Junior even liked me half the time, she laughed and said that was silly. Everyone likes me.

Embarrassment burns, thinking of the way he laughed about me behind my back yesterday. The day he was supposed to be pledging his love for me. And I wonder why I ever ignored my gut feelings about him.

Because you wanted someone steady in your life too.

I knew we didn't have an earth-shattering romance and that there were a few things that I didn't exactly *like* so much about him, but…I loved most things. Every time I tried to talk it through with my mom or even Kess, they reminded me that no one is perfect, we'd make beautiful kids together, and that Junior's financial stability would keep us comfortable forever.

My mom and Kess are good people, but I wouldn't say either of them have ever gone for what I'd call the *financially stable* choices in their own lives. I'm not sure why I took their advice to heart about this for my own life when I was vacillating on whether I should marry Junior or not, but I did.

I didn't say yes when he first asked me…or the next

two times. And when I was fairly certain I should say no, my mom and Kess pulled an all-nighter with me, talking out the pros and cons. All of this should've pointed to me saying no, but insert that old standby quote about hindsight here.

I glance back at Callum and my breath catches at the sight of him seated in front of those windows. Wow. He is a heavy dose of adrenaline rush. My hands shake slightly as I wash my plate and move on to the pan and spatula.

"I moved your RV," he says.

I turn to him again, excitement rushing back. His eyes skate down my legs the way they did when he first walked in. I'm pretty comfortable in my own skin and it's not like he hasn't seen a girl's legs before, but I still feel a flood of heat wind through me.

"You were able to fix her?"

His lips twist. "No. But there's a guy in town—Bill. I can have him take a look if you'd like."

"Oh. Yes. That'd be great. Thank you. I'm glad you were able to move it out of the snowbank. Thank—"

"You don't have to thank me for doing what anyone else would've done."

I frown. "Uh, no, I don't personally know anyone else who would've done everything you've done for me." I shake my head, going through the list in my head. "Even my Uncle Pierre who is very generous...I doubt he'd invite someone he didn't know to stay in his house overnight. And he'd never consider trying to move an RV."

A sound comes out of Callum.

"Wait...was that a laugh?" I pretend to be floored.

He rolls his eyes. "No," he mutters.

But I think maybe that's a smile playing on his lips.

It gives me too much of a thrill to see that.

"I'll call Bill and let him know your situation. It's no big deal."

I start to say thank you and instead say, "I appreciate that."

He grumbles something and I giggle. It dies as soon as I remember the pile of snow outside when I'm not wearing any pants.

"I don't suppose I could wear some of your sweats to go get my things?"

He nods and gets up. "You can take my coat…and boots. They'll be huge, but you won't mess up your—" He points to my lace boots by the door.

I smile at him and he hurries past me, setting his plate down and then leaving the room. He comes out a couple minutes later with a coat, boots, and sweats. I put the coat on first—it's the one he was wearing last night—and I inhale all the Callum goodness. Pine and leather and peppery—it's a flood of good smells is all I know. The sweatpants are next.

He watches as I slip my legs into them and roll the top down and the bottoms up. Next are the boots. I clomp over to the door and he looks me over, his eyes widening before he turns and points out the window.

"It's out that way, almost to the barn…"

"Okay."

"Would you rather I go out there? You look like you might trip in those boots."

"Nah, I'll be fine."

He pulls the door open and I walk out. About three feet out the door, I biff it face-first into the snow. Strong arms pull me up and I come up sputtering.

"You were right about the boots," I say, swiping snow off of my face and shivering.

"Let me help," he says.

"Okay."

He puts his arm around my waist and holds out his other hand, which I gladly take. Before I know it, we're moving and my feet barely touch the ground. When we reach the door to Jolene, he opens it for me and my feet slide out of the boots before I step inside. I look back at him—he's standing on the ground, hands on his hips waiting to see what I'm about to do next.

"Come on in," I say.

He hesitates and undoes his boots, stepping into Jolene. The space shrinks with him inside, but he looks good in here. He glances around, quietly taking it in.

"What do you think?" I can't resist asking.

"Classy," he says without hesitation.

A grin takes over my face, and I pat the counter proudly. "Isn't she? Jolene's come a long way."

"Jolene…"

"That's her name."

"Ah," he mumbles.

His fingers brush over the woodwork and I get the strong sense that he approves.

"You live in this?" he asks.

"I think I do now. Long term, it was supposed to be my office, but looks like it's going to be a lot more than that. Well, as long as it's safe. Did it seem like there were any leaks or anything?"

"Not from what I could tell."

"Thank goodness. I don't mean this in the ungrateful way it sounds, but…I wish I'd gotten pictures of her in the snowbank."

I'm sure I'll need them for insurance, but also, all the TikTok followers who have been with me on Jolene's renovating journey will want to see what she's going through now.

"I took a couple with my phone."

"No way!" I turn to him in surprise. "Brilliant! Thank you."

He rolls his eyes. "It was nothing. They're probably not any good. It was still dark out and it was lodged in a weird angle. The pictures helped me zoom in to see how to best get it out."

I put my hand on his arm and squeeze. "You're the best."

His Adam's apple bobs as he stares at me and then looks away, his cheeks turning ruddy. I drop my hand and feel my own cheeks heat. I go to the closet and pull out a bag, stuffing it with a pair of jeans, leggings, a shirt and sweater, socks, underwear, and my boots. In the bathroom, I grab my cosmetic bag and toss in a few other necessities, and I add it to the bag.

When I walk back toward Callum, he's looking at the books I have tucked into a basket.

"Do you like thrillers?" I ask.

He nods. "I do."

"Take any of those you haven't read. The one on top is a recent favorite."

He picks it up and looks at the back. I'm pleased when he tucks it under his arm.

"You ready?" he asks.

"Yes." I laugh. "Hopefully I can make it to the house to change in one piece."

"I'll make sure you do," he says with a sigh.

I flush again. "Thank—"

"Ahh—" he says, lifting his hand.

"You can't stop me from being grateful."

"I'm not," he says, sounding amused. "You just seem surprised by decency."

I swallow hard, feeling a lump rise in my throat.

"You're right," I whisper. "I think I am."

I walk toward the door and he opens it, moving out first and then lifting his hand up to help me out. I've stepped out of this thing a million times, but with his boots waiting for me in the snow below, I'm glad for his help. We make it back to the house without any altercations and I rush to get out of his boots and hurry to change, feeling the urgency to see Dolly growing with every minute.

Callum's waiting just outside when I step out in my clothes. He assesses my outfit much the same way as he did when I was in his clothes. His eyes on me aren't pervy, more like observant and curious. I can't tell if he likes what he sees or not, and for some reason, I wish I could.

As someone who was raised with *love, light, and sunshine, baby* as the family motto, I'm usually pretty chill. So I don't know if it's getting betrayed by Junior yesterday or the steady thrum of energy Callum Landmark seems to provide me, but I feel a little out of my element here. It's probably best that I figure out the RV situation and get it parked as close to Uncle Pierre's as I can get...just as soon as possible.

"She's that way, right?" I ask, pointing toward the barn.

"Yes, in the far right corner."

I nod and head in that direction.

"Bill can stop by in a few hours," he says, falling into step next to me.

"Great."

It's hard not to say thank you in there too, but he obviously thinks I overuse the words. I personally think you can never be too grateful, but I honestly haven't ever had a circumstance like this where someone else is helping me so much. I'm used to bending over backwards for people and then being teased for the way I am.

Ruby Sunshine Jones, always a ray of freaking sunshine.

Ruby Sunshine Jones, people pleaser personified.

Ruby Jones, *meh*.

I shiver slightly, wishing I'd kept Callum's sweater on over mine—it seemed to cut through the cold.

When we step through the gate, a brown and white goat runs over and a black and white cow isn't far behind. They come to an abrupt stop in front of us, causing me to almost fall again, but Callum puts his hand on my elbow, bracing me.

"Hi girls," he says softly. "This is Ruby. Be nice, okay?" He nuzzles the cow and she gives him the biggest melty eyes, while the goat leans against him and does everything she can to get his attention.

"Oh my goodness. They're too cute for words."

"Cute and rotten," he says. He pats the cow's head. "This is Irene. And her little sidekick there is Delphine. But don't be fooled. Delphine's the instigator."

Delphine leans more aggressively into Callum, and he surprises me by bending down and picking her up and hugging her like I'd imagine hugging a dog or cat. She nestles into him and he holds her close for a few seconds before setting her back down. She runs around him, happy now.

I laugh, too delighted and overcome to think straight. Is there such a thing as eye pheromones for what I just saw? I mean. That was the cutest thing I've ever seen.

A few of the other cows come over and Callum greets them by name.

Betty. Iris. Gladys. Ethel. Leona.

Some of them look so similar, I'm not sure how he can tell the difference, but I was able to tell between our emus, so I know it comes with knowing them well.

And the goats that run over to greet us are Jupiter and Moonbeam, but Irene stands guard near Callum, not wanting to share him. He tells her to be nice again and she looks up at him like *do I have to?*

"Yes, I'm talking to you," he says, and I laugh because he reminds me of myself communicating with my emus.

I feel a pang of homesickness, not for Utah, but for all the sweet birds I left behind. Mom and Dad had been threatening to sell the farm for a long time, and I'd been resisting them... I hadn't dreamed they'd sell the land along with it.

"They're beautiful," I say softly. "And spectacular names."

He chuckles and there must be ear pheromones too because hearing his laugh does this weird thing to my insides.

"If you want to introduce Dolly to them, I'd start with Irene and then Delphine," he says. "I can be there for it, and once they check her out, they should be fine with her out of the stall...as long as she's okay with *them*."

"Oh, you don't mind her being out of her stall? I can take her outside the gate, if that's better. She sticks close to me when she's out of her element."

"Whatever you're comfortable with," he says. "If she's going to be here for the day, she may as well get a good run in."

I'm glad he's so open to having an emu around even if only for the day, but all I can think about now is what are we going to do about tonight? And tomorrow?

I should've thought all of this through more carefully before setting off across the country without a plan. My life has completely turned upside down in the span of a day.

CHAPTER SIX

FAMILY MATTERS

CALLUM

I've seen Ruby flinch several times this morning and that fall in the snow couldn't have been great with her landing on the burns, but when I've asked if she's okay, she acts like it's no big deal. If I hadn't seen the pain on her face more than once today, I'd assume she's fine.

Wyatt calls as we're going to Dolly's stall, and I excuse myself and point Ruby toward the direction she needs to go. "Let me know when you want me to bring Delphine and

Irene in."

"Okay, I'll just feed Dolly and spend some time with her first."

I nod and answer the call. "Wyatt."

"Didn't anyone ever teach you to say hello?"

"It's unnecessary."

"To you maybe. But it always feels a little ominous to hear my name barked at me when I'm expecting a hello."

"I don't bark."

"Uh, check again, brother."

"What do you want?" I groan.

"Emma asked me about your *friend* this morning and I told her you don't have friends."

"Har-har."

He laughs and I absentmindedly pet Irene. We already talked about his engagement last night when I checked in with him, but I still feel bad that I missed most of the party.

"Any wedding dates I should know about?"

"Nah, still basking in the glow. Honestly, I'm just relieved she said yes." He laughs again and it's still surreal to hear him so happy. The guy fell hard when he met Marlow and her little girl Dakota. "If I can talk her into marrying me tomorrow, I'll let you know, but I have a feeling she's leaning toward something a little farther out."

I snort. "Go figure."

"So, tell me more about this *friend*. Emma said something about a Ruby? We don't know a Ruby…"

I roll my eyes and run a hand down my face while Delphine butts her head into my thigh.

"Pierre's niece—"

"*Oh*, so that's Ruby. Okay. I just thought you'd help her with her car and she'd be on her way. Is she hot?" He laughs and puts his hand over the phone, but I can still hear him through his muffled hand telling Marlow that I have a new *friend* named Ruby.

I shake my head and forge ahead, actually glad he called so I can get his advice. "She burned herself pretty bad. I didn't see the burns to know for sure how bad, but it was really hot cocoa and she had this dress on that seemed like it just kept pressing that heat into her skin."

"It's no joke, man. People come through the hospital all the time with burns from that kind of thing. Sometimes it can take weeks to heal…months even, depending on how bad the burn is. Why didn't you mention it last night? You should tell her to come in."

"I'd talked to Emma and I tried to get her to go in, but I don't think she's going to. Her RV broke down and she's got an emu here—"

"She's got…an *emu*. Are you serious?" His voice is incredulous and like he's barely withholding his laugh.

I'm already kicking myself for saying as much as I have.

"Wait, is she—did she stay at your place? Her and her *emu*?" Now he does laugh.

I lift my head to the sky and count to ten. I clear my throat to speak and he keeps going.

"This is too good. I'll bring some stuff over for her, man. We'll take care of her."

"I've got it—"

"See you in a bit."

The line goes dead and I stare at my phone, cursing under my breath. I should've never answered the call, but I thought Wyatt would be too high on his engagement fucking bliss to show his nosy-ass self. It's a good thing it wasn't Sutton or Scarlett. I would never hear the end of this. Theo and Wyatt are usually good for a little more subtlety than my oldest and youngest sibs, but from the sound of that…

"I think Dolly's ready for an introduction whenever your girls are," Ruby calls.

I look up and she's leaning out of the doorway, her cheeks rosy from the cold. My teeth grind together in an attempt to not react to how beautiful she is.

I lead Delphine and Irene just outside Dolly's stall and Ruby's grin widens as we come closer. She leads Dolly carefully outside and for a second, they all stand frozen. When Dolly takes another step out the door and into the yard, Delphine runs over and sniffs her and then runs back to report to me, her bleats snapping in rapid fire.

"Slow down, Delphine." I pet Irene standing solemnly next to me. "What do you think, Irene? Think you can let her pass?"

Irene lets out a long moo and I lift a shoulder to Ruby.

"I wouldn't leave them alone together just yet, but it seems like she's all in."

Ruby's eyes widen. "That was easy."

She laughs when Dolly leans down toward Delphine and they touch beak to nose. Delphine blinks and her floppy ears sway when she tilts her head, while Dolly's eyes stare fixedly on Delphine. All of a sudden, Dolly takes off and does this limp-noodle run around Ruby, never going far from her, but like she can't contain herself a second longer. Delphine follows as best she can, looking to me for assurance that this character isn't getting out of hand, and before I know it, I'm cracking up at these crazy-ass fools.

Ruby starts laughing too and it makes Dolly circle her faster.

"I'm not dancing with you today, Dolly," she says, waving her away. "Run your little heart out." She glances at me. "How do your cows and goats feel about music?"

My eyebrows lift. "They're for it."

She grins and pulls her phone out. "Don't judge. Dolly's partial to Cory Wong."

She waits for a reaction for me.

I shrug. "She knows what she likes."

"Are you a Cory Wong fan?" she asks.

"I've never heard of…them."

Her smile grows and she starts a song from her phone. "He's a guitar player and always has a great band."

It's a high-speed jazz funk that I have to admit is pretty damn catchy. As soon as Dolly hears the song, she pauses to look back at Ruby and I swear she smirks before she takes off across the yard, looking like a tipsy dancer. Irene harrumphs next to me like she's above it all, which makes Ruby cackle. Delphine tries to corral Dolly into one area, always the little enforcer when it comes to everyone but herself, but Dolly keeps doing her little run-dance, her eyes never wandering too far from Ruby.

"Lot of energy," I note.

"Right? You'll never lack exercise if you hang out with emus."

"You've always owned them?"

"For as long as I can remember. Uncle Pierre actually helped start the business—did you know that? Hence his restaurant, The Dancing Emu…an homage to the family business." She holds her hands out toward Dolly. "And this dancing delightfulness."

I run my hand over my jaw. "It all makes sense now."

"I've never gotten to go, never visited Uncle Pierre here in Landmark Mountain…he always comes to us for the visits."

"Good food."

I don't add that I'd enjoy frequenting The Dancing Emu

more if it weren't for the godawful karaoke that everyone in my family but me loves.

"Hey there," a voice calls and I groan.

I turn to see Wyatt walking toward us, the smile on his face too obnoxious for words.

"Wyatt Landmark, this guy's younger brother," he says, looking at Ruby but pointing to me. He waves a bag up in the air. "Heard you got a pretty bad burn last night and I brought some supplies over."

Dolly stopped running the minute Wyatt came into sight and she pops up between Wyatt and Ruby.

I snort. Serves Wyatt right, sneaking here under the guise of doctorly concern.

"Hello," he says to the emu, chuckling and backing up when she takes a step toward him.

"Oh, that's so nice of you," Ruby exclaims, turning her full-wattage beam on him and then me. "Dolly, step back."

Dolly listens, taking a step back, and Wyatt turns to me, sending me a look.

"That is an exceptionally well-behaved emu," he says. "Delphine and Irene could stand to learn a few things from... Dolly." His voice sounds choked, like he's barely holding back his laughter.

"Thank you," Ruby says earnestly. "But Delphine and Irene have been nothing but lovely to me and my girl."

Speaking of Irene, she's sidled up next to Ruby and Ruby reaches out to rub between her ears.

"Callum got me all set up last night with antibiotic cream and gauze—" Ruby says.

"I'm sure he did a great job too," Wyatt says, his eyes full of mischief when he looks at me.

"Wyatt's a doctor," I mumble. *And a nosy son of a bitch.*

"I brought an antibiotic cream that's more concentrated

than what you can get over the counter. Where are the burns?" he asks.

Ruby flushes and does a wave over her chest and stomach area.

Wyatt grimaces. "Brutal."

She nods.

"I'd feel better if you were seen by a doctor and it doesn't have to be me," Wyatt says. "My colleague Dr. Emma Langley is great. But at least try this." He waves the bag again.

"Okay, thank you." She smiles again when she takes the bag, and Dolly takes off in a spirited run.

Wyatt laughs, watching the way she runs off. "Dakota would flip over her," he says. He turns to look at Ruby. "How long are you staying? I'd love to bring my fiancé and her daughter over to see…Dolly."

I drag in a deep inhale, wishing I could bop my brother on the head. Could he be any more obvious? I can only hope that Ruby doesn't catch on to what he's up to.

Ruby's cheeks turn a deeper pink as she turns and looks at me. "I'm trying to get out of Callum's hair as soon as possible. The last thing he needs is us disrupting his peace."

Wyatt can barely pull off the frown he tries to manufacture, his laugh still too close to the surface. "Nonsense. Callum needs some excitement in his life. Can't you tell? If my family and I didn't drag him out occasionally, he'd never talk to anyone but these cows and goats."

I roll my eyes. "Better company than you."

He just laughs. "Ignore him. All bark." His eyes twinkle as he leans in. "And he's got plenty of room, as you can see. You'd be doing him a favor by sticking around for as long as possible."

"You should get that stuff on your burns," I tell Ruby. "Let it start working."

"At least say *please*, brother," Wyatt says. He grins at Ruby. "I swear he just gets bossier every day."

She laughs a little too much for my liking.

"Shut it." I point at Wyatt.

He lifts a shoulder at Ruby like *see what I mean?*

"I'll keep an eye on the girls if you wanna leave Dolly out," I add.

"It seems like they're all getting along okay." Her tone is reluctant, but I can tell she's thinking about trying it.

"They'll be fine." Just as I say it, Dolly walks over and stares at me, and then she moves so she's standing next to me. I make sure to stay still so I don't scare her off, and we quietly survey the land together.

Ruby giggles. "Well, she certainly seems fine. I'll be right back."

She walks away and Dolly turns and follows her to the gate, watching as Ruby walks away. Dolly then looks back at me like *are you really letting her leave us like that?*

"She'll be right back," I tell her.

Wyatt starts laughing and I try to ignore him, but the bastard makes it hard to do.

He slides his hands together, back and forth. "Well, I, for one, am *loving* this turn of events," he says.

"You need to get on back to your newly engaged life. It's giving you ideas that aren't there."

"Oh, I'd say the ideas are clearly there. The way she flushes every time she looks your way? The way your eyes haven't left her for more than a second at a time?" He gives my back a few hearty slaps and then squeezes my shoulder. "Can't tell me the ideas haven't crossed both your minds."

I turn back to see if she's in sight. "She showed up here in a wedding dress," I say under my breath. "Trust me, it's all in your head."

Wyatt looks stunned for a second, frowning as he looks back at the house. He starts to say something and clears his throat.

"I'm gonna head out. It's really nice to meet you, Ruby," he calls.

I turn and Ruby is heading our way, but still far enough out that hopefully she doesn't hear when Wyatt leans close to me and quietly says, "You better work your magic quickly then because I'm not sure I've ever seen you so mesmerized."

"Mesmerized?" I snort. "Get your deranged lovesick self off my property."

Wyatt just laughs harder, squeezing my shoulder one more time before he walks toward the gate. He holds it open for Ruby and they exchange a smile.

"Keep me posted on those burns, would you, Ruby?"

Her smile widens and she puts a hand up to her throat like she's overwhelmed. "I will. Thanks again for bringing this over for me," she says.

He nods and gives me another pointed look before he walks away.

And I know it like I know what the weather will be based on the clouds: It's only a matter of time before the whole family hears about this.

CHAPTER SEVEN

THE DIFFERENCE BETWEEN MINE AND YOURS

RUBY

So far, the people in Landmark Mountain have been very welcoming. Granted, I've only met two of the Landmark brothers, which made me feel like I was in my very own Nancy Meyers' movie, the way the two of them bantered back and forth. They are just so stinkin' beautiful that they don't seem real.

But then Bill comes over to take a look at Jolene and he's great in an entirely different way. He and his wife are fairly recent transplants to Landmark Mountain, he says, and he's burly, with a long white beard and smiling eyes. The good news is there are no leaks or major repairs needed that he can see, but the bad news is she needs a new battery, and it seems as if they're not just lying around at a nearby store. In fact, they're hard to track down, and the one we did find online is on back order.

When Bill leaves, promising he'll either keep looking or order the battery we found online by the end of the day, I don't know what to say to Callum. I'm glad my RV is not as in the way as it was last night, but it's still quite an imposition to just leave it parked out here.

I open my mouth to apologize again and he jumps in before I can.

"Wyatt was right," he says. "I've got the room and you're welcome to stay as long as you need."

My shoulders sag with relief and also embarrassment. I've felt a weird mixture of the two since I got here.

"Uncle Pierre won't be back until Thursday. That's too long for any houseguest. I can check into that place you were talking about—your sister's resort?"

His head tilts toward Dolly. "And leave her behind?" He grins to let me know he's teasing. "It's no trouble."

My phone rings and I practically wilt when I see that it's from my parents. I'm not ready to talk to them yet, but...

"I should take this," I say, holding up my phone.

He nods and I walk past the barn, Dolly on my heels.

"Hello?" I answer.

"My baby," Mom cries.

"Are you okay, Ruby?" Dad's voice is weary, and the guilt that I haven't called them before now outweighs the anger.

"I'm sorry I didn't call right away."

"We were worried sick." My mom sniffs. "Thomas told us where you are, but...we shouldn't have to hear it from him."

"*Pierre*. He changed his name almost two decades ago," I snap.

Dolly leans her head on my shoulder, sensing my anxiety, and I pet her.

"He'll always be Thomas to me." My mom sighs.

We'll never agree on this point. When Uncle Pierre came out, he changed his name from Thomas to Pierre and I think my mom had more issues about the whole thing than she wanted to admit. She thought it was ridiculous for him to change his name and refuses to call him anything else. I wish she'd respect his wishes and call him what he wants to be called. Her hippie vibes go south quick when it's too complicated for her to understand or if she doesn't agree with something.

"What happened, sweetheart?" she asks.

"Why didn't you tell me you were selling the place to Junior?" I ask. "I've worked so hard to keep it all afloat, and now it's just...his?"

"That's exactly why, honey. We didn't want you to have to work so hard, and the place would've been yours too, not just Junior's," Dad says. "You were about to marry him. What happened? The poor guy is a wreck. I didn't think you had this in you, Ruby Sunshine."

Wreck, my ass, but my dad's disappointment in me stings.

"We looked everywhere for you and he was already at the altar before we could let him know you were gone," my mom adds.

Normally, I'd feel terrible about any bride or groom being left at the altar. "I heard him talking about me...making fun of me." I grit my teeth so hard it hurts. "He was planning to only be married to me for a year," I say. "And unless my name was on the paperwork somewhere, he wasn't planning on that property ever being mine."

"What?" my mom says. "No, that can't be right. I'm sure you misunderstood. You're so sensitive, love. I'm sure he didn't mean anything bad. He *cried*."

"I didn't misunderstand him. He said I was *meh*, but that he wasn't ready to give up having me in…uh, you don't want to hear those details. And then he said the real prize at the end of the rainbow is the land. He was a much better actor than I knew. It was *all about the land*. Did you even ask him what he's doing with our emus?"

"We thought you'd be in charge of them," Dad says quietly, his tone completely different than before. "You already were most of the time anyway. You know we've never been good at all this. Thomas—Pierre—and your grandparents were always so much better…*you* are so much better at it. We thought you'd be happy about this arrangement. I-I had no idea Junior was—" His voice breaks. "I'm so sorry, honey. I don't know what to say."

"What *should* we do about the emus?" Mom asks.

I take a deep, cleansing breath, hoping that it will help, but the need to yell at my parents is still strong, so I just keep breathing.

"Ruby?" Mom says. "Do you think you can work something out with Junior about them?" She sniffles, and so help me, if she starts to cry, I really will lose it on her.

I'd like to tell the two of them to figure it out themselves since they did all this without discussing it with me, but that would most likely mean that they just wouldn't do anything about it. And the thing about my parents is, despite their faults, they mean well. They thought they were doing something nice for me. The problem is, they don't think things all the way through.

"I don't know, Mom. I'm not going back to him, if that's what you're suggesting. But Junior has never been a fan of the emus, and I can't imagine him keeping them for long. I suggest you try to find places for them as soon as you can."

"But we're leaving for our trip soon—" she starts.

"We'll see if we can," Dad cuts in. He chuckles nervously. "I don't suppose there'd be a place for them in Landmark Mountain?"

"Gee, Dad. Let me see if I can steal back the twenty-four emus we no longer own, transport them across the state lines, and find fifty acres to let them take over...I'll get right on that."

"Ruby Sunshine, it's not like you to sound so...harsh," Mom says.

"Twenty-five," Dad says.

"What?" Mom and I both say in unison.

"Twenty-*five* emus, not twenty-four."

I dig deep into my inner well searching for calm. If there wasn't snow on the ground, I'd go into a yoga pose right now, just to find some relief from this conversation.

"I took Dolly," I say.

She lifts her head when I say her name and I smile at her through my blurry eyes. My parents are talking about how problematic it is that I took Dolly when technically we don't own her anymore, the fact that they didn't realize I had her speaking volumes, and I tune them out as I take in the majestic mountains surrounding Callum's place. I happened to end up in a slice of heaven, and bringing any of my mess into this oasis feels wrong.

"I've gotta go," I say abruptly.

"What? We just—" Mom stutters.

"Love you both." I hang up before either of them can say anything else.

I don't have the strength to be the parent in our relationship today.

A few minutes later, I walk back toward the barn. Standing still that long made me chilly. Callum isn't where I last saw him, and I put Dolly in her stall and go into the house.

Laughter rings out and I pause in the doorway, wishing I could back out before I'm caught.

"Hello," an older woman's voice calls out.

I turn in her direction and recognize her and the others from Callum's pictures. His grandma, sister, and sister-in-law.

"I'm Grinny, and this is my granddaughter, Scarlett," Grinny says warmly. "And my beautiful granddaughter-in-love, Sofie."

Scarlett smiles and waves from across the room. "Hi. Welcome!"

Sofie smiles warmly. "Hey. It's great to meet you."

"So nice to meet you all." I sound more nervous than I want to, still shaken from that conversation with my parents.

My eyes meet Callum's and his expression isn't giving much away, but I get the sense that he's almost apologetic. Not sure why that would be.

"We brought some food over," Grinny says. "Heard Pierre's niece was in town. You look so much like your beautiful mother, dear...and I see your uncle in there too." Her eyes crinkle when she smiles.

"Thank you. I forget how long she lived here since she was gone long before I was born. I wasn't sure anyone would really remember her."

"I'm old enough to remember everyone," Grinny says, laughing. "Please tell her hello for me."

"I will."

"God only knows what my brother has tried to feed you," Scarlett says, poking Callum in the side.

He rolls his eyes, but it doesn't have the same edge it did when his brother was here. She leans on his shoulder and he puts his arm around her, tugging on the end of her ponytail. It melts my heart a little bit. I always wanted a brother or sister. Scarlett's eyes are full of mischief when she looks back at me.

"You are *stunning*," she says.

My hand flies to my neck and I flush. "Oh, thank you. Coming from you, just wow. Both of you. That picture of all of you at the wedding..." I shake my head. "*Breathtaking.*"

Sofie's eyes are shy now as she smiles. "Thank you so much. It was the best day."

"I'm glad we got over here." Scarlett pats Callum's chest. "Don't want this guy chasing you off."

He shakes his head and grumbles something, walking over to the counter to pour a glass of water.

"He *never* has company." Scarlett is still going. "And we rarely get people to stay in Landmark beyond the tourist season." Her smile widens. "Are you here to stay?"

"Uh...I'm not sure. I left in a hurry and don't have a good plan yet," I admit.

"Well, are you hungry?" Grinny asks.

"I...yes." I've been eating so carefully the past couple of months so we wouldn't have to do any drastic alterations on my dress that the thought of digging into this soup and salad with large buttery dinner rolls sounds divine. "Is that a pie I see?"

They laugh at my excitement.

There's a knock on the door and then it opens and more people flood in. They introduce themselves as they come in.

I'm on beauty overload. Seriously…this is the land of beautiful people. Sutton and his son, Owen, the next guy kisses Sofie before introducing himself as Theo, and a guy comes in and puts his arm around Scarlett's waist…Jamison. All bearing more food.

"You've gotta be kidding me," Callum mutters.

"Got room for more in here?" Wyatt calls when he comes in. He has a beautiful woman on one side, Marlow, and her mini-me on her other side.

"I'm Dakota," the little girl says.

"I'm Ruby," I say, as Callum mutters, "For fuck's sake."

His eyes grow wide as the little girl's mouth drops and he digs in his pocket and pulls out a dollar, handing it to her. He motions for Owen to come over and hands him a dollar too.

"Ignore my filthy mouth," he tells them. "Any day I get to see you guys is a treat, but your parents are suspect. This little impromptu party takes the cake."

Dakota wraps her arms around Callum's waist as he pats her back and looks around. "There's *cake*?"

Everyone laughs, me included.

"Ruby's a pretty name," Dakota says shyly.

"Thank you," I say, smiling. "Your name is pretty too, and so is your hair."

"Mama says it's grown a foot since we got here!" She frowns and pulls it around to look at the ends. "I forgot to ask you what that meant, Mama," she says to her mom.

She scrunches up her face, and Marlow tells her what it means.

Questions are thrown my way right and left, and we help our plates to the delicious food his family brought, as everyone moves around the open area. Conversation flows easily, especially after the food and a beer. Callum's the quietest of all of them, but he's relaxed and I can tell being around his family makes him happy. When he speaks, it's intentional and sharp-witted, and even when his words are sassy, it never feels unkind.

His eyes frequently meet mine, observing…assessing. Almost as if he's checking in to make sure I'm okay.

My cheeks hurt from smiling.

I like this family.

I should be sad today.

Rejected, but I'm not alone.

My life looks so much different than it did just yesterday. I'm not going to be a wife. I missed out on a tropical honeymoon, and I left the home I've always known and loved.

But for a few hours, we talk and laugh a lot, and things feel easier than they have for a long time.

CHAPTER EIGHT

THE SHINE IN SUN

CALLUM

The last of the family leaves after a long trip outside to see the animals, Dolly being a major hit with the kids, of course.

"Sorry about all that," I say, shutting the door and locking it. "We're a lot even when you've known us forever...coming in brand new, you must be exhausted."

"I love them," she breathes out. Her face is shining, and she laughs, tucking her feet under a blanket on the couch. "They are amazing. Every single person. I've always wanted to have a big family like that. It must have been so fun to always have a friend around."

"They're all right," I say.

She laughs and points at me. "You adore them. I saw it on your face the entire time."

I give her a droll look and she just laughs harder. I shake my head.

"And it seems like Sofie and Marlow...and Jamison too...they fit in so well. My cousins always tortured anyone new coming in to date their siblings. Was it always this easy between you guys?"

I nod. "Pretty much. Well, they all had issues with each other at first, but not with the family. Sofie and Theo grew up together, but then she was gone for eight years. She hasn't been back for long..."

"*Really.*"

I sit in the chair across from her, needing the distance. She's already like a beam of light in my house. I can't stare at her sunshine for too long, but it's almost impossible to stop trying. I clear my throat and nod, glancing at the fire.

"We all liked Jamison and Marlow before Scarlett or Wyatt did."

"No way. Even you?" She laughs when I shrug. "Well, they sure seem tight now. So cute together. Are Scarlett and Jamison engaged too?"

I shake my head. "Not yet. Only a matter of time."

"What about Sutton? Grinny said the two of you are the oldest and that Sutton's not married either, but is there someone special in his life?"

"No...Sutton was married before and now the two oldest Landmarks are holding on to bachelor status...forever, by the looks of it."

She starts to say something and pauses, her eyes darting to the fire.

I want to ask what she was about to say, but that's not my style. I've already said more than I normally do. I take a long swig of beer, blaming the chattiness on that.

My curiosity or attraction—whatever the hell this is—needs to be squashed before it even gets started. Nothing good can come from me being interested in her.

Joanna.

Chelsea.

Layne.

Bree.

All nice girls/women that I've gotten a little too attached to.

Joanna lived here and we dated off and on in high school. She was my first, and while I wasn't sure I wanted forever with her, I was disappointed when she left for college and never came back.

Chelsea was a tourist who stayed for six months longer than she intended to. I suppose it could boost my ego to think she lasted that long for me, but it's minuscule since she didn't end up *staying* for me.

Layne had family here and used to visit a few times a year. She wanted me to move to California with her, and I couldn't imagine myself there...honestly, I also couldn't imagine forever with her.

And Bree...she's one who has come through town the past three years for a week and expects us to pick up where we left off...which is mostly bed and a few dinners and drinks here and there. The last time, it just felt like a sad cycle, and I wanted to get off the ride.

It's not just them, it's me.

I know this.

I've made it clear to everyone in my life that Landmark Mountain is my home, and no one has made me want to change my mind about that. If I can't be enough to make someone want to stay, I don't need them. If that's close-minded and keeps me alone here forever, so be it.

I like my life.

But it's a little different with Ruby in my space. She's barely been here a minute, and already my head feels off-kilter.

For all the experiences I've had with women over the years, I haven't had them in my space. Joanna, Chelsea, and Layne were all before I lived in this house, but Bree—I guess I've known that was never going to be more than a tourist fling, and I don't want to invite potential drama into my home when that's all it is.

So yeah, looks like I will be a bachelor forever, and I'll keep my home my sanctuary, thank you very much.

I get up and toss my bottle into recycling.

Why the hell did I tell her she could stay as long as she needs? That was such a huge lapse in judgment.

"Did I say something wrong?" Her voice is tentative behind me, and I turn to see her concerned honey-brown eyes.

"Nah, I should just get to bed. You have everything you need? Are you still in a lot of pain with the burns?"

"I'm okay," she says. "Thanks." Her fingers fidget with her sweater.

I'm not sure why she looks disappointed, but I think about it all the way to the shower and the whole time I steer clear of my dick.

I lie in bed thinking about it, and toss and turn through the night with those eyes haunting my dreams.

Pierre can't get back in town soon enough.

The next morning, I walk out of the bedroom in my briefs, still absentmindedly scratching my chest when I collide into her soft body in the kitchen.

"Oh!" she yelps.

"The hell?" I grumble.

"I was trying to be quiet in here."

"Need some light?" I flip one on and wish I could turn it off immediately because her long legs are on full display. My already alert dick leaps to attention and her eyes drop.

She gasps and I turn quickly to get something out of the fridge as she starts talking a mile a minute. It's a good thing I put on underwear this morning, is all I can say.

"I-I wanted to do something nice for you," she says, shakily. "You've been so helpful, so I thought I'd get coffee ready and make breakfast sooner than yesterday—"

"Not necessary," I say.

"Well, it'll be ready in two minutes. You don't have to eat it if you don't want though…"

I close the refrigerator door and walk back down the hall to my room, cursing under my breath for the entire time I put my clothes on. When I come back to the kitchen, I see the scrambled eggs she'd been making in the dark and that there's a full pot of coffee waiting.

Her cheeks are rosy and she seems unsure of what to do with herself. She looks too cute for words in her short shorts and the loose sweatshirt falling over one shoulder.

"Thank you." I try to clear the gruff out of my voice, but it's no use.

"It's no problem," she says, waving me off. "I'm sorry I caught you off guard this morning. I should've had the lights on." She laughs. "I was using the flashlight on my phone." She shakes her head. "I don't always have the best ideas." She laughs again. "Uh, I thought maybe I could help you today. You could show me how to—"

"No need," I cut her off. "You should relax, go back to bed. You normally up by five?"

She wrinkles her nose and lifts a bare shoulder. My mouth waters. I soldier ahead.

"Later, you could go into town and see the shops…or Scarlett could set you up with a ski pass."

"Oh no. I'm not really in a place where I can—" Her voice fades. "Oh, *oh*! You need some space?"

Desperately.

"No, it's not that. You're not here long, may as well take a look around. See the sights."

I've never said *see the sights* in my life and I wonder if she can tell I'm talking out of my ass here.

She nods, but she seems nervous and again with that disappointed look. I'd feel bad if not for the fact that I can't even walk around with morning wood in my own home.

"Thank you for breakfast," I add.

"Of course. Thanks again for letting me stay here."

I sigh and nod, scooping eggs into my mouth. It's hard to be frustrated with someone who's so pleasant.

"Would you mind if I took some video footage while I'm here? The animals, the scenery…it's all so beautiful."

"I don't see why not." I take a long swig of coffee. "Good coffee," I say when I come up for air.

She smiles, pleased, and sips her hot tea.

I eat as fast as I can and am up and putting my plate in the dishwasher within minutes of sitting down. I feel her eyes on me as I put my boots and jacket on and nod before I go out the door, feeling immediate relief from the separation.

Going through my everyday rituals, I occasionally catch glimpses of her. She's a flash of color that I don't normally see around here. Her hair is flying under a bright blue and yellow striped beanie with a white fluffy ball on top, and her outfit matches...tight blue leggings and boots and an over-sized blue sweater. When she comes out pointing a Nikon at the cows and goats, Dolly at her side, I'm tempted to pull my phone out and take a picture of her.

Of course, I don't. Too busy for that.

But she's painfully distracting.

The animals are drawn to her like bees to honey, swarming around her. Many times over the course of the day, I hear her laugh bubbling out, and I want to go see what made her laugh, what she finds entertaining.

Of course, I don't.

I work through lunch and ignore the hunger, choosing to chop wood instead. It has to be done, and a couple of hours working on this instead of eating won't kill me. Ten minutes in, and I've shed my flannel. My arms burn with the exercise and I sweat through my Henley, tempted to take it off too. When I have a nice pile of wood, I drive the ax into a log and grab my shirt, wiping my forehead with it.

The sound of a click makes me turn and Ruby is there with her camera. She lowers it guiltily and grins like *Oops, caught me*. She's surrounded by an entourage of my animals, looking like a honey-haired version of Snow Fucking White. She doesn't seem fazed by it; in fact, she looks right at home.

I swallow and wipe my face again as she turns and takes off in the opposite direction.

"You hungry?" I call out. "There's leftover soup or I could make sandwiches."

"Don't worry about me," she says over her shoulder. "I had a snack earlier."

She walks to her RV and I watch as she takes pictures and

then goes inside, and she's in there so long, I start to wonder if she'll ever come out.

That night I order pizza from The Gnarly Vine and we dig into it. I'm hesitant to start conversation because A) I hate pointless chatter, and B) it's already feeling entirely too cozy in here for my liking.

But I think the silence must make her uncomfortable.

"Pierre called this afternoon," she bursts out, startling me.

I pause before my next bite.

"How's he?" I ask when she doesn't say anything.

She clears her throat and picks at the cheese on the pizza. "He feels really terrible about being gone, but...he needs to stay another week."

Her eyes fly to mine, her apprehension making more sense.

"I'll talk to Scarlet tomorrow about staying at the lodge... you need your space back." She finally takes a bite of pizza. "Oh, this is *so good.*"

"Stay."

Her gaze is intense when she looks at me again. "I'm already mortified that I've—"

I hold up my hand and she stops. "Stay. Really. I have the room. There's no need to move unless you'd rather have a change in scenery."

"I think this scenery is perfect."

My lips twitch as I try to hold in my grin. "Good. It's settled."

Her shoulders relax and she grins. "Thank you."

I sigh, falling into my pretend annoyance about how thankful she is about everything, but smile back. "You're welcome."

It's quiet for a minute as we both dig into our pizza.

"Do you sell milk and cheese somewhere? I saw the glass bottles out in the barn."

I nod, finishing chewing before I answer. "A guy will be here on Wednesday morning to deliver it to the stores that carry it around here. And then I get the next batch ready for the farmer's market. Usually I do that every week, but Theo and Sofie asked if they could do this Saturday. I occasionally do another market that's a half hour from here on Sundays."

"Sounds like you stay busy."

"A little too busy, but I like the work."

"If you ever want to add some sparkle to your packaging, I'd be happy to design something."

"Some *sparkle*?"

She giggles. "You make that sound like a bad thing. I happen to be decent at branding...not that you need help. Yours is—"

"Just okay. I know." I make a face. "It could stand to be updated. And everything grew bigger and faster than I expected...not that I've got a huge thing going on here, but it's all I can handle on my own."

"I'm shocked you don't have more help around here. I really don't mind helping, you know. I'd enjoy it even."

I try to read her, see if she really means this or if she's just being nice. "So besides helping raise emus, you do branding on the side?"

She lifts a shoulder. "Sort of." She makes that crinkly face that's so adorable it makes my heart pinch every time she does it. "I documented my remodeling project on TikTok and it sort of...blew up. Before I knew it, people were asking for merch and I was getting free products from all kinds of companies. In my spare time, I worked on T-shirts and stickers and mugs, mostly cutesy, yet *classy*," she holds up a finger to emphasize classy, "RV and design-related."

"Don't get me wrong, I've never heard the words, *classy RV-related,* but since that's the first word that came to my mind after seeing your RV, I'm curious."

She laughs. "Well, thank you."

"How do I see your stuff?"

Her cheeks bloom with color. "Uh…just look up Ruby Sunshine Jones on Tiktok or Instagram."

"Ruby Sunshine Jones," I echo. I can't hold back a grin. "Well, that makes a helluva lot of sense."

CHAPTER NINE

CHOCOLATE

RUBY

Over the next week and a half, Callum and I find our routine. I get up at 4:45 and have breakfast ready for us before he comes out fifteen minutes later. Despite his protests, he thanks me and scarfs it down. He's been fully dressed since that morning I saw him in his briefs. Good thing. The sight of him first thing in the morning, that very large and very appealing...no, not appealing...I mean *distracting* body part he's got going on is not something I could handle seeing every day.

It's just too much on the eyes and honestly, must be too large to be comfortable, but I can't say I'm not curious about who he wields that thing around. Try as I might, I haven't been able to suss out any girlfriends or even potential ones, and that's just hard to imagine.

Callum Landmark is a total babe and he's not getting the full recognition he deserves, being out here all by his lonesome.

I may not want a man in my life for the next jillion years, but I can still appreciate this man's allure.

While he works, I've been creating content. So far I've only posted a few times since I got here, and my followers are heartbroken about Jolene's misfortune, but they are *obsessed* with the new scenery. And I think I'll be getting that battery sooner than expected, thanks to the posts.

There were a bunch of questions in the comments wondering about my wedding content and the lack thereof, but I haven't answered any of that yet. I also haven't answered Junior's calls.

He keeps leaving messages like it's urgent that I call him. Like I *owe* him a conversation. He might be right, but I'm just not ready to talk to him.

So far I haven't ventured into town and we haven't gone anywhere, and the strange thing is, I haven't missed it. I was on the go so much at home, working on the farm all day, posting on my social media accounts, planning the wedding, and then going out with Junior at night…I didn't realize how tired I was.

Most days Callum or I make a light lunch and then I try to beat him into the kitchen to make dinner, but last night, he did, surprising me with a delicious mushroom risotto. We chat, okay, it's mostly me chatting, by the fire after dinner, and then I fall into bed and sleep harder than I've ever slept in my life.

It's not what I expected in coming to Landmark Mountain, and certainly not at all how I thought I'd spend my honeymoon, but each day, I wake up with anticipation and a little more energy than the day before. The burns on my chest are angry reminders of my first night here, symbolic of the state I was in when I arrived, which in some ways feels like an eternity ago. Hard to believe it's not even been two weeks.

This morning, Callum surprises me by being up before me, already making breakfast when I go into the kitchen. I pause at the sight of him and he barely glances up, his sleepy voice sending a shiver down my body.

"The truck will be here soon."

"Oh, I forgot today was the day."

He nods and flips the eggs onto a plate that's already filled with toast and fruit. I take the plate he offers and he finally meets my eyes. The intensity mixed with—amusement maybe?—leaves me breathless.

"Didn't know I had a superstar in my house," he says.

That husky tone of his just…well, chalk it up to one more thing about him that distracts me. I can't believe the women in this town aren't beating the door down to get to him.

My head tilts as I stare at him and then hurriedly look away.

"I couldn't sleep last night, so I finally downloaded Tiktok and watched…some of your…whatever you call them."

"Toks," I say playfully.

"Dumb name."

I lift a shoulder.

"But you're good. *Really* good. I like how you explain your processes…and your videos are quality."

He doesn't go on more about it, but his simple statements feel like the highest praise I've ever gotten from anyone, ever. And I'm closing in on a million followers, so that's saying a lot.

"*Thank you*," I say. "Really…that means so much."

He covers his hair with a beanie. "I'm not telling you anything you haven't heard. People love you. Hundreds of comments on your posts…"

"You don't seem like the kind to throw around compliments freely," I admit. "Junior hated it."

"Hated what?"

"That this is how I became successful."

"Not the first time I've thought Junior must be an idiot."

My cheeks and heart…and the rest of me…warms.

"You're not wrong," I say quietly, my lips lifting in a smile.

He just stares at me for a moment and then turns and walks out the door. He does that often too, just leaves without warning. My phone buzzes as he walks out and I check my texts.

UNCLE PIERRE

I can't wait to see you. I'll be in town by seven tomorrow night. Meet me at the restaurant?"

I'll see you there. Can't wait!

I'm so excited to see him and the restaurant too, but I have to admit, I'll be sad to leave this place. It's been the perfect oasis to get back on my feet after nearly wrecking my life.

I take extra pictures and video footage throughout the day, not just for me, but I get a lot of Callum too. When he originally said someone was picking up the milk and cheese last week, I had no idea two semitrucks would show up. I enjoy watching the loading of the trucks, seeing the bottles all lined up, and the assortment of cheeses. It's all a much bigger deal than Callum made it out to be.

He seems relieved when the truck pulls away, and I wonder if this is when he'll finally stop and take a break, but no, he moves to the ax and chops wood for a couple of hours…which is insanely mesmerizing to watch. Delphine, Irene, Dolly, and I keep a close eye on him the entire time he works. I will miss this too, the ax show *and* the cows and goats.

I haven't had the nerve to tell Uncle Pierre about Dolly yet. Now that I know we're meeting at the restaurant, I realize I'll either need to ask Uncle Pierre for a ride or Uber the mile or so into town and I can't exactly haul Dolly into the back of a car with me. Callum has mentioned that Dolly can stay here even after I go stay with Uncle Pierre, to which I said I'd pay to board her here, but I still wish I had a better solution than depending on Callum any longer.

I should've mentioned her long before now, but I'd rather talk about all of it in person rather than say it over a text or phone call. Uncle Pierre is excited about my surprise visit, but I'm not sure how he'll feel about the rest of my surprise.

Or *surprises*.

Dolly…and I don't want to leave Landmark Mountain. It's been great for my social media, but even better for *me*. The pressures of keeping up my family's business while growing my own, all while planning a wedding—I had no idea how exhausted I was.

Forcing myself away from Callum and his ax, I go inside

so I can make sure my last night here is productive. Callum has refused board for Dolly and while I know my incessant chatter must be driving him up the wall, he's barely acted annoyed at all. Even his grumbles have gotten less frequent. It's probably wishful thinking, but I think he might even kind of like having me around.

Nah, definitely wishful thinking, but at least he's been nice about the whole thing.

His refrigerator and pantry are a dream. Well-stocked and organized. For dinner, I make a spicy tofu curry with red peppers and mushrooms over rice and a huge salad. The only thing I find for dessert are ingredients for a chocolate pie, so I make that, taking my time with the homemade crust since it's been a while since I've had the time to bake.

When he comes in to take a shower before dinner, he pauses as he walks toward the stairs. "What smells so good?"

"It's a surprise."

"That's the best thing I've ever smelled."

I laugh, taken by the excitement in his eyes. He turns and walks toward the oven and I step in front of it, catching us both by surprise when our chests collide.

"What is it?" His voice is low and makes my belly do this weird little dance.

"Nuh-uh-uh," I sing, shaking my head. "No peeks."

He tries to turn on the light to the oven and I dodge, blocking his hand. He grabs my wrists and holds them up, both of us laughing by now, but it dies quickly as our chests rise and fall against each other. He drops my wrists and steps back, leaning against the island. His eyes take a long stroll down my body—it's not the first time he's done this and yet, he hasn't made a habit of it either. More often than not, I've wondered why he looks at me so little, but now, I feel the power of it and know he was doing me a favor.

I feel like the wind got knocked out of me.

"Are you just gonna stand there staring at me until I take it out?" I finally say, my voice more of a squeak. I clear my throat.

He smirks. "I might."

I point at him. "You need a shower."

His nose crinkles and he lifts his shirt like he's about to smell himself and decides otherwise. His smell does not bother me one bit. I find it intoxicating if I were to be honest with myself right about now, but I know he usually showers before dinner…and it seems like before bed too, now that I think about it.

He lifts off of the island without another word and trudges down the hall.

"Brownies?" he calls.

"Nope."

"Damn," he mutters. "Cake?"

"Nope."

After it's baked, I tuck the pie behind the bread box to cool and hide from Callum, while I make the whipped cream and tuck it in the fridge and then shave chocolate shavings from the bar I found in his pantry into a small glass bowl. His family might not think he's a good cook, but his kitchen has everything I could ever want. I don't use much of the chocolate bar, hoping he wasn't looking forward to eating the whole thing later. I haven't seen him eat many sweets except when the family was over, but the way he perked up over the smell of baked goods has me wondering if that's his soft spot.

His family stops by often and they call every day—I've even talked to them on the phone myself. I haven't heard from my parents since I told them about overhearing Junior, and I've always considered us close, but Callum's family has a different level of closeness and I find it so endearing.

Scarlett asked me to go to lunch with her and Sofie and Marlow yesterday, but I told them I couldn't get away. In truth, I wanted to be sure I was helpful around here just in case Callum suddenly needed it, but I think he probably would've enjoyed the solitude. I'm supposed to have lunch with them on Sunday at the lodge.

Callum comes out wearing a taupe Henley and darker brown sweats, his hair dripping and tucked behind his ears. His eyes are predatory as he stares across the kitchen at me.

"Chocolate chip cookies?" he asks.

I laugh. "Wow. I think this is the most I've heard you talk since I got here."

He frowns. "I've talked."

"Mm-hmm." I point at the table. "I put dinner on the table tonight."

His face lights up and then falls.

"You don't like curry?"

"I love it. I just don't see the dessert."

I laugh harder, loving this side of him. We sit down and he passes the rice for me to help my plate first.

"Thanks. This looks amazing," he says.

"You're welcome. I wish I could repay you for all of this…" I look down at my plate and then add the curry on top of the rice. "I don't think you could know how…healing it's been to be here."

When I look up, he's watching me, the bowl suspended in his hands. He clears his throat and finishes putting food on his plate.

"I'm glad. Broken hearts suck," he says simply.

I take a bite and chew slowly, thinking about what he's said. "I don't think I've ever had my heart broken," I admit finally. "Have you?"

His expression is one of surprise and then he takes a bite

of the food and closes his eyes, letting out a long groan. I shift in my seat, uncertain of all the sensations he's setting off in my body with that sound. Being around this man is a new experience for me, that's for sure. I wish I could figure out what it is about him that makes me feel so...alive.

"That is delicious," he groans.

My cheeks flush with the praise and the sound of his voice. "I'm glad you like it," I say softly.

He's quiet as he takes a few more bites, but his eyes close with rapt appreciation with each new taste. He finally sets his fork down and looks up at me, startling me with his focus.

"You haven't had your heart broken?" he asks.

I shake my head.

"What was the deal with Junior?"

"If I'd felt what I should've felt for him, I would be heartbroken."

He studies me, waiting for me to continue, and when I don't, he says, "Did you know you didn't love him?"

"I was worried that I didn't love him like I should, but since I've never felt more for anyone than I did for him, it seemed...well, I had a lot of sleepless nights about it." I rub my finger over the rim of the plate and think about all those sleepless nights. "I talked to my mom and cousin about it a lot, and I tried to postpone the wedding a few times, telling Junior I didn't think I was ready."

"What did he say?"

"It made him mad, and he said that we'd spent too much on the wedding to change it...and he couldn't get time off later in the year because of work. But I knew none of that was true. His family was paying for the rehearsal dinner and that was it. I either paid for everything myself or it was donated by sponsors as long as I made posts about it."

"The night you got here, you said something about him marrying you for your property."

I make a face. "I can't believe that wasn't even two weeks ago. I sure made an embarrassment of myself that night, didn't I?"

"Don't do that," he says, leaning in.

"Do what?"

"Put yourself down."

My face heats and I stare at my plate to distract myself from his intensity. "I overheard him making fun of me with his groomsmen before the wedding. It was humiliating, and yet, every mile I drove away from him, I felt like I'd been given a gift in seeing his true colors. There were red flags all along, but I assumed it was my eccentricities that were always going to be problematic in a relationship. Truth was, he was just a jerk. And I hate that he has our land, but I'm making my peace with that. What I can't make peace with is that he has my emus."

He clenches his jaw. "You said he hates them."

"He does."

"Then we need to figure something out."

I laugh and shake my head. "You've done enough, believe me. What else can I do for you, is what I want to know?"

He shoves his hair back as it falls forward. "Can you give me a haircut?"

CHAPTER TEN

THE HILLS ARE ALIVE WITH THE SOUND OF SILENCE

CALLUM

"I give *killer* haircuts," Ruby says a little too exuberantly.

My eyes narrow as she bounces in front of me. She's wearing this grey matching sweater and leggings getup that is staggering from every angle. It takes a force I'm not sure I possess to keep my eyes trained on her face and not the tits that are now at eye level. They're true perfection. Even better than that chocolate pie she made, which was right up there with magnificence. Best damn pie I've ever had, but her tits make my dick weep, and that's just the truth.

Her neck and shoulders are graceful, her long, toned legs a distraction in themselves. But the view in the back is gonna do me in. Since the moment I saw the way those ribbed sweater leggings are hugging her curvy ass, I've been at odds with maintaining eye contact and trying to catch a peek of her backside.

And it's not like her eyes are any safer.

They're warm and sparkling with energy and passion.

"Don't worry." She laughs. "I'm good at this. It'll be great."

She sets up the scissors and comb, a little pucker in her brow, her teeth worrying her lip as she concentrates.

Her lips. I could get stuck on them all day.

My sigh is more than a little exasperated.

She looks up at me, amused. "Oh, come on. It's not as bad as all that huffing and puffing you're doing over there."

"I'm second-guessing this decision," I mumble. "You look eager to chop."

She grins and walks around me, assessing my hair.

"I'm trying to decide if I should go drastic or just take a little length off and thin it out some. You have such great hair. But you're covering too much of this face." She bites her bottom lip again and my jeans tighten.

Not the best idea I've had, this haircut...although it sure feels fun right now. She's leaving tomorrow, why not torture myself tonight?

She spritzes my hair with the spray bottle she rushed to get from her room once she knew I was serious. I had no idea females carried around all these supplies. I thought we'd use the scissors I keep in the kitchen.

Her next spritz lands in my eyes and she gives me a mischievous look when I blink up at her.

"Oops," she says.

"Mm-hmm."

She giggles and I search for things to think about to offset the rager in my pants, somehow landing on rank cheese and Delphine's gas. It only minimally helps because once Ruby's hands slide through my hair and she steps in closer, all bets are off. I barely breathe for the next few minutes as the sound of the scissors takes over, and then she starts humming a perky melody and that's all I hear. She smells like a heady combination of vanilla and chocolate that sends my senses on overdrive. My hands itch to reach out and swipe her hair over her shoulder, to trail my fingers down her neck and bury my face in her breasts.

I clear my throat and shift in my seat.

"You getting antsy?" she asks. "I'm sorry I'm in my own little world with your hair. I hope it's okay that I'm going for it." She laughs and shoots me a slightly guilty look before staring at my hair again with an almost wistful expression. "And it is looking *so good*." Her teeth press into her plump bottom lip and I can't look away. When she realizes I never answered, she pauses and glances at me. "Are you okay?"

"Yeah," I rasp out.

She swallows hard and I follow the movement her neck makes, only to be drawn to her pebbled nipples right in front of me. They weren't like that a second ago. My jaw clenches and I close my eyes. What is this anguish? Am I really this bad off? This desperate for a woman that I can't even function like a normal human being? What is wrong with me?

My eyes remain closed, although the images my mind creates aren't any purer.

It's been almost two weeks under the same roof with

Ruby, and granted, I haven't ever lived with a woman or spent this many consecutive days with one since…college…if then? But that's no excuse for the gutter my head is in.

She leans in and I catch an extra trace of her sweet fragrance or maybe that's just her skin. My eyes fly open and she's between my legs, so close my hands could simply lift up to get two handfuls of her faultless ass.

Fuck. Me. Everything my brothers have said about me is true. I'm a fucking caveman.

I exhale raggedly, sweat breaking out.

"Are we almost done?" I ask, cringing inwardly at the raw need in my voice.

Her hands glide through my hair and I feel like the goats when they're leaning into a good ear scratch. My hair feels a helluva lot lighter.

Ruby smiles down at me. "You look sleepy."

"I assure you, I am not."

I don't miss her sharp intake of breath, her chest rising and falling as we stare at each other. Her eyes dance like she has a secret.

"I'm done," she says softly. "Go see what you think."

I stand up and her mouth parts for a second as she looks me over. We hang there suspended, and for a moment I wonder if she's feeling this charge between us too. She blinks and clears her throat before dusting hair off my shoulder.

"I'll sweep this up. Go look," she says.

Dismissed, the mood is broken and I'm certain any contrived feelings I imagined were all in my head, particularly the one without brain cells. I'm grateful she turns to get the broom because I have to adjust myself before I'm able to walk. My thoughts are an eternal string of curse words as I trudge up the stairs, through my bedroom, and into my bathroom. I could've gone to the closest bathroom, but frankly, I need the distance. Being on the same floor as her right now feels too close.

I shut the door behind me and lean against it, barely sparing a glance at the stranger in the mirror. I walk over to the counter, sagging against it as I tug my shirt over my head and open my fly. I let out a long hiss as I wrap my fist around my fevered dick and simply grip it as tight as I can. A long guttural moan escapes when I slide my hand up and down once and then again in quick succession…and one last time. It's embarrassing how fast I make a mess, how endless my release feels as I squeeze my eyes shut and still see Ruby Sunshine Jones shining through.

I've been about to explode since the first night I met her.

And me trying to be decent and not jack off to thoughts of her while she's in the other room is probably what backfired on me tonight.

In my defense, which I don't really feel worthy of, but here it is: I didn't realize when I opened my home to her that she'd be staying this long.

No excuse, Landmark, I tell myself. *Just get through this night and she'll be out of here tomorrow.*

I wash my hands and chest and catch a better look in the mirror. Holy hell. I still have the scruff on my face—I rarely let it go into a full beard anymore, but I can't be bothered to shave every day either. But it's been a long time since I've been this clean-cut. My neck is exposed, my eyes and jawline more defined, and I look a good five or six years younger.

She's right…she's good.

I put my shirt back on and hear something in the other room that makes me freeze. My heart is already pounding from my session with my dick, but now it tries to gallop right out of my chest.

"Hello?" I call.

She wouldn't have heard me, right?

I open the door and Ruby is in my room, hustling toward the door to the hall. She turns and stares at me, eyes wide, her face pink.

Fuck.

"I'm sorry," she pants. "I was just—I wanted to see if you liked your hair…and your bedroom door was open, but I shouldn't have come—"

Her cheeks burn even hotter and oh yeah, she heard. She knows exactly what I just did. I cross my arms over my chest and she gulps.

"I'm not exactly used to company," I say gruffly.

Deafening silence.

And then…her shoulders shake as she starts to laugh. She slaps her hand over her mouth, her eyes widening as she can't seem to reconcile her laugh with her mortification.

My lips twitch as I try to hold in my own hysteria, but when it bursts out of me, my laugh so loud it bounces off the walls, Ruby jumps…which only makes us laugh harder.

I run my palm over my face, certain my own cheeks must be on fire, and Ruby fans her face as she tries to catch her breath.

"I'm…sorry you heard that," I finally say.

"What? No, no," she sputters. "Are you kidding? I've tried so hard to be quiet myself, but it's so stinking silent out here in these mountains." She gasps, as if she realizes too late what she's admitted.

Well, well. My hands go to my waist, head tilting as I study the way her chest starts splotching all the way from the cleavage that's peeking out of her sweater to the very tips of her ears.

"How many times have you tried to be quiet?" My voice is calmer than I feel. Measured and every word distinct.

Not sure where I get the nerve to go there, but we're in uncharted territory already, and frankly, I need to know her fucking answer.

"Every night," she whispers.

My fists clench and her eyes drop down my body. My dick wrestles against my zipper.

"And every morning," she adds.

It's like the bathroom didn't even happen. I'm hard as steel just like that.

She sucks in a deep breath and when her eyes meet mine again, they're glassy. Her nipples are peaked, and the way her chest is rising and falling—I might be oblivious about women ninety-eight percent of the time, but I'm an observer, and I know what I see in front of me right now...

Lust...

Desire...

"Are you normally...quiet...so often?" I ask.

She runs a hand over her arm and shivers, and I love every second of the effect I'm having on her.

"No," she says, her eyes widening. "I'm not. I don't know if it's all this mountain air and the solitude and freedom and relief and the lack of orgasms before...or you cutting wood and stuff." The words fly out of her and she puts her hands on her hips, like she's suddenly inspired. She opens her mouth to keep going and I interrupt.

"Me cutting wood and stuff?"

She puts her hand on her head and blinks at me then swoops her hair up so it's off of her neck. "I'm wishing I didn't have this sweater on right now," she says.

"You can take it off if you need to."

Another sweet gasp from her and I want to suck up each one of them.

I'm the one left gasping for air when she lifts her sweater

over her head. She's wearing a white fitted tank underneath, so it's not revealing quite as much as I thought might be coming, but the sight is still glorious. Her tits are highlighted with the deep V, the dip between calling out to me. And I'm able to see the outline of her nipples so much better.

I watch every breath she takes, entranced.

"Much better." She sighs, as if she's not making me salivate right here in front of her. "I shouldn't have said that about you cutting wood, it's just..." She lifts a hand, her shoulder lifting. "Well...I just never knew, that's all." She shakes her head, licking her lips. "I never knew watching a man who looks...like *you*," her cheeks deepen with color again, "chopping *wood*, could be my catnip." She fans her face and laughs.

I press my lips together to keep from laughing...and to keep from stalking over there and kissing the blush right off of her.

"Your hair looks really good," she says softly, her voice shy again. "Do you like it?"

"Not as much as I like hearing you talk about my wood," I say, enjoying that gasp and her laugh.

She points at me and tries not to laugh, but it's no use. I wait for any move, any hint that she might want me to step closer, but she takes a step back.

"Now that I've thoroughly embarrassed myself, I'm going to bed," she says, her lips puckered with restraint.

I want to tease that grin out with my tongue.

"Okay," I say instead.

She nods. "Night, Callum."

"Night, Ruby."

She walks into the hall and toward her room.

"Ruby?"

"Yeah?" She pauses but doesn't turn.

"You can be as loud as you want."

Her shoulders lift and she turns to look back at me. I'd give anything to be able to read her mind right now.

"You too," she whispers.

Fuck. Me.

CHAPTER ELEVEN

VIRAL

RUBY

What was that?

That's the question that's been chiming through my head all night long.

Like a gong: *What. Was. Thaaaaat.*

I didn't sleep at all.

When my ears weren't straining to hear what might be going on in Callum's room, I was reliving our conversation over and over…and over and over…and didn't even have to touch myself to feel the thrumming pulse between my legs.

I can't believe any of it happened. I flip-flop between being so embarrassed I can't think straight to laughing hysterically in my pillow. From thinking I can never look Callum Landmark in the eye again, to talking myself out of going back to his room and seeing if I imagined the whole thing.

There were a few seconds that I thought for sure he was going to kiss me, but he *didn't*, so now I'm almost positive I've romanticized the whole interaction.

The guy was just worked up for some reason and needed a release, pure and simple.

I obviously get it, the way I've been so hyperfocused on my own orgasms since I got here.

I'm not normally anything like this, and cannot *believe* I admitted any of that out loud when I've barely even acknowledged it to myself, but Callum…he's a hot, healthy, virile guy who keeps a lot inside.

It's no surprise the man has needs.

And I'm sure what happened last night had absolutely nothing to do with me.

My phone vibrates on the nightstand, interrupting my *how could I have said all that to Callum* loop. I'm so eager to shut off my brain, I don't even look to see who it is.

"Hello?"

"It's about time you answered my calls."

Junior.

My lip curls. "If I'd known it was you, I wouldn't have."

"What happened to us, Ruby? You break my heart on my wedding day and then talk to me like you're the one who's been wronged?"

I exhale toward the ceiling so the long gust doesn't deafen his eardrums in the phone. Not because I'm full of generosity where Junior is concerned, but because I want him to hear my next words.

"Since I was only going to last for a year and was *meh* anyway, I'm certain your heart is very much intact." If my voice could cut iron, it'd be in shreds right now.

He curses under his breath. "Ruby, look, you misunderstood me. I didn't know you heard that, but…I can see why you'd think—"

"Don't you dare gaslight me now, Junior Fitzgibbons. Why did you call? You got everything you wanted. Did you call to gloat or what?"

"Of course not, Ruby." He sighs, still sounding like the wounded one.

I throw the covers back and start pacing the floor, my anger building with each step.

"I wish you'd talked to me instead of just…bolting," he says. "I would've explained…"

"Yeah, you would've tried to bullshit me back into your bed, and you know what, Junior? It was never any good, so it wouldn't have been worth it!"

"What do you mean it was never any good?" His voice takes on an edge. "Don't pretend like we didn't have—"

"Honestly, I didn't really even try to pretend, that's how *bad* you were at paying attention to me *not* being satisfied in your bed," I yell.

My eyes widen as I freeze, and then I tiptoe to the door and quietly open it. Callum is standing in his doorway, dressed for the day, looking all kinds of hot with his new haircut. His eyes do a quick sweep of me in my barely-there shorts and tank before lifting to my eyes and staying there.

I scrunch my face together and whisper, "Sorry."

He shakes his head slightly and points at the phone.

"You okay?" he asks.

"Who is that?" Junior yells on the other end.

I nod to Callum and back into my room, shutting the door. Embarrassed, I slump down at the foot of the bed and try to get control of my emotions.

"Dammit, answer me, Ruby. Are you cheating on me?" Junior says.

I start laughing and it sets Junior off more. He yells and carries on and when I finally stop laughing, I hold the phone out until he finishes.

"Are you done?" I finally say.

"Is that why you left? You had a boyfriend on the side? Dammit, Ruby. Whatever game you're playing, it's time to come home," he says.

"You have a lot of nerve," I seethe. "I don't have a home to come back to." I'm surprised I'm able to say that as calmly as I do, because saying it out loud makes me want to cry. "And you're crazy if you think you have a chance with me ever again. You ruined any hope of that when you bashed me to your friends on our wedding day...and you solidified it even more when you didn't make sure my name was on the deed to the land you stole."

"I thought we were getting married. Come home and we can work something out with the land," he says.

"You think I trust your word at this point? What is this about, Junior? I don't want anything to do with you. I heard how you really feel about me—I don't know why you're pretending you want anything to do with me."

"That's what I'm trying to say—I didn't mean it. It's just...it's how guys talk to each other."

"No, I don't believe that."

He lets out an exasperated sound. "Ruby! Quit being so fucking stubborn." Another long huff of air and his voice is softer when he comes back on. "The emus are lost without you."

I close my eyes and a tear rolls down my cheek. "They are? Who's taking care of them?"

"I'm trying to hire a few people and it's been a goddamned disaster. You know I'm not good at any of that."

"Call my parents. They'll help figure it out."

"I've tried. They're not taking my calls either. I think they've left town. I really need you, Ruby."

I groan, looking up at the ceiling. "Call Kess and she'll know how to reach them."

"Ruby, it's—"

"I've gotta go. Do me a favor, Junior."

"*Anything*," he says passionately.

"Lose my number."

He's saying something when I hang up on him.

And then I put my head in my hands and cry.

Not for Junior.

For the emus.

I try to call Kess myself, but she doesn't answer, so I leave an impassioned voicemail for her asking her to please check on the emus and help Junior with them until he can find someone to take care of them.

Before I hang up, I add, "I don't know what to do, Kess. I can't afford the land it would take to keep them, at least not right now, and I can't deal with Junior. My parents created this mess and need to figure it out, so if there's any way you can track them down, I will owe you forever."

She calls back within five minutes. "Sorry, I was in the shower. Your parents are already on their road trip. Your mom said it was going to be epic."

I groan.

"Are you really not coming back?" she asks. "I miss you."

"I miss you too. I just need some time. But I can't really imagine being there anymore, not with the way things are now."

"Yeah, I get that."

"And you're not going to be there for much longer anyway…"

She sighs. "Maybe I should reconsider transferring to UCLA in January."

"Don't you dare. You can't wait to be in California. You're not staying in Utah longer for me…especially when I'm not even there!"

"I'll help with the emus for as long as I can, but I think you should talk about it with your followers. They'll help you. Who knows, maybe you'll find a place to live. At the very least, they'll help you get back on your feet. It's not like you to just give up."

"Ouch." But I nod like she can see me. "You're right. I could be doing more."

"I mean, you're a runaway bride who doesn't even seem hurt. You're the strongest person I know," she adds.

I make a face. "I think I might be broken, not strong," I admit. "And I think I wasn't particularly hurt, except for my pride, because I didn't love Junior the way I should've."

"You tried to tell me and Aunt June that," she says. "We should've listened."

"It wasn't up to you to decide any of that." I fall back on the bed. "I better go. I need to get ready and create some kickass content that'll change my situation."

"That's the spirit," she says, giggling. "Love you, Ruby."

"I love you too. Thanks for calling me back…and for checking on things over at the farm."

"I'll let you know how things are looking once I'm there."

We hang up and I message my parents, asking them once again to please check on the emus and to help me figure out what to do about them. I take my time getting ready. I'd intended on making an extra special breakfast for Callum on my last morning here, but it's better this way. I humiliated myself last night and this morning…it's definitely time for me to go.

When I go downstairs, the house is silent. There's a pot of coffee and the scrambled eggs are covered on the stove. I heat them a little and eat quickly before going outside. I stop in my tracks when I see Callum outside.

Chopping wood.

I fan myself and then I hold my phone up and hit record.

And after I feed Dolly and try to avoid running into Callum, I step into Jolene and edit the video.

It starts out with a video of my emus at home, and the first seconds say: *When I realized my fiancé didn't want me…*

And the next video is Callum's ripped arms and chiseled body as he chops wood. Over that, I write: *I needed a change of scenery.*

It's not my typical content, but it's effective.

Two hours after I've uploaded it, I've got five hundred thousand views.

A few hours after that, two million.

Callum's gone viral.

CHAPTER TWELVE

YOU KNOW WHERE TO FIND ME

CALLUM

Good God, the things this woman is doing to me.

First of all, I slept with one eye trained on my door, hoping against hope that she'd pay another visit to my room.

Didn't happen.

And then I overheard her telling—I'm assuming her ex— that she hadn't been satisfied in bed…and that stayed with me all day.

Now what she said last night about the *lack of orgasms*

before makes a lot more sense, and it will probably keep me up again tonight as well.

How can someone who looks like Ruby not be getting worshipped on the regular?

Not to mention, she's *great*.

I don't even like people, but I like her.

I'm not surprised that she's been scarce today. I had a feeling, after our night and the way she wilted when she realized I'd heard her this morning, that she wouldn't be her extra bubbly self who wants to help in whatever way possible.

Still, it's almost dinnertime before I see her again.

When she comes downstairs looking dressed to kill in tight jeans and a pale pink sweater that shows a little skin on each shoulder, I fight the urge to haul her fireman style to my room and show her a thing or two about getting satisfied.

Her expression is sheepish when she looks at me. "I'm sorry to ask this of you," she says, "but are you *sure* it's okay if Dolly stays here? At least until I can talk to my uncle about it."

I frown. "I wouldn't have offered if it wasn't okay."

Relief floods her face. "Thank you. Thank you for everything, Callum. Staying here has been"—she shakes her head—"I can't even tell you...it's been healing and restful...and your company has been really nice."

I nod and try to smile, but then preoccupy myself with picking up her bag. For some reason, I have the strange urge to convince her to stay a little longer.

"I'll be back to take care of Dolly, so you don't have to worry about any of that."

"Enjoy your time with Pierre. Just text me if you ever want me to feed her. I don't mind doing it. I'm out there all day anyway."

She smiles. "Thank you."

"Hey…how are the burns today?"

Her nose crinkles. "You're so sweet to check on that each day. There's one area that's going to take a while to go away, I think. It's not hurting quite as much though."

I nod. "Let me know if you need any more of the stuff Wyatt brought over and I can bug him about it."

"You're the best, Callum."

She steps forward, and my heart trips over itself. Her hands rest on my shoulders and she leans in and kisses my cheek.

She smells so sweet, and her lips feel like the softest bit of heaven on my skin.

"If you think *I'm* the best, you need to meet more people," I say under my breath.

She giggles, stepping back and looking up at me. "Nope. You can't convince me you're not the biggest teddy bear in Landmark Mountain."

I lift an eyebrow and shake my head. "You haven't been anywhere but right here. Of course I'm the best when all you've seen is Bill…and cows and goats…"

"Don't forget your whole family," she adds.

"Right," I say, suddenly at a loss.

In a big family, it's normal to be compared to your siblings all the time. At least I guess it is since that's how it's been with ours. I've never minded it. Everyone in town, and even within our family, talks like it's a given that Sutton is the man in charge. He's a judge, he gets shit done, everyone listens to him. Wyatt is the smart one who saves lives. Theo is the charmer who saves animals, and Scarlett is the beautiful life of the party who is such a people person, she could've run the lodge by herself at sixteen if Granddad hadn't been such a control freak.

And then there's me, the grouch who dabbles in an

organic dairy farm. Or to the critics, the owner of the geriatric bovine retirement home.

The only thing people take seriously about me is that they'd rather not get stuck next to me at a party because I sure as hell won't be bothered to make small talk.

I've been content to have the focus on everyone but me. That's the way I like it.

But there's something about hearing that Ruby prefers *me*.

I don't know why it makes something warm settle in my chest.

"I've been working on a few branding ideas for you. Maybe I could show them to you sometime soon...I need to make a few more tweaks before I'm ready to show you."

"That's...thanks. Yes. I'd love to see."

There are a few beats of awkwardness as she moves past me.

"Is Pierre picking you up?" I ask when she reaches the door.

"No, I called an Uber driver."

"*Ruby*, I could've dropped you off. I'm supposed to meet Grinny over at The Pink Ski anyway..."

"Oh, it's okay." She laughs and she's more nervous than I've seen her in days. "I've already put you out enough."

"It's no trouble, Ruby. If you need a ride or even to borrow my truck—just ask. As you know, I'm a homebody. I'll be at the farmer's market on Saturday, but other than that, no big plans."

"Except your date with Grinny tonight," she says, smiling.

"Except that." I grin.

She glances at her phone. "The driver's here. I better hurry." She walks to the door and looks at me over her shoulder. "This isn't goodbye—I don't know why I'm sad all of a sudden."

"You know where to find me." My voice is hoarse and I clear my throat before adding, "See you around, Ruby Sunshine."

"See you around," she says.

"I can't stop staring at you!" Grinny says, clasping her hands together. "Your hair hasn't been this short since high school. I absolutely love it."

I laugh. Doesn't surprise me one bit that Grinny's thrilled about my haircut. She's never given me a hard time about my messy hair, but she's strongly hinted at how she misses seeing my eyes. They've never been in hiding, so the only assessment to be made is that she thinks my hair is too long.

"You don't look like a serial killer at all," she says.

I laugh. "That is some high praise," I tease.

Her shoulders shake as she laughs. "You know I never thought you did anyway, but when Scarlett told us what Jamison had said about you looking like a cross between a model lumberjack and a serial killer, it sorta stuck, didn't it?"

"Idiot," I grumble.

She gives my shoulder a nudge.

"Language," she says, laughing again.

I pull into the parking lot, glad Grinny made a reservation. The place is hopping as usual this time of year.

"Go ahead and order dinner if you haven't eaten yet," she says, as I open her door and help her out of my truck. "I took a nap, so I'd be good company this late." She pretends to be offended when I chuckle. It's only seven fifteen. "But you know me—my appetite is conditioned to eat by five, so I'll be eating dessert." She laughs and pats my arm.

"I think I will. Sorry, I couldn't meet you earlier. My packaging for the milk and cheese came in and I knew if I didn't work on that until it was done, I wouldn't be ready for the farmer's market."

She waves me off. "I'm just lucky to see you at all. I'll take all the time with you I can get."

I know she only means it in the sweetest way, but I feel the guilt nonetheless. Grinny has never asked much of us kids beyond wanting to spend time with us. I see her a couple times a week, usually just the two of us for lunch or dinner once a week and then the family dinner on Sundays, but with Granddad gone, I should be spending more time with her. There's usually a random time thrown in, something unplanned, whether it's running into her at the store, or her stopping by to say hello to the animals.

I squeeze her hand and she beams up at me.

A few girls are coming out of the restaurant as we're walking inside and they stop and stare at me. It's so strange, I turn around to see if someone's behind me, but it's just us on the sidewalk. I take the door and it seems to jar them. They stumble out and one of them says, "I can't believe it. He is *so hot.*"

I glance at Grinny and her eyes are wide and twinkling.

"Sounds like I'm not the only one who thinks you're handsome," she says.

I groan and that just makes her laugh harder.

When we step inside The Pink Ski, Sally Shire walks forward, her arms outstretched. Grinny hugs her and when she steps back, Sally's mouth drops.

"Callum Landmark, is that you?"

"Has no one ever seen a haircut?" I say under my breath.

"Not on *you* very often, that's for sure." Sally doesn't miss a beat. She hugs me tight and steps back, her hand on my jaw as she reaches up to study my face. "I think I know now why you've been hiding this face—you didn't want to show your brothers up!"

She and Grinny cackle.

"Like that could ever happen," I say.

Sally's eyebrows lift. "You're all exceptionally good-looking men, but I gotta say, the perfectly *coifed* model lumberjack look works for me." She winks and then laughs again when I groan.

"Is there anyone in town who *hasn't* heard that line?" I ask.

"Oh, quit your grousing," Grinny says.

"Jamison described perfectly what everyone in this town already thought," Sally says, leading us to a table. "Do you want your usual drink?"

I nod.

"Yes, please," Grinny says. "And I'll only be getting dessert, but Callum will be having dinner."

A table of tourists are loud as we're walking by and then they go silent. Sally glances over and makes a face so I look too. It's a table of five women and every single one of them has their phones up. I can't tell if they're taking a picture or all on a video chat.

It's always been strange to me how everyone is on their phone all the time, but this seems extreme.

But to each their own. I guess if it makes them happy, so be it.

Sally leaves us with the menus even though we know it by heart. I still look at it like it will tell me something new.

"The girls and I will be stopping by the farmer's market

on Saturday. We need to stock up for Thanksgiving," Grinny says.

"I can't believe it's already almost Thanksgiving."

"Just next week," she says. "Should I set an extra place setting for Ruby?"

I frown. "Why would you do that?"

"Well, she's *living* with you. Seems like the considerate thing to do."

"Oh, right. No. She left tonight. Pierre is back in town, so she'll be staying there now."

She makes a face. "Well, that won't be comfortable for either one of them. Have you not been to Pierre's before?"

I squint down at the table trying to remember when I would've been at his place. "Not that I recall. Does he still live way down Heritage, in that last house?"

"No, he hasn't been there for a while, although I believe he still owns that place and rents it out in the busy seasons. He's been in the same condos as Wyatt for years now."

I run my hand down my jaw. "I'm not sure Ruby was aware of that. Fairly certain she's not."

She lifts her shoulder. "You have all the room in the world, and the perfect place for Dolly," she says nonchalantly. "No reason she should uproot that sweet bird all over again."

"Mm-hmm," I mutter.

"What?" she asks innocently.

"I see that look in your eyes, Grin."

"I don't know what you mean."

"Put all of that matchmaking out of your mind."

"She's such a lovely girl," Grinny tsks. "Why *wouldn't* you pursue someone like her? I know you like the ladies… that's still true, isn't it?"

I snort. "Yes, I still like the ladies."

"Well then. Ruby is absolutely delightful. And she seemed very fond of you. Why not ask her out?"

"Besides the fact that she's not a local? She's also nine years younger than me...*and* she hasn't been out of a relationship for long."

That's downplaying it, I know, since Ruby was literally a runaway *bride*...but that doesn't feel like my story to tell.

She shakes her head, her smile widening. "Those are not issues at all. Except for her not living here." She leans in closer. "You just need to give her a reason to stay."

"Not what I excel at," I grumble.

"Nonsense. You are so good at—" She pauses and turns to look at me before glancing at the table across from us. "Are those girls taking photographs of you?"

I glance over at the table and see the back of five heads, their phones held up high, as they selfie themselves and...me.

The fuck?

CHAPTER THIRTEEN

WAKE-UP CALL

RUBY

"It is so good to see you, Uncle Pierre." I reach across the table to squeeze his arm as he smiles at me. "And I love The Dancing Emu. *Absolutely love it.*"

His eyes crinkle at the sides as he looks around his restaurant. It's bustling around here, and there have been times he's had to go take care of business throughout the night, but we've still managed to have the best visit.

"I can't tell you how wonderful it is to have you here," he says. "I feel terrible that I wasn't here when you needed me."

"No, please don't. There's no way you could've known I was going to bail on my wedding and come here."

He makes a sad face, his large brown eyes full of concern. "Now that I hear the details about Junior, I'm relieved you didn't marry him. He sure played the martyr card that day. What an *ass*."

"No one deserves to be left on their wedding day, but…"

"*Junior* did," Uncle Pierre jumps in. "Don't you dare feel bad for him. I'm having a hard time not being angry with your parents about signing away that property when it should have been yours. That will take me a while to work through. Believe me, I let your mother know my feelings." His eyes lift to give me a pointed look. "But anyone who belittles you the way Junior did…it's just not acceptable." He shakes his head and sucks a breath between his teeth. "If I'd heard the things he said and you *didn't* leave him, I would've hauled you out of there myself. I'm still irate that he used the word *meh* regarding you. There is nothing about you that is not fabulous."

"Says my uncle." I laugh.

"Not even. It's just the truth." He leans in and whispers. "Table to your left, four tourists. Not one of those men can take their eyes off of you. Same with these two on the other side. I'm starting to get jealous," he says drily. "Junior deserves to be single and sad about it for the rest of his life."

"Speaking of single…is there anyone special in your life?" I ask.

"No, no." He shakes his head, but the way his expression changes makes me push.

"No one?"

"No one worth fighting for," he says, the lighthearted tone he's had all evening sounding flat now.

"Sounds like there's a story there."

"Just a little good old-fashioned rivalry and denial," Pierre says, shrugging.

"Ooo, do tell."

"Nothing to tell, trust me. Jack over at The Gnarly Vine likes to pretend my adorable place and I do *not* exist...like his elegant establishment with its wines and charcuterie boards and his sickeningly perfect white wavy hair are too good for little ole me." He puts his hands under his chin and gives me a fake smile.

I frown. "You are six feet of fine, Uncle Pierre. Jack's perfect white wavy hair can't have anything on you. And what you've done to the place—I've only ever seen pictures of what it was like before, but this...it's amazing! Easily the most charming place I've ever seen. The detailing in the woodwork, the enchanted forest feel...I absolutely love it. I'm sure Jack is just jealous of his competition."

He rolls his eyes. "Doubtful. His place is pretty great." He leans in and whispers, "Callum checks in with me before he places an order at The Gnarly Vine to see if I want anything and then drops mine off before he heads home...it's a great arrangement."

My cheeks heat just hearing Callum's name and how thoughtful he is.

Uncle Pierre smirks and looks around the restaurant once more to make sure no one is listening before he whispers, "Jack is none the wiser. He makes the best wood-fired pizza, but you did *not* hear that from me. On the rare occasions he comes out of hiding in his kitchen, he claims I'm an over-grown hobbit."

My eyes widen. "*Rude*. But…if this is what a hobbit's house looks like, count me in."

He sits up straight and his head falls back as he laughs. "Exactly. I couldn't have said it better myself." His face is wistful as he glances around his restaurant. "I'd hoped your mom would be running this place with me one day, but… when our parents divorced, she went with Mom…even though she didn't want to. It was complicated. You knew Grandma well, so I'm sure you have some idea of how difficult the situation was." He crinkles his nose. "But then your mom met your dad and he stole her heart."

"I don't understand why she never came back, not even for visits," I say. "It always sounded like she loved growing up here."

"She did," he says softly. "I think she loved it too much. Your dad had that land in Utah, so that's where they settled, and once she started doing her thing with the emus there…I knew then she wasn't coming back."

"Do you miss having emus?" I grin, hoping it will pave the way for the Dolly conversation.

I had no idea I'd have such a hard time bringing her up.

"Yes, but mostly no," he says. "It was hard when Dean and Frank died, really hard. They were all I had left of our emu family. But once this place took off and I made the decision to move into my condo, it got so much easier."

I'm nodding sadly until he says that last sentence. And then I think surely I've misheard.

"What did you say?" I lean in. "What about a condo?"

"Oh, just that it helped so much to leave the Heritage house. I'm much happier in my condo now."

"You sold your *house*?" My voice shakes slightly and Uncle Pierre's brow furrows as he reaches over and squeezes my arm.

"Oh honey, sorry, no…" He laughs and gives my arm another pat before taking a drink. "That house is still ours. I'm not pulling a June on you." He rolls his eyes. "I love my sister, but sometimes…I don't know where her head is. Don't you worry—when and if we decide to sell the property, it'll be a family decision. Anyway…I rent out the house, pretty much full-time to long-termers. The guests that are there now are staying a month, but often I have people in there for the season." His lip pokes out as he nods proudly. "I've done a lot of work on it and it's beautiful, if I do say so myself. Boho chic, original woodwork, but everything else is modernized. If you'd like, I'm sure I can get you in there to see it."

"I'd love that."

"Your mom might have told you the barn was destroyed in a snowstorm a few years back."

I sag against my barstool. "No, she didn't."

"*That* was a sad day. A huge chunk of our history gone, just like that. I haven't had the heart to rebuild it…or the time," he says, chuckling softly. "I wish you could've seen it though."

"I wish I'd found a way to get here sooner. I've always wanted to visit…"

"You had your hands full taking care of the emus. I swear, you were running that farm when you were five years old."

I laugh and nod. "You're not wrong. And seeing how busy you've been here, it means all the more that you've always made time to come to us."

"I gave up on begging my sister to bring you or to let you come on your own." He gives me a look. "But I can't believe you didn't *know* I'd be at your wedding."

"I should've. I've been on autopilot for a long time now. The business…" I shake my head. "I—"

"Excuse me, are you that girl on TikTok with the RV and

emus?" Two girls my age or a little younger stand near our table, looking excited.

One of them is wearing my *Own Your Emotions* T-shirt.

I flush. It never fails to both thrill and embarrass me when I get noticed in public. I'm used to it happening at home and even in the bigger cities in Utah, but I can't believe it's happening *here*. Landmark Mountain is small and cozy, but the amount of traffic to get here tonight was intense. I've heard we're deep into tourist season, and after tonight, I believe it.

"That's me," I say, laughing. "I'm Ruby."

"Oh my God. I knew it," the girl says. "It's great to meet you. We are huge fans...I'm Ana and this is Mae. When we saw The Dancing Emu, we had to come here. I can't believe you're here! This is my favorite shirt," she gushes.

"Will you be restocking the Emused hoodie?" Mae asks.

"Definitely."

"Yay," Ana says. "I love your RV stuff too, but the emus get me every time. Would it be okay if we get a picture with you?"

"Sure." I look at Uncle Pierre. "Would you mind taking our picture?"

He looks delighted as he shoots me a look and holds out his hand for their phones. "Of course I don't mind. I'm the proud uncle," he tells the girls.

"And the owner of this place," I add.

The girls get on either side of me.

"We love this place," Mae says. "Oh my *God*, I can't believe we're meeting you!" she squeals.

I laugh. "It's great to meet you both."

Uncle Pierre takes a few pictures and then tells them to check to see if they're okay.

"Ooo, I love that, a professional photographer uncle too," Ana says.

Uncle Pierre cracks up over that.

"These are so good," Mae says, looking at her phone. When she puts her phone in her bag, she glances around the restaurant. "So, is this where that hot guy you posted lives? Wow." She fans her face. "Whew." And then she makes a sympathetic expression. "I was sad to hear you're not with your fiancé anymore, but good riddance if he didn't appreciate you, know what I'm saying?" She leans in closer. "And I can see why you'd move on with that guy."

"Oh, I haven't moved on with anyone," I jump in.

"Well, you *should*," Mae says. "He's giving me total Conrad Fisher vibes."

Ana frowns. "He's like a thousand times better looking than Conrad Fisher. And a *man*."

"I *know*," Mae says emphatically. "I said the Conrad Fisher *vibe*. That aloof, moody, so hot-they-can't-even-be-bothered thing that we love."

I try so hard not to laugh.

"Who is Conrad Fisher?" Uncle Pierre asks.

Thank you. I wanted to ask, but I'm glad he beat me to it.

"*The Summer I Turned Pretty*?" Mae says.

"Oh." Uncle Pierre still looks confused.

I file it away to look up when I get home. I haven't had time to watch or read anything in such a long time.

"Thanks again. I'm glad you're as nice as you seem in your videos," Ana says.

"She's the best there is," Uncle Pierre says.

"Thank you. That's really kind." I wave as they walk away and look back at me one more time.

"And you're famous," Uncle Pierre says, clapping. "June

said you get recognized all the time in Utah, but I love seeing it with my own eyes right here!"

"Semi-famous in a very niche category." I laugh.

"You cannot possibly downplay that. She was wearing your merch!"

I put my hands on my cheeks to cool them off and it's a good thing, because his next words are, "They were talking about Callum, weren't they?" He holds up his hands. "I promise you I'm normally up-to-date on all your posts, but I got a little behind with being out of town. What have I missed?" He does a little shimmy in his seat.

"Nothing." But my face flames even hotter as I think about the night before. Those sounds he made. God. It was…I put my glass of iced water against my cheek and take a deep breath, looking around to make sure there are no Landmarks nearby. "Yes, I posted a video of Callum."

"He is exceptional, isn't he? They all are." He sighs. "But those oldest two get my heart rate pumping a little extra. I don't know what it is exactly—Wyatt and Theo are gorgeous and absolutely wonderful, but Sutton and Callum…" He shakes his head. "They couldn't be more different from one another." His eyes bulge comically. "Sadly, they're as straight as that shelf hanging over there." He points to the bar and I turn to look, nodding in approval when I see how straight it is. "One of the few times I've ever used a leveler." He winks. "So tell me everything."

"Uh, there's really nothing to tell," I say.

It's not like I can tell him I can't stop touching myself since arriving at Callum's house.

And I've heard what he sounds like when he comes.

And I've grown to love waking up at 4:45 in the morning because I know I'll get to see him first thing.

And his excitement over chocolate pie is the cutest thing on EARTH.

"What is that smile?" Uncle Pierre smirks. "Spill. I'll understand, trust me. I've had my fair share of crushes on older men...how much older is he than you?"

"Nine years. But I wouldn't say I have a crush on him." *I totally have a crush on him.* "Callum has been amazing. I don't even have enough nice things to say about him. The way I showed up here and he opened his home to me...longer than he expected."

Uncle Pierre cringes, mouthing, *Sorry.*

"No, please don't keep apologizing. I threw everything off with my escape." I laugh. "But he's been so...chill about the whole thing. Even about Dolly, which could've sent him—"

"Who's Dolly?" he interrupts.

"Oh...yeah. Dolly." I make a face. "So it was really hard to leave all my emus...I still don't know what to do about it and have got to start figuring it out, but...there was one emu I couldn't leave. Dolly. She's here with me...I'd thought she could go in your barn, but...you don't have one." I laugh awkwardly.

"Oh, honey," he says. His face quickly brightens. "But Callum has plenty of room? And she's getting along with his crew?"

I nod, unable to keep the huge smile from taking over my face at the thought of Dolly with the cows and goats. "She fits right in. If I gave in to what I wanted to post every day, it'd be a gold mine." I laugh. "I've taken it slowly since I've been his surprise guest, but it is nonstop fun over there with the animals."

And like those girls said, the hotness factor is off the charts with Callum around.

"I'd love to see that," he says, chuckling. "I'm not asking this to put any pressure on you, because goodness knows, I'd love to see you stay right here forever...but do you have any idea of what you're doing next?"

I fall back against the back of my stool. "My battery still isn't in for the RV, and I can't exactly travel with an emu. Not for long anyway. Callum has said she's fine staying there, but he can't possibly be okay with that for any extended period of time." I lean against my hand, suddenly more overwhelmed than I've been since I got here. "Everything I've made has gone to keeping the farm going...and the wedding." My eyes get blurry as I try not to cry. "Which feels really stupid right about now."

Uncle Pierre has scooted closer and his own eyes fill as he listens. He's always been so sweet, so empathetic.

"Junior isn't going to take care of the emus, so I need to figure out good homes for them...and a place to live."

"You're welcome to stay with me as long as you like," Uncle Pierre says.

"Thank you. I know you mean it too, but you're not even in the house anymore...how much room do you have at your condo?"

He opens his mouth and closes it, waving his hand. "We'll make do. And the house is booked solid for the next nine months with different renters, but I'll cap it there. You can move in there late-summer and in the meantime, we'll work on barn plans."

"No. I can't ask you to do that." I shake my head. "I love you for offering, but I—"

"I insist," he says. "Sweetheart, we will work it out. Don't you worry. Now that I've got you here, I really don't want to let you go. Come see my condo. We'll figure it out."

His condo is beautiful. Clean, decorated so cute, and only

one bed in the place. And it's not that I'm picky, but his couch isn't even a full-sized one that I could stretch out on.

When I set my overnight bag next to the couch, he shakes his head and moves it toward the bedroom. "You're in here."

"Uncle Pierre..."

"I don't want to hear it," he calls over his shoulder.

I'll stay here tonight, but tomorrow I'll have to come up with a new plan.

CHAPTER FOURTEEN

CLARIFICATION

CALLUM

RUBY

I'm sorry to waffle on this, but I'd like to take you up on that offer to check on Dolly tonight. I'd really hoped I could get back over there after we left the restaurant, but Uncle Pierre and I stayed later than I expected and just got to his place. We've had a lot to catch up on.

I read her text a few times before answering, trying to read through the lines to see if she's upset or surprised about Pierre's condo.

Finally, I text back.

I'd be happy to.

RUBY

Thank you so much, Callum!

I groan, swiping my hand down my face. Why does an image of her smiling at me, thanking me for the umpteenth time as she tugs her sweater over her head fill my head so clearly?

It hasn't been long since I got back from dinner with Grinny, and I can't believe how empty the house feels without Ruby. I hurry out to the barn to check on things, stopping to see Dolly last. She comes up and nuzzles my hand, but keeps checking the door to see if Ruby is there.

"You'll see her tomorrow," I tell her.

Dolly does her drumming sound.

"Yeah, I miss her too," I say softly.

Dolly amps it up and I nod.

"I know. It's weird how she fills up the space with all that…joy. Didn't know I was into that sort of thing," I admit.

Dolly comes over and stares at me, unblinking for a few long beats. When she moves in closer, I don't know whether to back out quickly or to stay as still as possible. I opt for the latter, and am in for a sweet surprise when she turns and rests the side of her face to my chest.

"Well, this is sweet," I whisper.

I reach up and pet her the way Ruby does and she stays there next to me for a few minutes. When she backs away and walks to her bowl to take a drink, I clear my throat.

"I'll see you in the morning, Dolly. Sleep well, okay?"

She looks up at me and her neck bobs like she's agreeing with me. Holy shit, I wouldn't have been able to leave her behind either.

After I've gone inside and showered, I climb into bed and pick up my phone. I can't sleep and it's late enough that I think maybe Ruby and Pierre have gone to bed by now. But just in case she's concerned, I shoot her a text.

> Dolly is doing just fine. I get why you love her.

RUBY

> I love her so much. Are you saying this because she's the cutest thing you've ever seen?

. . .

She's cute, but no. She kind of…
hugged me.

RUBY

NO WAY. I can't believe it! She's only ever
done that with me! I'm gonna cry.

Don't worry. She still loves you most.

RUBY

No, I'm not jealous. That's just so sweet and
I miss her.

She misses you too. Kept looking to see if
you were coming.

RUBY

You're breaking my heart.

> She's fine.

RUBY

I'll be over as soon as I drop Uncle Pierre off at The Dancing Emu. We're having breakfast early, so I should be there in plenty of time to feed Dolly.

> Take your time. If you're not here by the time she usually eats, I'll feed her.

RUBY

You're the best, Callum.

> So you say. Sweet dreams, Ruby Sunshine.

I want to say *Think of me in your quiet time*, but…I don't. My thoughts sure go to what she might be doing alone in her bed though.

The next morning, I drag. I'm slow to get breakfast done and even after a second cup of coffee, I'm achy and just can't seem to get going. When Delphine and Irene start misbehaving, the void of Ruby around here is even more noticeable.

She'd be cracking up and distracting them out of their mischief.

When I round the corner a few hours later and see her walking toward me in her tight jeans and a light brown down jacket that matches her eyes, I instantly feel...*relieved.*

It's short-lived because when I grin at her, she returns it, but it's dim. It doesn't reach her eyes and she looks worried.

"What's wrong?" I ask.

Her brows crinkle in the center.

"Am I that obvious?" She laughs, but it's forced.

"Yes."

She exhales and points toward Dolly's stall. We walk there and I wait for her to start talking. She's quiet until she sees Dolly and then she talks to her, petting her and putting her food out. As Dolly starts eating, Ruby looks at me again.

"I had a great time with Uncle Pierre. And he's so willing to do whatever he can, excited that I'm here and all that. Which is just..." She puts her hand on her heart like she's moved.

"But?"

"His circumstances are just a little different than I realized," she says. "He doesn't even have the barn I've heard about all my life...that housed all the emus." She makes a face. "Which I should've never assumed was still here, but...I had no idea that was gone or that he'd moved into a one-bedroom condo."

I grimace. "I was afraid you might not have known that. Grinny told me last night about the condo—I didn't realize he didn't still live in that house on Heritage."

"And I talked to Junior yesterday," she adds.

My blood does that slow roll into a boil the way it's done since I first heard what an ass he is.

"As soon as my RV is fixed, I need to get back to Utah and see what I can do about the emus."

I knew her visit was temporary, but still, I was hoping it wouldn't be this soon.

"I just have no desire to be there…at all."

This perks me up. "Really? You're not missing home?"

"Not even a little bit." She glances at me shyly. "I *really* like it here."

My heart gallops out of my chest.

Her cheeks flush. "I mean, last night, seeing how cute everything looks decorated for Christmas…and The Dancing Emu is amazing…"

"Oh, right." Does my disappointment show that she wasn't talking about me when she said that? "Yeah, the town goes all out for the holidays."

"But I don't trust Junior to take care of things on the farm, and my cousin Kess promised she'd look after them, but she's in school full-time and will be moving to California in January. She doesn't really have the time to focus on this too."

"Does Junior want you back?"

Of course, he does, what am I saying?

She gets a strange expression on her face and shakes her head. "No. I mean, yes, he's pretending to be all sad about things, but I think he's really just embarrassed that I didn't marry him. He says I'm overreacting…and that what I overheard him say was just…the way guys talk."

"What did he say?" I grit out, already knowing I won't like it.

This woman thinks the best about everyone and everything. For her to walk away from him, he can't be a good guy, that's all there is to it.

She takes a deep breath and Dolly comes over by her, like she can tell Ruby is unhappy about something.

"I heard his friend Mitch ask if Junior was really ready to be married. Mitch is not the best." She makes a face. "And Junior said outright that it was only for a year." She pets Dolly, her eyes distant. "I like his friend Charlie a lot more, even though what he said that day sounded pervy." Her cheeks get pink and she glances at me, embarrassed. "Charlie said if *he* had me in his bed, he'd keep me for longer than a year." She starts talking faster and has no idea how I'm fuming. "And what Junior said next is what I've repeated to my family because it was just so…I don't know…degrading? But really, the whole tone of the conversation was just as bad."

"What. Did. He. Say?"

Her eyes flicker to mine in surprise and her mouth parts. "Uh, he said, 'Meh,' which really isn't the worst thing someone could say about me, but…*meh? Really?* That's what he says about me to his friends on our wedding day? And then he sort of corrected his statement by saying, 'No, she *is* a great lay,' and that he wasn't quite ready to give that up." She rolls her eyes. "But the damage had been done, right? Not what anyone wants to hear from their future husband. And then that the real prize is the land he's getting…that the wedding was just a formality. He had the audacity to laugh about my parents' peace and love bullshit and how they believed the land was mine too, but that my name was not on the deed. And if all that's not bad enough…they laughed about Dolly and called her an idiot."

She turns to look at me, fire in her eyes now, and I have to bite back a grin. "That's the line that sealed it for you, isn't it?"

"You're damn straight it is!" She puts her hand on Dolly's

back. "She's the smartest emu I've ever met, and I've met a lot."

"Ruby?"

"Yeah?"

"That is *not* the way guys fucking talk. My brothers and I talk about everything…well…*they* talk about everything with me," I pause and she smiles, "and they'd never talk about someone they love like that. Ever. We wouldn't talk about anyone like that. It's sweet that you're fired up about Dolly, and it's understandable to be upset about his fuckery with the land, but the way he made you feel small, the way he laughed about you…*that* is inexcusable, and reason enough for you to stay the hell away from him."

Her eyes fill with tears.

"Do you hear what I'm saying?" I say softly.

She nods and when a tear drops down her cheek, I catch it with my thumb and wipe it away.

"He didn't deserve your sunshine," I whisper.

She gulps and another tear drips down her cheek. Dolly's drum starts sounding off and Ruby pets her.

"I'm okay," she tells her. "Thank you, Callum," she says shakily. "That…really means a lot."

Her face clouds over and the next thing I know, I'm pulling her to my chest and holding her tight. When it seems like her tears have stopped, I lean back and look at her.

"Your sadness kills me," I tell her.

"This is…the happiest I've ever been," she says, more tears dripping down.

I can't help it. I chuckle and she laughs through her tears.

"I mean it. No one has ever made me feel," she pauses and swallows hard, "as cherished as you just did."

"Don't settle for anything less," I say. "Okay?"

Her intake is shaky, but she nods. "Okay."

"Now…this living situation with your uncle. I think you should just move back into your room here. What do you think?"

Her mouth drops again. "Uh. I think you're being too nice."

"Dolly would be miserable if you lived with Uncle Pierre."

She laughs, wiping her face again. "It's only until my battery comes."

There it is, that reminder that she's still leaving after all this. I barrel through anyway.

"All the more reason to keep her happy before you take her on the road again."

She pauses, contemplating what I've said. "Are you one hundred percent sure you're okay with this?"

"Wouldn't have said it if I wasn't."

"Right." She grins. "I guess I could stay. This will make it easier for me to help you with the farmer's market this week-end. Nuh-uh," she says when I start to protest. "That's the condition I'm bringing to this. If I stay, I'll be doing a lot more to help out around here."

I shrug. "Or you could also use this time to chill and catch up on whatever you need to…maybe sleep in once in a while." I smirk when her eyes narrow.

"Nope," she says.

"Suit yourself."

There's no sign of tears now. Her smile is like a rainbow breaking through a storm.

"I will…roomie," she says.

I snort and we walk out of Dolly's stall. I feel much better than I did earlier, happy to say I'm not getting sick after all.

"I'm gonna call Uncle Pierre and let him know the new plan."

"He's welcome over here anytime too, just...make yourself at home."

She pauses and looks over to smile at me, her eyes intense as she nods. "I'll tell him you said that."

The day flies by. In the afternoon when my energy is lagging, Ruby comes walking out in the pasture with Dolly.

"Will it bother you if I play some music?" she asks.

"No."

Even though I'm prepared for it, I startle when I hear the music boom through the speakers. Dolly takes off like a shot and Ruby follows after her, Dolly's manic dance next to Ruby's graceful leaps are a sight to behold. I laugh until my stomach hurts and I watch spellbound, as they move across the field. Delphine and Irene stand next to me, watching too.

"What do you think of those two?" I ask them.

Irene harrumphs and Delphine burrows her head into my pocket, nuzzling my side.

"Yep, agreed," I say, giving them both a treat. "You said it better than I ever could."

CHAPTER FIFTEEN

SMALL TALK

RUBY

"How'd you ever do this without me?" I ask Callum, as we pack up the displays for the farmer's market.

We sold out of everything, and there was a long line the entire day.

"After today, I'm not sure," he admits. "It's usually busy, but that was nonstop. You were a huge help."

"Your haircut seems to be a big hit too," I say slyly.

He gives me the side-eye before walking to the truck. "I think you've found your new vocation."

"Not even close. You're just good material to work with."

"You make me sound like a piece of wood." His ears turn pink and I love that I can see when that happens now, thanks to his haircut.

"Here we are, talking about your wood again," I tease.

His chuckle is low and makes me squeeze my legs together. My own cheeks turn pink with my boldness and I turn away so he can't see how flustered I am.

I check under our area to make sure we haven't forgotten anything and nearly run into Callum when I turn back around.

"Oh, 'scuse me," I whisper. "Thought you were by the truck."

His gaze sweeps over my face, pausing on my lips and then back to my eyes. "You up for Sunny Side with everyone? I let Pierre pick the place since he doesn't get to many restaurants besides his own."

"I've never been. I'm excited. I really want to try The Gnarly Vine and The Pink Ski too. I love all these cute names. At home, we had Frankie's and Diner K...which are fine, but they don't have the same pizazz as Sunny Side and all the others. Sunny Side is my favorite for obvious reasons." I do jazz hands every time I say *Sunny Side* and he chuckles.

That low, raspy chuckle has become my favorite sound. It's like an instant flood of endorphins every time I hear it.

We start walking to the truck and when I get in, I shiver. Callum looks at me as he turns the ignition. We had little heaters outside, but there were times when my hands were still chilly.

"You're cold." He frowns. "If you're with me next time, I'll bring another heater." He pushes the button to turn on my seat warmer.

"I'm okay. I wasn't cold while it was happening. Now that the rush is over, I'm noticing it, but I was fine."

He nods. "Okay, good. You'd like Tiptop too," Callum says. "Not as cutesy a name for a restaurant around here, but that's because my friend Blake named it instead of his wife Camilla. She would've been more creative if she'd been around when he first opened."

"I haven't heard about that one yet. I guess now that I've been here for two weeks, it's time to branch out a little."

"You mean I can't keep you all to myself anymore?" he asks, glancing at me.

My mouth waters and I swallow hard. "Is that what you've been doing?"

He smirks and shrugs. "I prefer to think of it as allowing you time to recover from your...strenuous circumstances, but...yeah, I was hogging you."

A delighted laugh bursts out of me and it makes Callum's smile widen. My heart practically thumps out of my skin.

"I needed the downtime more than you know," I say. "If I hadn't run into your snowdrift when I did and had this peaceful break—sort of like a forced vacation—I think I would've shut down or gotten sick. I was headed toward losing it for a while there...haven't really admitted that to myself before now, but it's the truth. It's been a long year." When I look at him, he's listening intently, his eyes warm. "What are you thinking right now?"

He smiles. "I'm thinking that only you would think getting up at 4:45 every morning for the past two weeks is a *peaceful break*."

I crack up at that. "I meant it!" I insist.

"I'm glad you found your way here, Ruby Sunshine."

Happiness buzzes through me and I smile all the way to Sunny Side. It's adorable inside with yellow and white booths and turquoise accents. The Sunny Side branding is stellar with its yellow sun and clean black lines rising over the horizon. Callum's family and Uncle Pierre are already there when we arrive, filling a long table and the surrounding cluster of booths. The place is humming with their chatter. Everyone says hello. Scarlett, Sofie, and Dakota come hug me, and I look around for Marlow.

"Your mom's not here?" I ask Dakota.

"Not yet. She and my Wyatt wanted to go to the farmer's market, but the baby is making Mama's stomach feel yuck."

"Oh no. I'm sorry to hear that," I say, swooning at how she says *my Wyatt*.

"Me too. It sounded very awful hearing her frow—throw up," she corrects herself, her little nose scrunching up.

"Poor Lo," Sofie says. "Hopefully this phase will pass soon. She wasn't sick for long with you, peanut," she tells Dakota. "Let's hope that carries over."

Dakota sighs and nods like a grown-up and then her whole countenance changes when she sees Callum. She wraps her arms around his waist.

"I didn't see you yet!" she squeals.

She lifts her arms and he picks her up without hesitation, giving her the biggest hug.

"You doin' all right?" he asks when she pulls back and pats his face, studying him carefully.

"Your face isn't hiding," she says. "Where are all your hairs?" She pats his face again. "There's not very many on your face, and"—she tugs his hair—"short," she says matter-of-factly.

"What do you think?" He makes a funny face and she cackles. "Should I grow back my hairs and keep this face hidden?"

"No," she says, laughing harder when he makes another face.

"You sure?"

"I'm sure." She tries to catch her breath, still giggling as she pats the top of his head. "You're pretty, Uncle Callum."

He groans. "Thank you, Kota," he forces out, shooting me a look when I giggle.

A few people I don't recognize are sitting next to Grinny and Sutton, and the adorable elderly man next to Uncle Pierre stands up when Callum and I walk over.

"You must be Ruby," he says, holding out his hand.

It's more of a squeeze than a handshake, both of his hands encircling mine. My heart has already melted.

"I've heard so much about you," he adds. "I'm Pappy, Jamison's grandpa...and I'm a lucky guy because this crew around here has welcomed me in too. Here, have a seat."

He motions for me to take the seat next to Uncle Pierre.

"It's nice to meet you," I tell him. "I don't want to steal your seat though!"

He chuckles. "I've been wandering to each table saying hi. I think I left my jacket at that table, so I should probably get over there." He beams at me and walks over to Grinny and Sutton's table.

Scarlett and Dakota go back to their seats next to Jamison.

"Pappy's adorable," I whisper to Sofie.

"Girl. He has every female in Landmark Mountain heart-eyed. He's that amazing all the time," she whispers back. "*Almost* every female."

"How could anyone resist?" I ask.

She shakes her head, her expression turning mischievous when she looks over at his table. He's saying something to Grinny, his smile wide, and she flushes and shakes her head, looking more serious than I've seen her.

"It takes a very strong and stubborn woman to resist," she says, chuckling.

"Oh…is something…are *they*—" I stare at Grinny and Pappy and think nothing in the world could be cuter than the two of them together.

She leans in closer. "Between you and me," she whispers, "they both loved their spouses so much, and Pappy's wife has been gone longer than Grinny's husband, but he still talks about her like she hung the moon. It's incredible, the love there. But…" She pauses and then smirks. "I don't know. I could be imagining it all, but they danced at my wedding and…I think I saw something there. Grinny is the nicest, most loving human *ever*, but she gets a little…agitated when Pappy is around."

"But they'd be *so cute*."

"Why don't you join us, Sofie? There's room," Uncle Pierre says, pointing at the chair across from him.

Callum and I are still standing and I don't want to make it look like I'm waiting to see where he sits, even if I am, so I sit down next to Uncle Pierre.

"Oh, Theo's already ordered my pancakes over there. I better go sit with him. I'll be back though," she says, smiling at me.

Callum sits across from me and a cute older lady walks up to the table, pulling out the chair next to Callum. I've noticed her before now, flitting all over the restaurant like a butterfly.

"Grinny told me and Helen you were beautiful, Miss Ruby, and she wasn't kidding," she says, reaching across the table to lift a lock of my hair. She rubs my hair between her fingers and makes a clicking sound with her mouth. "I used to have hair like this," she says.

"Your hair is beautiful," I tell her. And it is. It's not long, but it's thick, and she has great style.

She waves me off and flutters her eyelashes at Callum. "She's sweet too." She winks. "You should keep her."

His eyebrows lift. "Hey, Peg."

"Hey, good-lookin', the haircut is sexy as all get-out."

"Thanks," he says, lifting his eyes to mine.

I'm pressing my lips together to keep from laughing, and Uncle Pierre has already laughed out loud at Peg twice. It doesn't seem to register with her.

She turns her attention back to me. "What are you, 5'9"? 5'9 1/2"?"

"Uh, I think I'm 5'9", yes."

She puts her hand on her heart and shakes her head reverently. "I wanted to be 5'9" so badly. As it was, these short little legs of mine had to work overtime."

"Oh, for goodness' sake, Peg, ease her in slowly," a woman says behind me.

I look back and it's the woman who was sitting with Grinny and Sutton. She has short, permed hair and she's leveling Peg with a look.

"Settle down, Helen," Peg says. "I was just admiring Ruby's long legs. If we can't appreciate one another's strengths, what are we even doing on this planet?"

"If only you'd appreciate strengths beyond the superficial," Helen says primly.

"I appreciate all the strengths," Peg insists.

"Mm-hmm," Helen tuts, but when her gaze turns to mine, it warms. "Hello there. I'm Helen."

"Nice to meet you, Helen," I say, smiling up at her.

"We call Helen, Peg, and Grinny The Golden Girls around here," Uncle Pierre says. "Where you see one, you'll usually see the others."

"Unless I'm with a fella," Peg says, leaning in. "Getting

some lovin' when I can just makes me a better friend all the way around."

"Peg!" Helen says, while Callum and Uncle Pierre laugh.

"You know it's true." Peg laughs. "I become quite cantankerous. Nobody knows that better than my girls." She glances back at Grinny's table. "Speaking of cantankerous, Grinny—"

"Is just fine," Helen finishes, her eyes wide and focused on Peg.

"Right," Peg says, giggling. She glances back at their table again. "That Pappy is a fine specimen. And the only man I've ever come across that hasn't—"

Helen leans down and pats Peg's hand. "Why don't we let them order?"

Peg looks up at Helen and smiles at her and then around the table. "This one tries so hard to keep me in line."

"It's impossible, but I do try," Helen adds.

We all laugh and Peg stands up and moves next to Helen, putting her arm around her. And then she points at me and Callum.

"The two of you would make *outrageously* beautiful children."

"For fuck's sake," Callum grumbles under his breath, shooting me an apologetic look, while I try not to turn bright red.

She's still going. "I never had my own, but I love this boy like he's my own grandson, and I tell you what…he was the most *gorgeous* baby. Most come out looking like little old, wrinkled men, you know? But not the Landmark babies. And especially not this one."

"I knew Callum was your favorite," Sutton says from the other table.

Peg laughs and shakes her head.

Grinny looks over then and her eyes narrow on Peg.

"What are you saying over there, Peg?" Grinny asks.

"Just how beautiful the Landmark babies are," Peg says, full of innocence.

"And in particular, Callum," Sutton adds, smirking at Callum.

Grinny's head tilts and she slowly nods. "He *was* exceptional."

Peg lifts her hands like *See?*

"Still is." Grinny winks.

Amen.

"Wonder what happened?" Callum mutters.

"I heard that, Callum Henry Landmark, and you cannot tell me you don't know how handsome you are!" Peg cries. "Why, I saw people taking pictures of you when you walked by the other night…when you walked in here today too, now that I think about it. There were some girls talking about how *hot* you are…"

Callum frowns, and I shift in my seat. Ana and Mae talked about how hot Callum is—could it have been them? Is it possible that people are recognizing him? No, that wouldn't be happening so fast. Would it?

"I'm so sorry I'm just now getting over here," a woman says, pulling a small notepad out of her apron. "Hi, I'm Jo," she says to me, blowing a strand of hair out of her eyes.

"This is my niece," Uncle Pierre says proudly.

"Oh my gosh, it's so nice to finally meet you!" she says. "I'd heard about you…nothing gets past the gossip mill in Landmark Mountain…"

Her glance at Callum makes me think she heard about me staying with him for sure.

"But I didn't realize you were June's daughter! I can totally see it now," she says. "Your mom was always so pretty. How is she?"

"Thank you. She's doing well. Doing the RV life right now." I smile back at her, feeling somewhat awkward.

"Well, tell her hello from me. I'm quite a few years older than her…actually babysat her and this one a time or two." She smirks at Uncle Pierre.

Someone yells from the kitchen and she looks back.

"That didn't sound good. What can I get for you?"

"I haven't looked at the menu yet," I say apologetically. "What do you recommend?"

"The pancakes are great anytime," she says. "Or the burgers."

"Love the burgers," Sofie says from the other table.

"The omelets are great too," Sutton adds. "And the French dip."

"I feel like the French toast never gets enough credit," Uncle Pierre says. "Or the tomato basil soup."

"Everything sounds so good," I say. "I've had a lot of sweets today, so maybe I'll try your grilled cheese and tomato basil soup?"

"Solid choice," Callum says.

Jo nods, grinning, and looks at Callum. "You switching it up today or do you want your usual?"

"Usual, please."

"Coming right up. What about you, Pierre?"

"Hmm, I need to get here more often. It's so hard to choose," he groans.

"Want me to surprise you?" she asks.

He points his menu at her and beams. "You know me so well."

She grins back and takes our menus before walking away.

"She's nice," I say. "Everyone I've met so far has been."

"I love Jo," Uncle Pierre says. "She and Mark opened this place when I was in high school and I came almost every day for those four years. Did my homework and had lots and lots of talks with both of them. They were, oh, I don't know, eight or nine years older than me, and I thought they were some of the coolest people ever. Still do," he says, grinning. "Jo was the first person I came out to. It wasn't *that* long ago, but we didn't personally know another soul around here who was gay. Tourists, on the other hand, were an education." He lifts his eyebrows. "Jo stood by me, even offered to be there when I told my parents. Held me up when it didn't go so great."

The flicker of pain that crosses his face makes my heart hurt. From conversations I've picked up over the years, I know that my grandma never accepted Uncle Pierre after he told them, and it's what finally came between my grandparents.

"Jo's good people, she and Mark both are." Uncle Pierre clears his throat and makes a face. "Sorry to get heavy on you guys."

"I like hearing the real shit," Callum says.

Uncle Pierre points at him. "One of my favorite things about you. No small talk for you."

Callum tilts his head in acknowledgment.

"Since we got right into it and aren't small talking, anything I should know about you?" Uncle Pierre asks Callum, back to sounding playful.

Callum looks around and leans in, his elbows on the table. Uncle Pierre and I both lean in too, the curiosity growing by the second.

"I think I'm one of the few people who saw Ruby in her wedding dress," Callum says softly, his gaze searing into me.

I gasp and clutch the closest thing on the table, a napkin.

"And that image will be imprinted in my mind forever," he adds.

My mouth drops as I stare at Callum and I turn to look at

Uncle Pierre when he squeezes my knee. His mouth has also fallen open. He turns to stare at me and then back at Callum.

"Damn," Uncle Pierre says, with nothing short of reverence. *"Damn."*

I can't even string together coherent words after that.

CHAPTER SIXTEEN

YOU'VE MADE AN IMPRESSION

CALLUM

I was just trying to have an honest moment, didn't mean to shock both Ruby and Pierre into silence. I figured if anyone wanted to know how beautiful she looked in her wedding dress, it'd be her uncle.

It's a shame everyone missed seeing her in it, and yet, I'm not complaining about that at all.

If she'd gotten married that day, it wouldn't have brought her here.

To me.

She's *not* here for me, but having her at my place the past couple of weeks has made that blurry.

When Jo sets down Ruby's food and then brings out my usual, which is the exact meal Ruby ordered, her eyes meet mine and her cheeks flame brighter. It hits me how over-whelming this whole interaction must be for her. First, Peg talking about what gorgeous children we'd have and then me saying the image of her in her wedding dress is imprinted in my mind. I grimace and her eyebrows lift in question.

But then something else catches her attention and it's like a thunderstorm covers her face in an instant. I actually grip the table to brace myself.

"Ruby?" I ask.

"*What are you doing here?*" Her teeth are gritted, her tone so unlike the Ruby I know, I'm ready to toss this table out of the way to check on her.

"There's my girl," a voice says behind me. "I'm here to bring you home."

Everything inside me tenses.

"Oh, you have got to be kidding me," Pierre says.

Conversation slowly halts around us.

I turn to see a guy in a tucked in button-down shirt and crisp jeans secured with a belt. His hair is parted on the side and he looks like he'd be *pissed* if anyone tried to mess it up. His squirrely grin is centered on Ruby and doesn't falter even slightly at the iciness she's sending his way.

I hate him instantly.

"Chat with me outside?" he asks, that same ingratiating smile holding steady.

"No, thank you, Junior," Ruby says.

Her words are polite, but her tone is *fuck the fuck off.*

Junior's exposed teeth clench slightly, but that's the only change in his demeanor.

"I came all this way, babe," he says, upping the smile another notch.

My eyes narrow on him and a growl comes out of me without warning. He glances at me in surprise. His Adam's apple bobs as he tries to hold on to that smile, but it's a little weaker when he turns to Ruby again.

That fucking pleases me.

"I didn't *ask* you to come all this way," Ruby says.

I grin and the fucker looks at me again, clearly disoriented now.

"Babe, come on. We need to talk. I-I miss you. Please."

"No, Junior. I don't know why you're here, unless it's to tell me you're giving my land and emus back."

Splotches of red fill the center of his cheeks and his fists clench before he shakes them out and laughs like Ruby's just told a joke.

He steps closer and puts his hand on the table, leaning toward her.

"Babe, *please.* Let's talk about this. I'm lost without you, *Dolly* is lost without you—"

"I am *not* your babe," she interrupts, "and since Dolly is living her best Colorado life right now, I'd say she's very much *not* lost without me."

All pleasantries fade and Junior just looks angry now. His fist lands on the table hard enough to make the silverware rattle, and he glares down at Ruby. I choose that moment to stand up. Normally, I make a conscious effort to not intimidate people with my size, but in this case, it's satisfying to see the way he swallows hard and takes a step back as he looks up at me.

"It appears you're not wanted here. You should go." I

don't mean for my voice to come out quite so ragey, but I guess it can't be helped.

"Ruby," Junior squeaks. "Outside."

"*Did you not hear what she said?*" I keep my volume down, but it's still forceful.

Junior flinches, but his jaw clenches and he nods. "I did, but I really need to talk to her."

Ruby's hand touches my arm. "Thanks, Callum." She squeezes my arm and I look at her. She smiles gratefully and some of the tension inside of me eases. "I'll handle this," she says softly.

We stare at each other for a few seconds longer before I nod and take a step back. She glares at Junior and walks outside, with him following close behind.

"I wanted to step in, but it was too exciting to see what you were about to do," Pierre says, fanning his face. "He looked *terrified*." He grins but watches worriedly out the window. "I should go out there to help her now, though, shouldn't I?"

"She said she'll handle it," I say.

"Right." He nods.

"Who is that?" Sutton asks.

I know by his tone that if we weren't in a public place, he'd have more choice words than this, but being a judge, he's always mindful.

"Her ex," Pierre says. "A real snake, if you ask me."

Sutton moves to our table as we all watch what unfolds outside. From what I can tell, Junior is doing all the talking, while Ruby stands there getting angrier and angrier. I don't take my eyes off of her in case she gives me a sign that she needs backup.

"They were engaged to be married," Pierre says softly, "and he made my sister and brother-in-law think he was buying their land to save their finances and the farm...that Ruby would own it...but it was all a lie. Ruby overheard him telling his friends that her name isn't even on the deed."

"Where is this property? Has she seen the paperwork?" Sutton asks.

Pierre frowns. "I—you know, I don't really know? I doubt it actually. She left town so fast, none of us saw it coming." He chuckles. "The joke was on Junior because he came out in his expensive wedding suit looking all smug, and Ruby was long gone."

He makes a face when we're quiet.

"Don't make me feel bad for thinking that is justice right there," he groans. "I'm not the worst—I felt bad for the guy...until I heard what he'd done."

"Sorry, I'm just thinking," Sutton says.

"What are you thinking?" I turn back to look at him for a second before returning to Ruby outside.

"Well, without seeing the paperwork, it's hard to be certain about anything, but I'd imagine there's a lawsuit in there somewhere...maybe some fine lines that need to be dissected." Sutton leans in, his voice so low that only Pierre and I can hear, he says, "With the way that guy just talked to her, I don't trust him, and I've learned to listen to my gut."

"I just got chills when you said that," Pierre says. "You've never led me wrong. When I ran that contract by you with that company that wanted to franchise, you said something didn't feel right about them, and you were spot on. I never told you this, but they filed bankruptcy last spring."

Sutton nods briskly. He's in judicial land right now, all business.

"Do you think Ruby would be open to me looking into this?" he asks.

"100% yes," Pierre says.

Sutton asks for details about where Ruby lives, the county, and a few other things that Pierre does his best to answer.

When I see Junior get in her face and Ruby starts to cry, I push past both of them and hurry outside. I don't shove Junior or knock him out the way I want to, I just put my hands on both of his shoulders and move him back by about two feet. He's so stunned, he stops his rant and I turn to face Ruby.

"I know you had it handled, but...he made you cry," I tell her.

Her eyes are bleak and glassy as she looks up at me. "Would you get me out of here?"

"Gladly."

I take her hand and we walk to my truck, which seems to jar Junior into action again.

"Ruby," he says, panting behind us. "Think about what I said. Okay? You know I'm right. You can't just leave all those animals, it's not right. I went about this the wrong way, but I'm not heartless—"

I turn and Junior's chest runs into my hand. "You've said your piece. It's best if you get out of here. Now."

His face curls up. Not attractive.

"What are you gonna do?" he snarls. "Beat the shit out of me? Run me out of here? I'm not intimidated by—"

I turn my back to him and open the door for Ruby and she gets inside. And then I walk around to my side and look back at him.

"You're not worth my time. She wants to talk to you? She'll reach out. Meanwhile, get lost."

He sputters, looking like the cowardly little shit he is, and I drive Ruby back to the house.

There's no satisfaction in it though, because she cries the whole way.

When I put the truck in park, I turn to face her.

"What can I do?" I ask.

"He's right. I have to go back," she says.

That is the last thing I want to hear.

"You want to be with Junior?"

I sound calm, but inside is an inferno.

She gives me a sharp look.

"What?" she sputters. "*No!* Did you *hear* him? *See* him? I would rather move to the other side of the world to a hideous place with no trees or mountains or-or flowers and have no friends or any comforts whatsoever than to spend *one more second* with that lying, *tiny*-souled man."

She flings her tears away and glares at me.

I stare back at her for a beat, my lips twitching.

"That was very specific," I say.

She rolls her eyes, fighting her own smile.

"And very heartfelt," she says, less heated now.

I hold out my hand and she takes it, and for a moment, I just sit there enjoying how right this feels.

"Tell me why you have to go back," I finally say.

CHAPTER SEVENTEEN

NEVER HAVE I EVER

RUBY

Where do I begin?

I lean my head against the seat and then shiver.

"Do you think you could…make me some of your hot chocolate first? I've been thinking about having it all day…in front of your fireplace. I don't think I've ever fully warmed up from the farmer's market."

He curses under his breath and hurries out of the truck.

I've barely opened my door and he's there, helping me out of it.

"I'm fine," I tell him. "I shouldn't have asked—"

"We don't say *shouldn't* around here," he grunts.

I smile, but he's already hurrying me into the house.

"Here, take this." He hands me the blanket that's become my favorite.

I sit on the floor in front of the fireplace, wrapping the coziness around me as I watch him.

"Thank you."

Callum has a roaring fire going within minutes. He pauses next to me once he's done.

"Maybe a bath would warm you up more while I work on the hot chocolate," he says. "If you want to take a longer one, I'll get my shower too."

"That's a brilliant idea."

He moves into the kitchen to set out the ingredients. I want to turn and watch him in there too, but I don't. I study the fire for another moment and then hurry upstairs to run my bath. A few minutes later, I hear Callum in the room across the hall and get warmer than I've been all day when I imagine him in the shower.

Thoughts of Junior screech those lusty thoughts. Seeing him again. Seeing the *real* him…I was given such a gift when I overheard him trashing me. That's been the overriding thought, far more than any sadness: I dodged a major bullet.

The pleasure is real when I step into the bath. This day feels like it's been at least three, and after a long day on my feet out in the cold, I can't think of anything better than this right here…except that fire downstairs and the broody man who stoked it.

By the time I step out of the tub, I'm content. Smooth and

silky and smelling like my brand new cherry body wash, the chill is gone.

I dig through the drawer and pull out something I haven't worn around Callum yet—one of the long sleep shirts I designed that has an emu with parted hair and glasses and says Emunized. It hits me mid-thigh, and I glance in the mirror to make sure it's not too obvious that I'm not wearing a bra. I take the clip out of my hair and give it a good shake, bringing some of it around the front to cover my breasts in case it is apparent.

There's always the blanket down there too, if I need backup coverage.

I don't usually care about this in the mornings, but I guess it's because I'm half asleep then.

I slide into my slippers and walk downstairs, grinning when I see Callum in the kitchen. His hair is wet and he's wearing a white Henley with grey sweats.

Mouth-watering.

He looks me over and his low chuckle makes my stomach clatter to the floor.

"I like the shirt."

"Thank you." I curtsy.

He points to the fire. "Best get in there so I can fulfill your wish."

For a moment, I forget what I'd said about drinking the warm beverage in front of the fire and I imagine him leaning over me, his muscles straining as he drives into—

"You okay?" His head tilts.

"Oh…yes." I hurry to the fire and sit in front of it, pulling the blanket over my legs.

Callum isn't far behind, placing a tray of hot chocolate carefully beside me.

"I can't believe you'd ever trust me with hot chocolate again," he says.

"It's me that I don't trust, and neither should you." I point at him.

He sits next to me and picks up one of the mugs.

"I trust you," he says. When I smile over at him, he adds, "And I didn't make it as hot."

I laugh and his smile is sweet as he takes a sip.

"I don't suppose that bath changed your mind about going back," he says.

I stare at the fire wistfully and shake my head. "No. And, to finally answer your question...I have to go back to see what I can do for the emus. When Junior told me the ways they're showing signs of distress, I was ashamed that I've stayed away this long. I've hoped my parents would step in, even though deep down I knew they wouldn't."

"Do you believe Junior's telling the truth?"

"I don't know," I admit. "But I can't, in good conscience, ignore that he might be."

"What will you do if he's right?"

"I need to find homes for them, one way or the other. I don't trust him to do that. If I had my wish, I'd keep them forever. Uncle Pierre said we could talk about building a new barn on his property, but there are renters in his house for the next nine months, and I wouldn't feel right taking that over until I have enough to pay him well. Which would take time. So I think the best option is to find homes for them. I can post about it and then go through a heavy vetting process."

"And, what—you'll just make nice with Junior in the meantime?"

"I don't know if that's possible," I admit.

I crinkle my nose and pick up my hot chocolate, leaning over the tray and blowing carefully before taking a sip.

"This is so delicious," I sigh. "And the perfect temp. Thank you. I really wanted it so bad on that first night and then I had to go and ruin everything by spilling it."

He chuckles. "I'll make lukewarm chocolate for you any time. But back to the emus…what if—"

He pauses for so long that I set my mug down and turn to face him, my legs crisscrossed under the blanket.

"*What*?" I ask.

He takes a lengthy swig of the hot chocolate and I grin when he sets the mug down and has a ring of whipped cream over his top lip.

I don't know what comes over me.

He just looks so unbelievably cute.

I lean over and wipe the whipped cream off with my thumb and then lick it clean. His eyes dilate, his tongue coming out to swipe over his lips.

"I just forgot every thought I've ever had," he says gruffly.

Everything inside of me spikes up—heat, adrenaline, lust.

"I haven't forgotten you were crying not that long ago though," he says.

He turns to face me. His knee bumps the tray, and he moves it so it's still within reach but not between our knees anymore.

"What if I went back with you?" he asks.

My heart gallops away with me, but everything else comes to a standstill. I stare at him until he starts to fidget.

"Not a good idea?" he asks.

"I just—what do you mean?" I frown. "How would that even be possible? You have so much going on here."

"I have people I can call when I need extra hands. It would take some rearranging, for sure. I'd have to enlist my family's help. If anything went haywire, Theo would know what to do. And Sofie's Aunt Hilary and her wife Abby often take care of Sofie's horses and they're really good with them. Different responsibilities with the cows and goats, but they'd pick it up fast. They've offered to help if I ever need a break. I've rarely taken one, so I think my family would bend over backwards to be helpful and say, "*Please,* get out of here," if I ever asked."

My eyes fill with tears and panic flashes across his face. I reach out and grip his hand.

"Or I can try to do whatever you need from right here," he hurries to add.

"You'd really do that?" I ask, my voice cracking. "You'd come with me? *Callum.*"

"Oh," he says, relieved. "Of course. If you think it'd help."

I lean up on my knees, pushing the blanket out of the way, and move until I'm as close as I can get without being in his lap. I put my hands on either side of his face, and time halts when he looks up at me. His hands fist my shirt at the waist and that alone makes me breathless.

"What did I do to deserve you?" I whisper.

And then he kisses me.

For all his rough edges—his deep, grumbly voice and the calloused hands and hard muscle—his lips are the softest, and his tongue is the sweetest.

Does he ever know how to use his mouth. It decimates me.

I can't get close enough and he must feel the same, because his hands drop to my backside. He moans his approval and tugs me until I'm straddling him, his hands staying put as he squeezes my cheeks and kisses me.

My head falls back when I feel how hard he is against me,

the thin layers between us making it *gloriously* evident, and his mouth trails down my neck.

I whimper and he rocks up, and it feels like heaven hitting me in the perfect spot, but in the next second, he picks me up and sets me across from him.

We stare at each other, chests rising and falling.

His eyes trail down to my bare legs, my blue lacy boy shorts showing.

"*Fuck*," he mutters.

Does he not want me?

Oh God, this is so embarrassing.

"I want you so bad I can't think straight, Ruby," he says, swiping his hand down his face.

I don't think I said anything out loud, but maybe he can see the mortification all over my face. Or maybe he's just saying how he feels…I really hope it's that.

"But you've been through a lot. Seeing that bastard talk to you the way he did today and now here I am, mauling you in my house not long after. That's not much better. You were *crying. Hard*," he adds.

The relief I feel from him saying he wants me is acute.

"Please, maul me," I say.

My lips part when he looks at me.

His eyes take me in, my face, my mouth, the nipples that are straining against my shirt.

"Please," I whisper.

"You sure you mean that?" he rasps.

"Oh, yeah, I'm sure," I tell him emphatically.

He's on his feet in seconds, bending down to lift me up like I weigh nothing. He groans again when my shirt rides up and his hands are on my bare skin.

"Did I already say I like this shirt?"

"Yeah."

His grin is feral as we rush up the stairs.

"I'll make you more hot chocolate later," he says.

I laugh and he kisses it away, the hunger for each other taking over. He moves through his bedroom, setting me on my feet in front of the bed, his lips never leaving mine. His kisses make me dizzy, but he still keeps a little distance between us and I want more. I tug his shirt up and he pulls back, his hair messy from me holding onto it.

"So, when you said *please maul you*...were you saying you want to have sex with me? Or do you mean more of a make-out session...without some layers?" He tugs his shirt over his head and runs his thumb over my top lip.

I take a moment to appreciate the view.

"The first option," I tell him, and then lean over and kiss his chest, my tongue swirling around his nipple.

He moans and the sound grounds me, knowing he's feeling this pull between us too.

"You do the best things," he whispers.

"I think I've found the secret to getting you to talk more." I smile against his skin.

His hand grips my jaw and I look up at him.

"I don't want you to regret me, Ruby."

"That would never, *ever* happen," I tell him.

He lifts my hand to his mouth and kisses my knuckles, his gesture chaste but the look in his eyes so far from it.

He bends slightly to reach the bottom of my shirt and lifts it slowly, like he's unwrapping a present, but when he lifts it over my head, his expression is not what I was hoping for.

"*Ruby*."

I point at his face. "Not quite what a girl wants to see when a guy looks at her breasts for the first time."

He makes a sound with his mouth, his brows so furrowed

in the center, I want to smooth away the crease. He grips my arms as he studies me.

"Of course, you're the most beautiful woman I've ever seen," he says, offhandedly.

"No need to flatter me," I tease.

His eyes flash to mine and his jaw tightens as he straightens, one hand dropping off of my arm and moving to my chin.

"I never flatter," he says. "Understand?"

I blink up at him. "Okay."

"You're *beautiful,* everything about you. I've thought it since the night I saw you in your wedding dress, and every day since. I think it even more right now. But your burns still look as painful as they did two weeks ago."

I put my hands on his chest, still trembling with excitement to be touching him like this.

"They look worse than they feel, I promise."

"Which ones hurt the most?"

I show him. His eyes are intense as he looks me over, and then he reaches out and softly slides his thumb over my nipple.

Slowly, *reverently.*

The contact scatters goose bumps across my skin and his eyes meet mine.

"Are you still cold?"

"Not even a little bit." My teeth press against my bottom lip as he tugs my nipple between his fingers. He moves to the other side and does the same. He leans down and lightly blows across the worst burn in the center of my chest and then straightens, sighing.

"I really don't want to hurt you," he says regretfully.

I try not to show how disappointed I am, but honestly... I'm not gonna *force* him to have sex with me.

"So, there'll be a little change in plans for our first position," he continues, the slow smile spreading across his face *wicked*.

A thrill shoots through me. "First position? You're already planning on us doing this more than once? Presumptuous." I laugh.

"Fuck. *Yes*." He leans in and kisses me and just as I'm about to climb the man, he pulls back.

I groan and he chuckles.

He palms his dick and my eyes widen as I get a better look at what he's dealing with.

"On the bed," he whispers.

I gulp and then do as he said, crawling across it.

"Fuck, you're perfect," he says.

His hands close around my backside and my eyes close as he kneads my cheeks. I'm hesitant to move because it feels so good.

"Will you be comfortable resting your head on your arms and leaving this right here?" He gives my bottom a slap and I yelp, my laugh dying as he leans in, his hardness pressing between my cheeks. Desire rushes through me. "Ruby?"

"Uh, y-yes." I lean my forehead on my arms, feeling more than a little exposed to have my hind end hanging in the air. But the way he's touching me—*yes*. The next second, I gasp when he pulls my lacy boy shorts off.

I turn back and look at him and his eyes are gleaming as he stares at me. He tilts his head to meet my eyes and looks so serious I almost ask what's wrong.

"This ass has been front and center in my dreams." He squeezes each side and his teeth press against his lower lip. "I need my mouth on it."

I squeak, my head falling back down to my arms. The things he does and the way I love it—kissing and sucking and biting, greedy and playful with the occasional slap. I didn't dream I could lose all inhibitions this way, but I do.

And then when his tongue swipes along my core for the first time, I'm so worked up, I think I might flood all over him. He groans like he's ravenous, his hands moving my cheeks apart, giving him even better access, and his tongue goes crazy.

He sucks and licks and flicks and is so tuned into me that when I breathe even slightly different or whimper or moan— he really loves it when I moan—he goes in even more intently.

I never imagined I could have an orgasm this way, but then again, I've never experienced anything close to this.

And oh, how he proves me wrong.

When he finally flips me onto my back and shoves his sweats down, his long, thick erection bobbing, I eagerly lean up on my elbows and watch as he gives his tip a hard squeeze, and then slides his fist over himself once.

This is it, I think, *he's finally going to ravage me with that thing.*

But no. He widens my legs and leans down, licking me again.

"I want to see your face when you come this time," he says, his eyes hooded as he looks up at me, his tongue getting back to work.

His fingers dip inside and never have I *ever* come so hard in all my life.

CHAPTER EIGHTEEN

SELF-PRESERVATION

CALLUM

"Please," she whimpers, even as she's still fluttering against my tongue. "*Please*, Callum."

She tastes like cherry sunshine.

I have found my nirvana.

I press a kiss against her clit and she shudders.

"Tell me what you need, Ruby Sunshine," I say, moving up over her.

She reaches up and tries to tug me down, but I brace

myself. She looks like an angel in my bed, her skin shining, her cheeks flushed. And my God, when she comes, watching her knocks me sideways.

"I need you," she says.

"You've got me."

"*Inside me*," she insists.

She latches her legs around my waist and I tug her up to meet me instead of lying on her. She frowns slightly and I shift her legs so she's straddling me. My dick jolts against her and she gasps.

"I'm ready for our third position," she whispers.

I smirk. "But we haven't even tried our first yet."

She leans back so she can see me better, and I laugh at her expression.

"So, that was…not our—? I thought you were done," she says.

"Are you not satisfied?" I tease.

My hands go to her ass again. I'm obsessed with it. When her burns are healed, I'll go crazy with her tits, but I'll still be obsessed with this ass.

"I am so satisfied, but," she rubs against me and I suck in a breath with the feel of her sweet wetness against my dick, "I want you to be too. And you cannot possibly be done with that thing so hard—"

"That *thing*?" I laugh. "You mean my dick?"

Her look is shy, and her cheeks flush darker as she laughs too. "Yes."

"I'm more than satisfied," I tell her. "I loved everything about that." I kiss her nose. "And I like it when you say *please* too."

Her lips stick out and I lean in and line the edge of her lips with my tongue, loving the way she rubs against me again, almost as if she can't help herself.

I reach over and grab a condom, sliding it on while she watches. She licks her lips and my dick twitches against her.

"Are you comfortable?" I ask.

"Yes." Her hands find my hair again and it does something to me, the way she tugs it with ownership.

"Good. First position," I whisper. "Close and face to face, but your chest should still be okay this way."

She sighs. "You really are perfect."

"Hardly," I scoff. "But let's get this as close to perfect as we can."

My hands slide up to her hips and I lift her over me.

Worry flashes over her face. "I don't have a ton of experience with…um, positions, so don't expect perfection, okay?"

I keep her hovered over my tip. "I just don't want to make your burns worse, that's all I meant. I already think you're perfect."

She bites her lower lip, her eyes watering. "You really are," she whispers. "Callum. I can't wait another second."

I couldn't hold back if I tried when she says that. I line her up and push in just a little bit.

"*Oh*. It's already so good," she says in awe.

"It *is*," I grit out.

"More," she whispers.

I nudge in deeper, her walls tight and the best thing I've ever felt. I close my eyes when I swell harder inside of her. She gasps and clenches around me.

"Ruby," I say between my teeth. "You're making it really hard to take this slow."

Her hips do a lazy swivel and she grins when I curse.

"Nothing about us has been slow," she says, leaning her head against mine. "Even though it's felt like a slow fire burning me up, just being near you."

I love hearing the word *us* on her lips. And everything she's saying, everything about this.

"God, Ruby. You're right about that." My voice sounds strangled.

I go a little deeper and her mouth parts.

"You're...really big," she says, her teeth pressing into that bottom lip.

I lean in and nip it myself. "It'll fit, don't worry. Just breathe. Am I hurting you?"

"No. It's taking me a minute to adjust, but I love how you feel."

"We've got all night. There's no rush."

"I want all of you." Her hips swivel slowly around me and the sensation makes my vision blur.

I hold onto her hips and sink all the way inside her.

"*Ohhh*," she whimpers.

We pause for a few seconds, staring at each other.

She puts her arms around me and then flinches when she presses her chest against mine. She makes a face and pulls back slightly.

"Are you okay?" I ask.

"I'm better than okay," she says. "Besides wanting to suction my chest to yours, I'm perfect." She grins. She leans her forehead against mine and inhales. "I've never been so filled up. You...it's...*so* good."

"Did you touch yourself this morning?" I ask, thrusting up once.

She gasps and her walls flutter around me. "I had to, knowing I'd be around you all day. Did you?"

"I have since you heard me a couple nights ago." I lead her hips, rocking her back and forth. "At first it felt wrong to do that when you were...heartbroken in the other room."

"I'm not heartbroken, Callum. Can't you feel this? I'm so far from heartbroken."

"I definitely feel this." I press into her harder, starting a slow, steady build.

Her rhythm matches mine and I have to fight so hard to make this last.

"After nearly losing my shit when you cut my hair," I say between thrusts, "I realized it'd keep backfiring on me...if I didn't..."

"So...it was self-preservation?" she asks, her breathing becoming shallow, her chest rising and falling faster.

"Something like that."

She leans in and kisses me softly before giggling.

"What?"

"I really didn't expect you to be chatty during sex," she says, putting her hands in my hair and tugging. "I freaking love it."

"With you, I finally have something to say."

Her eyes get glassy again and she gasps when I pick up the pace and rock into her so deep it makes us both tremble. For a few minutes, the only sounds are our ragged breaths and moans, and the sounds of her taking me in.

I've never heard anything better.

When I hit a particularly great spot, her head falls back and I kiss her neck, sweet and salty now with our increasingly frantic pace.

"I *love* first position," she gasps when I lift her and slam her back down, over and over again. "And-how-you-make-me-feel-every-thing," she chants with each plunge over me. "Mmm, oh—*Callum*..."

I feel it before she cries out, the way she grips me tighter and tighter, her inner walls determined to wring every ounce of pleasure out of both of us. My whole body is in a state of euphoria, an indescribable rush taking over as we shudder, my lips finding hers as we crash together.

When we've caught our breath, we stare at each other. Her expression is shy and sweet, excitement firing off behind those eyes.

I've never met another person like her.

"You still okay?" I ask.

"I'm so good." She sighs. "Thank you," she whispers against my lips, giving me a soft kiss. "I finally get what the hype about sex is."

It doesn't surprise me that Junior had no clue about how to make her feel good. Just more to dislike about the arrogant bastard.

But I can't say I mind her looking at me like I've just blown her mind.

She sure as hell has blown mine.

"So, what is your type?" she asks.

She's on top of me now, her hips circling over me, her tits hypnotizing me with their tantalizing sway.

"My type?"

"Yeah…I'm trying to imagine what kind of woman has been here. Scarlett talked like you *never* have women around, but that's hard to imagine."

"That's what you're thinking about right now? I must not be doing this right."

She laughs and her pussy squeezes me. I suck in a breath and she grins, knowing exactly what she's doing.

"You're doing this so right that I never want it to end," she says.

Our bodies are slick with sweat and we keep pausing

when it feels too good, enjoying the push and pull of nearly falling over the edge. We've been hovering over it for a while now, and this in-between place is fucking blissful.

"Thought it might be my only chance to really get you talking about the deep stuff, while we're having sex," she adds.

I lean up slightly, still conscious not to touch her burns, and tickle her side. She bounces around on me, laughing, and my dick gets a little too happy. I move my fingers between her legs and am satisfied when I hear her sweet sounds. I rub little circles over her and she hums, her eyes closing briefly. She fights to open them.

"I love feeling you get close. I see it here," I press my free fingers on the pulse in her neck. "And feel it here," I tap her clit and she shudders, a moan falling out of her, "and here," I flex inside of her.

"Callum," she pants.

"I never have women here," I tell her. "And after tonight, I can't imagine anyone else but you in my bed at all."

Her mouth parts and when I drive into her with a few hard strokes, her thighs start trembling around me.

"Still feel like talking?" I ask.

She bites her bottom lip and shakes her head, and my hands grip her hips as we lose all inhibition, our bodies taking over.

CHAPTER NINETEEN

IDEALISTIC, IDYLLIC, INCREDIBLE

RUBY

The sun is brighter than ever when I wake up. My body protests slightly as I stretch and I grin, my body feeling every place Callum has been. My replay of the night screeches to a halt and I sit straight up, realizing how late it must be.

I jump up and get through a quick shower in a daze.

I didn't even hear Callum get up this morning. He must be exhausted. We were awake most of the night, talking and laughing while our bodies just kept coming together in the most incredible ways.

This is what I've wanted in my life, but I didn't believe it really existed. Not for me, anyway.

When I was questioning whether I should marry Junior before our wedding day, these feelings I'm having for Callum and the explosive sex we had *four* times during the night, are exactly what I knew was missing.

At first I thought I'd be giving up something if I married Junior, but then it seemed like I probably had an overly idealistic view of marriage that no one would ever be able to live up to.

My parents are happy together. It's not that I haven't seen a good relationship. I'm just different than them. To anyone who doesn't know us well, it could seem as if I'm as carefree and free-spirited as they are, but compared to them, I'm pragmatic and straitlaced.

I've been the practical one in the family, making sure the never-ending business expenses of our emu farm were covered, as well as basic things like money for groceries. I love my parents dearly, but there have been many times I've felt like the parent. Instead of worrying about the past due balances I found piling up years ago, I figured out a way to pay them.

In a way, I guess that practicality crossed over into my relationships too, and I settled for something that was convenient.

No one is happier than I am to admit how wrong I've been about how much more a relationship could actually be.

I'm trying not to get ahead of myself here and immediately jump into something with Callum beyond our night together, but it's hard because he surpasses anything I could have imagined. I can't unknow the fact that I *can* have explosive sexual chemistry with an incredible man.

My phone rings and I grab it, answering before it rings again.

"Hey," Kess says. "I just wanted you to know I was out at the farm yesterday and I'm here now too, and everyone looks good. There are a few emus who seem lonelier than I remember them being before, but they look healthy."

"I can't tell you how relieved I am to hear you say that." I hurriedly get dressed and fall back on the bed, looking up at the ceiling. "You think they'll be okay for a few more days until I can get there?"

"For sure. I'll miss you at Thanksgiving, but I'll look after them. It's more about when I leave for school in January that I'm worried about."

"Thanks, Kess. I'll be there long before then. Just not sure when my RV is going to be ready…"

"I've got you," she says.

"Thank you, thank you. This helps so much."

"Love you, Ruby. I'll FaceTime you later if you want to see them for yourself. I just need to charge my phone or I'd do it right now."

"No, that's perfect. Let's chat later."

My exhale is ragged, but I feel so much lighter when I stand up again.

Now, any jitters I'm feeling are more about seeing Callum this morning.

Before I go downstairs, I look in the mirror and tell myself, "It's okay to have sex and even these feelings…with no strings attached. I can just accept it for what it was—the best night I've ever had."

But even as I say it quietly in the bathroom, I'm aware

that my heart crossed over into unknown territory even before last night.

Callum owns a piece of me. There's no denying it.

I go downstairs as he's coming inside and he pauses before taking his coat off and hanging it on the hook near the door. I watch him shyly, trying to get a read on how this morning-after will be. His expression is solemn compared to the playful, sexy smirk he wore throughout the night. When it's silent during his walk toward me, I press my nails into my hands to resist the urge to start rambling nonsense and instead, I stand there quietly.

When he reaches me, he stares at me for a moment before pushing my hair off my shoulder, his fingers brushing over my neck. And then he leans in and kisses my cheek. My eyes flutter shut with the nearness of him, and nerves and infatuation ping-pong around my insides.

"Mornin', Sunshine," he says gruffly. "You doin' okay today?"

"I'm so okay it's not even funny." I clear my throat and press my lips together, barely holding back a laugh. "How about you?"

His eyes smile first, crinkling at the edges, before the slow grin crosses over his face. His hands land on my hips and he tugs me flush against him.

"The only thing wrong with today is that I had to leave you in my bed," he says against my lips.

He kisses me so thoroughly, my knees go weak.

Yeah, I'm doing better than okay.

When we eventually pull apart, he gives me that slow grin again and I try not to dissolve into a puddle.

"Feel like going out for breakfast? I wasn't sure how long you'd sleep, so I went ahead and fed Dolly after I milked the girls."

"Thank you. I definitely overslept."

"I feel bad that you haven't even been to Happy Cow yet. And that's why no one ever said I was a great host," he says.

"Uh, you're the *best* host. You didn't even know you were having a house guest...much less a couple weeks' worth of this." I point at myself and his huge hands on my hips tug me closer. "And I haven't felt like I was missing a thing—the farmer's market was great, Sunny Side was great...I adore The Dancing Emu. The downtime has actually been exactly what I needed. I was burned out."

"You had a lot of responsibility on your shoulders, didn't you?"

I nod. "Knowing what I know now, all the time and money I put into saving our farm feels like it was for nothing, but I wouldn't change anything...well, except for agreeing to marry Junior in the first place."

His jaw clenches. "Do you think it's safe to say you can have Thanksgiving here?"

My cheeks heat as I smile at him shyly. "You really want me intruding on your family's Thanksgiving?"

"After last night, I think it should be obvious that I want you intruding on my everything."

My insides burn hotter. This man.

He smacks my backside. "Come on. It's time to acclimate you to Landmark Mountain."

"The farmer's market wasn't enough?"

He looks like he ponders it for a moment and then lifts his shoulders. "It was a good start, but there are a few other places I need you to see. You haven't even been to our family's resort yet. Well...it's Scarlett's now and Jamison's...and Jamison's brother, Zac."

"I'd love to see it. Uncle Pierre has mentioned the resort before and then told me when Zac Ledger bought it." My eyes widen. "Does Zac ever come to town or do Jamison and Scarlett just handle the business?"

His expression is somewhere between a smirk and a scowl. "He comes occasionally. You a football fan or is it specifically Zac Ledger?"

I shrug. "Is it wrong to say both?" I laugh when his scowl deepens. "I mean, he has nothing on you, but...he *is* the GOAT."

"He's all right." His smirk is back. "Okay, he's great. Good guy, sweet wife, best little girl ever...you'll love the guy." He pretends to be annoyed, but I just laugh at him. "Professionally though, I think Weston Shaw is about to turn everything upside down."

I must look perplexed because his eyes widen playfully.

"From The Mustangs?" he adds and when I bite my bottom lip, he shakes his head. "Not a Mustang fan, I take it?"

I make a face. "Sorry. Are they doing well?"

He kisses the tip of my nose. "They are. But it's just as well you don't know about Shaw. He's in the same state and single."

I laugh. "Trust me. A football player is the last thing I want."

"Yeah? You asked about my type, but I never found out about *your* type."

I put my hands on his bulging biceps and squeeze. "None of them have anything on you, Callum," I say softly. "I didn't know a man like you existed."

He groans as he leans in to kiss me again. "You're making me want to forget all about taking you out. Tomorrow, Happy Cow, maybe dinner at Tiptop? Today, frequent visits to my bed?"

I put my hands on my cheeks to cool them down and

press my lips together to keep from laughing. "How about today and tomorrow, all of the above? Happy Cow and then—"

"Such a multitasker." He lifts me up and places me on top of the island. "I need a little taste to tide me over..."

My mouth parts and when he sees the lust in my eyes, he grins and starts undoing my pants. I lift up and he undoes my pants, cursing against my skin when he sees me.

"So damn pretty," he whispers.

His tongue is flicking over my lace before he even tugs them out of the way, finding my wet center. He hums against me and it feels so good I can't think straight.

My hands fall back behind me as I whisper his name, his hands holding my hips steady as his mouth works me over. The need for him builds until I'm delirious, my eyes rolling back as he sucks me senseless. When his fingers slide inside and out, his mouth never letting go, I lose my mind. I fall apart, and it feels endless. When I open my eyes again, he's watching me and he places one more kiss there before standing up, his lips shining from me. I'm dazed and weak and euphoric as he puts my panties and jeans back in place.

He leans on the island, his arms on either side of me, and he looks a little drunk himself.

"I could do that forever," he says.

"I would not complain."

He smirks at how my voice trembles. Or maybe it's pride about how he just rocked my world. Either way, it's such a good look on him.

The thick bulge in his pants distracts me, but when I reach out to undo his pants, he intercepts, lifting my hand and kissing my knuckles.

"I promised you breakfast. This can wait." His voice is husky as he adjusts himself.

My mouth waters, so ready for him. But he turns and walks toward the door, grabbing my coat off of the hook and holding it out for me. I slide into it with his help, still shaky from the way he so easily makes me fall apart.

CHAPTER TWENTY

SILENCE AND SWEETS

CALLUM

Something strange happens as we're walking on the sidewalk outside Happy Cow. A few tourists stop and take pictures of Ruby and me, squealing when they see us. And then a whole other group of girls come up and ask us to sign their T-shirts.

I glance at Ruby in question and then take a shirt from one of the girls, recognition striking when I see the familiar emu Ruby had on her nightshirt.

"You want her signature, not mine." I hold the shirt back out for the girl to take.

"We want *both* of your signatures," one girl gushes. "I've watched the one of you no less than a hundred times."

Ruby looks a little bit sick when I look at her again.

"I'm so sorry. I, uh…I posted footage of you chopping wood," Ruby says under her breath, biting her lower lip. "I've sort of neglected my account since I posted that…just preoccupied with other things, but I know it took off." She makes a face at me but signs the shirt and a few pieces of paper and then smiles at the girls.

"That's what's going on?" I sign the shirt too and then the papers.

Is this what was happening the other night when I was out with Grinny? I thought I was imagining things.

"You have two and a half *million* views!" The last girl says, beaming up at me. "I never knew chopping wood could be so *hot*. Do you do it every day? Any chance we could see you in action?" She winks and then bats her eyelashes, and I shake my head, turning to look at Ruby.

I have no idea what to do with this.

Ruby finishes signing and lifts her hand in a wave. "Thanks so much for your support, guys!"

Then she takes my arm and hurries me down the street.

"Are you mad?" she asks.

"No? Of course not. I—I'm just…so, what's the big deal about chopping wood?"

She pulls me into the alley near Happy Cow and pulls out her phone. She laughs and covers her mouth, and her eyes are wild when she looks up at me. "It's you. You chopping wood is a big deal. Trust me." She cracks up again. "You've gone viral, and so has another post I've done while I've been here."

I stare at her. "What does that mean exactly?"

She cringes. "It means you might be getting stopped frequently for a while. I'm so sorry, Callum. That's gotta be the last thing you want…"

"Is it helping your business do well?" I ask.

A little crease forms between her brows. She looks down at her phone again, her fingers moving quickly before she pauses, and a flood of expressions cover her face in the next few seconds: surprise, awe, and then I think she might cry.

"I've sold more in the past two days than the entire time I've been running this business."

"Well, then that's worth it all, right?"

Her face crumbles and she leans her forehead onto my chest, sniffling before she says, voice wobbling, "You are the very best man, Callum."

I lift her chin up and kiss her sweet lips. "No, I just have a soft spot for you, Ruby Jones."

She wraps her arms around my neck and kisses me. It's so effective, I want to have my way with her right in this alley, but given that she's some kind of social media star and it's broad daylight, that probably wouldn't be the best idea.

"I'm wishing I'd taken you up on staying in bed," she says when she pulls away.

"Our outing can be brief," I say, smacking her ass when she giggles.

Mar is saying bye to a customer when we walk in, and her mouth falls open when she sees me. I see her eyes clocking my hand on Ruby's shoulder and I leave it there, not minding what the hell anyone thinks.

"Callum Henry Landmark," she says, holding both hands out in front of her like she's dizzy. "Am I seeing things? You haven't been inside Happy Cow since 1972."

"Happy Cow didn't exist in 1972, and neither did I," I grumble.

"I know…but it's *still* been that long since you've stepped foot in here," Mar says, cackling.

I roll my eyes good-naturedly and nod at Lar, who steps out of the kitchen and yells out a hearty hello.

"I thought I was hearing things when Mar said your name," he says. "And to see you here with a lady. It's a grand day."

I just lift an eyebrow. I might rarely come here, but I spent a lot of time with Lar and Mar when I worked on Theo's place. They brought treats and also worked their asses off. Great people. They never shy away from stirring the pot, but I love them just the same.

"This is Ruby Jones," I say, my hand falling to her waist.

She looks up at me and smiles and then says hello to Lar and Mar.

"You're Pierre's niece that I've been hearing so much about?" Mar asks Ruby.

She looks surprised. "Yes, I am. You've heard about me?"

"Girl, I daresay we heard about you within an hour of you getting to town. People around here like to keep tabs on things." She winks at Ruby. "For weeks now, I've heard this guy's been keeping you all to himself," Mar teases. "You're beautiful—I can see why. There's a bet going on at Sunny Side to see who will be the next Landmark to get married. You guys are going down like flies."

Ruby glances at me, mouth parted and her cheeks flushing.

"Welcome to small-town life," I tell Ruby.

To Mar, I say, "And you wonder why I never come in…"

She laughs, knowing I'm messing with her, and then she points her finger at me, her easy grin disappearing, and I dread what's about to come out of her mouth next.

"This should've been the first place you brought her."

Not as bad as I expected.

"She hasn't even been to the resort yet, Mar. And how 'bout you don't scare her off?" I stare her down and she blinks, her smile spreading over her face again.

"It sure is good to see you both," she says warmly.

"Good to see you too. Got any apple turnovers?"

"You know, I believe there's one left." She looks down at the pastry case and points it out.

"We'll take it and a few chocolate croissants." I look at Ruby. "And anything else you want to try…"

"I'll be good with what you picked. Sounds delicious."

"But does anything else look fun?" I ask.

I hear a gasp and look up to see Mar blinking rapidly and fanning herself. "Did you see this coming, Lar?" she says, bumping his elbow with hers. "The silent studly one is pulling out all the right words. I am *literally* swooning."

Ruby grins and leans on the counter, shooting me a sexy look over her shoulder. "So am I."

Besides my one body part growing hard as a rock, the rest of me softens into mush.

"I like this girl, Callum," Lar says.

Ruby laughs and my heart does that crazy flutter it's been doing since I met her. I like her too. A whole helluva lot.

"What is that?" Ruby points at the pastry next to the eclairs.

"That's a tarte tatin—it's like an apple upside down cake," Mar says.

"It's beautiful," she says. "Let's try that. And then that should be plenty."

"It's one of my favorite things," Mar says. "And if you like strawberries…I don't always have these strawberry tarts here, but I just felt like making a batch. They've been getting rave reviews this morning."

"We'll take it," I jump in. "You want to pick out your coffee, Sunshine? I'll have the light roast." I nod at Mar, who has paused her bustling and now stares at us as if she's in a trance.

"Make that two, please," Ruby says. "With room for cream and sugar in mine, please."

Mar sighs and blinks slowly, shaking her head. "The two of you have made my morning. He calls her *Sunshine*, Lar. Just pick me up off this floor right now because I am weak in the knees." She points at him. "We've gotta head to Sunny Side before the day is over…place our bets." She turns and gets our coffee, humming as she works. "It's the quiet ones that knock us off our feet, isn't it, Lar."

"I wouldn't know," Lar says pointedly before he places the pastry in a box. He grins up at me and jumps when Mar swats him with a towel. "What? You've never called *me* quiet. Is that why you're so chatty? Because I'm knocking you off your feet?"

He yelps when she reaches out and twists his nipple, but he just laughs and tugs her in for a kiss. She pretends to protest, but it's obvious she loves every second of it.

"Now I *am* kind of ticked you didn't bring me here sooner," Ruby teases, bumping her shoulder against me.

I wrap my arms around her, pulling her back against my chest. When I kiss her temple, it surprises me that I've done it, but it feels so right, I lean into it and so does she.

"You okay with this?" I whisper in her ear.

I feel her cheeks lift with her smile.

"You should just know by now that when it comes to you, Callum, I am better than okay."

CHAPTER TWENTY-ONE

WE'LL GET THERE

RUBY

We drive down Heritage Lane, which is the cutest main street I've ever seen. I already thought so, but it's like the quaintness smacks me upside the heart every time I venture out. Everywhere I look is decked out with Christmas decorations and the occasional shop holding out with a combo of fall decor for Thanksgiving. Callum points out a few places he thinks I'd like.

I sip my coffee and moan into the cup.

Callum looks over at me and grins. "Good?"

"It's *delicious*."

His eyes are heated as they drop to my mouth. He reaches out and wipes some of the foam from my lips and licks it off his thumb.

"Not as good as you," he says.

His low, husky voice, paired with those twinkling, smiling eyes, sends a throb between my legs.

"Why don't you pull out one of those pastries? See what you think," he says.

"Which one is your favorite?" I ask.

"All of them."

I laugh and pull out the apple turnover he ordered and hold it up for him to take a bite.

"Ladies first." He grins and shakes his head when I try to make him go ahead.

I take a bite and gasp. "Oh, wow. That is exceptional."

He looks so pleased and nods. When I offer him a bite next, he takes one and then says, "Go ahead, you finish it."

"There's so much in here, I want to try everything. Is this your favorite?"

"I love all the apple stuff, yeah. But the chocolate croissants are a close second." He chuckles when I give him another bite of the turnover. "There's the lodge," he says, pointing to the grand resort highlighted by the mountains surrounding it.

"It's stunning."

The ski lifts are filled with people, and traffic is backed up. The parking lot to the lodge is full.

Callum glances at his watch.

"It's a busy time to be over here. I usually hit Happy Cow early if I want to avoid this."

"You mean you *have* been there more recently than 1972?" I tease.

He laughs. "Aren't they a trip? Mar gives me a hard time if I'm not in there once a week. I haven't been since you got here…therefore, the dramatics."

"I loved them. Is there anyone in town I should avoid? Everyone I've met seems so nice."

"Nah. Cecil is an old codger—he owns the grocery store —but you'll have him wrapped around your little finger in seconds flat. He gets meaner as the season gets busier, but I can't say I blame him for that."

Someone passes and waves when they see him. He lifts his hand and nods. It happens more than once and makes me smile every time.

"I didn't check to see if Scarlett is free. Want to stop in and say hey anyway?"

"I'd love to."

"You haven't met their dogs yet either, have you? Lucia and Delgado."

"No."

"You're going to flip when you see how cute they are." He swipes a hand over his face. "Seems like you should already know everyone in my life. I can't fathom that I've known you for such a short amount of time."

"I can't either. I've never…" I crinkle my nose and almost lose my nerve to say more, but then decide to go for it. "Does it scare you for me to say that I've never felt like this?"

I lift my coffee to my lips, partially to hide behind it. But I don't turn away from him and since we're stopped at a light, he's laser-focused on me.

He reaches out and puts his hand on my thigh, squeezing it. "When it comes to you, I think the only thing that could scare me is if you weren't feeling the same way as I am, which is something so fucking big, I can't put it into words. And the thought of you not staying, *that* scares me," he adds.

Traffic starts moving and he squeezes my thigh again, keeping his hand there as we continue down the street, barely making any progress.

"I shouldn't have said that last part. I never want you to feel pressured to stay," he says.

"Would you mind if we go to the lodge another day? I don't think I can keep my hands off of you for much longer."

He looks in his rearview mirror and ahead to the oncoming traffic and suddenly cuts into the right lane and turns down a side street.

"You're reading my mind, Ruby Sunshine."

He makes a few more turns and I lose all sense of direction, but everywhere I look is something else beautiful. I feed him more bites of the turnover and have to restrain myself from groaning with each bite of the chocolate croissant. I can't tell for sure—I think we're going away from his place, but he gets past the traffic and winds back through side streets until I recognize where we are again. Still, it's a surprise when we're on his street and driving down his driveway.

"It might take me a while to figure out how you got us back here."

He grins and picks up the pastry box. "A while, I like the sound of that."

I can't contain my huge smile as we get out of the truck and Callum groans when I stop to pet the cows and goats and Dolly when they all rush toward the fence.

"Cockblocks, every single one of you," he mutters, but he doesn't hesitate to scratch Irene's ears as she nuzzles up to his hand.

The air is buzzing between Callum and me, so even when I'm giving Dolly and Irene and Delphine love, I'm aware of his eyes on me. The way my legs and arms feel like they're underwater, buoyant and every nerve ending crackling with awareness.

Someone waves in the distance and starts walking toward us. A really attractive woman. I stand up straighter when she calls out and Callum turns and waves.

"That's Hilary," he says softly.

When she gets closer, she smiles at me and lifts her hand up in another wave.

"You must be Ruby," she says. "I'm Sofie's aunt and she said you and I would hit it right off. She couldn't say enough nice things about you."

"Aw, she's so sweet. I kind of blew into town and created a lot of chaos, but everyone has been so welcoming." I laugh but cringe when I hear it out loud because it's the truth.

"Seems like the perfect amount of chaos from what I can tell," Hilary says, looking between Callum and me with a smile.

"Hilary stopped by this morning and helped feed everyone. She wanted to get more comfortable with everything before I go to Utah with you." He lifts his chin toward Hilary. "You don't have anything to worry about. You're a natural."

Hilary does a dramatic fake flip of her short blonde hair on either side and laughs. "Why, thank you. I even helped milk the girls this morning and didn't get kicked once." Delphine sidles up next to her and Hilary pats her on the back. "That guy works his ass off," she says, pointing at Callum. "After all you've done for Sof on that barn...I'm absolutely thrilled to help you out any chance I can get." She pauses and looks at me. "Did he tell you he designed Sofie and Theo's barn? It's a work of art. You can probably imagine just by looking at his house."

"No, he didn't tell me that. I'll have to see it. I do love his house…and his barn," I say.

And pretty much everything I know about him so far.

"Thank you, ladies," Callum says softly, continuing to pet each animal that wanders over. "They're comfortable with you," he tells Hilary. "You've done great today. Abby did too, from what I saw." He looks at me. "Hilary's wife was out here early this morning too."

"That's so nice of you both," I say.

"Like I said, we'd do anything for Callum. Gladly. And this is fun." She smiles when Dolly shakes her feathers. "I took Abby home about an hour ago to help Sofie with the horses. I grew up here, but Abby didn't. We just moved here recently to be close to Sof, and it's been great. I wasn't sure Abby would take to small-town living, but she's loving every second." Hilary grins.

"Well, I can't wait to meet her," I tell her.

"You can meet her at Grinny's on Thursday," Callum says.

"Oh, you'll be with us on Thanksgiving?" Hilary does a little dance. "That's great. Hey, Grinny won't tell me what I can bring. Do I just wing it?"

Callum chuckles. "She struggles to delegate. There will be way too much food there, so only bring something if you want to." He glances over at me and goose bumps skitter over my skin.

"Why don't you guys go do something fun?" Hilary says. "I can stay. I can even do the nighttime routine if you want. I took notes on everything you told me. If I forget something, I can always ask."

"Really? Going out for breakfast was a treat. I'd rather take you up on the nighttime routine when I'm out of town," Callum says.

She waves her hand. "I've already said it at least ten times. I'm happy to do this. I've got you covered when you travel and I'll feel more confident if I've tried it out while you're close by."

He nods. "I get that. Thanks, Hilary." He reaches out and squeezes her shoulder and she beams up at him. "You'll call the second you need anything?" he asks.

"Promise," she says. "But I don't think I'll need anything." She grins and turns around to walk back toward the barn. "Have fun, you two."

Callum looks at me and holds out his hand, weaving his fingers through mine.

"Still want your hands on me?" he asks under his breath.

"Desperately."

"Cannot happen soon enough for me," he says.

When he shuts the kitchen door behind us, he tosses the pastry box on the island and starts removing his coat and boots. I do the same and then he moves toward me and pulls my sweater over my head. My button-down shirt is next. He laughs when there's a thermal under that.

He pulls my hand and leads me to the stairs, up to his bedroom, and takes his phone out of his pocket, placing it next to the bed. His expression is shy when he looks at me again.

"I really like having you in my space," he says. "Didn't think that was something I'd ever say."

I walk toward him and put my hands on his chest, leaning up to brush my lips against his. When my hand touches his face, he covers it with his.

"Your hands are freezing. Want me to warm you up in the shower?" he asks.

"That sounds perfect. I'm just trying to not get all of this too wet." I point to my chest. "Which will be easier to pull off in your swanky shower made for like a dozen people."

He winces. "I hate that you're still hurting. I'll make sure we're careful."

"I swear it's feeling so much better." My head falls back and I groan. "So much for my intention to seduce you into bed. We get home and are sidetracked by smelly animals and the unsexiest talk ever."

He stills, his eyes boring into mine. "Does it scare you when I say hearing you call this home might be the sexiest thing I've ever heard?"

My heart thunders against my rib cage, and I shake my head. "Not even a little."

He lifts my last shirt carefully over my head, pausing to kiss my bare shoulder.

"I've never been with anyone without a condom," I say against his neck. "And I've been on birth control for a long time."

"Never?" he rasps. "I don't know why I said that. I wouldn't care if you had been, as long as we're going into this knowing we're clear of everything. I haven't either…and I'm free of all the things," he adds and shakes his head. "Did that make sense? I can't think straight when you're touching me."

I grin, leaning over and nipping his bottom lip. "Same here. All clear." And then I turn and look at him over my shoulder as I walk toward his bathroom. "Whoever gets naked first gets to come first."

"Oh, are those the rules?" His voice is raspy.

His pupils dilate as I take off my pants and reach into the shower to turn on the water. His hand slides under my lacy panties and he squeezes, cursing under his breath.

The water runs, and the steam warms the room. I'm overheated anyway, with his hands on me. Senses on overload as he dips his fingers inside. The way he turns me around and lowers to his knees, watching my reactions as he chases the sway of my hips with his tongue diving deep…it's too much and it's just right.

The rules go out the window and I fall apart before my panties ever fully hit the floor.

But there's nothing compared to feeling him bare inside me. *Nothing.*

CHAPTER TWENTY-TWO

HAPPY THANKSGIVING

CALLUM

"Are you *sure* it's okay that we're not taking more than this?" Ruby asks.

She's balancing two chocolate pies on her lap, and a fruit salad is held in place between her knee-high boots as we drive to Grinny's on Thanksgiving.

"Yep, still positive."

"Uncle Pierre is bringing a few things, but I should've made more of an effort." She sighs, fidgeting and looking sexy as all fuck in her soft amber sweater that matches her eyes, tight black jeans, and her hair up in two messy buns.

"I promise what you're bringing is perfect," I tell her. "You look beautiful. I like your hair like that..."

"Thank you." She blows a curl away from her eye. "You didn't give me much time to get ready this morning, so I had to get creative."

I hum, unable to apologize for the way I made her scream with pleasure this morning. I can't keep my hands off of her. We took care of the animals yesterday, but every chance in between, I had her up against the wall in the barn and the shower and in the bed in her RV...and a couple times in the kitchen. It was a day I'll never forget.

But every day with her feels that way.

This morning was even better.

She gives me a stern look when she catches me staring at her.

"None of those bedroom eyes until we're back home and far, *far* away from your family. They're already going to take one look at me and know what we've been doing!"

I squeeze her thigh, loving the way her breath hitches when I slide closer to that sweet divide between her legs. I press my thumb over her with just enough pressure...

"If they don't know by looking at you, they'll for sure know when they see me," I tell her.

I can't help but laugh when her expression changes to horror, but I continue rubbing and her mouth parts. When she whimpers, I pull over to the side of the road and turn to face her. I move the pies to the floor next to the fruit salad and her eyes are glazed as she looks at me.

"Callum, I cannot go into your grandmother's house looking like I've just had an orgasm."

"Wouldn't it help you relax a little bit?"

She makes a face and then laughs as she nods. I don't waste time. I unzip her jeans and tug them down enough to get my hands beneath her pretty underwear. She moans and her head falls back against the seat when I make contact with her bare skin. Her teeth clamp down on her lower lip when I groan at how wet she is. My fingers dip in and out and it sounds obscene in the contained space of my truck. When I tap and rub her sweetest spot with my other hand, she gasps my name.

"Don't stop," she whispers. "Mmm, please."

"I'm not stopping. I love it when you let go. There's nothing better."

She moans again, bucking against my fingers, as I keep up a relentless rhythm.

I feel it when she's close and my dick jerks in my pants, desperate for her. It's a balancing act to not come in my pants, watching her this way, feeling the way her walls clamp down on my fingers, pulsing, pulsing, pulsing.

"I could come just watching you. You're the sweetest fucking thing," I whisper.

"I love the things you say," she cries. "I'm close again." Another wave sends her flying and her eyes squeeze shut, and I watch, entranced as her hips lift, trying to get as much of me inside her as possible.

It's like fireworks detonating inside her, and I continue to rub her bud until she sinks back into the seat, spent.

Her gaze is hooded when she looks at me again, still catching her breath.

"It's like I can't get enough of you," she says. "Nothing has ever been like this." She shakes her head, dazed. "I had no idea."

"I didn't know it could be like this either, Sunshine. You blow my mind."

She lifts an arm and it's floppy. "I'm weak." She laughs. "But I saw some wet wipes in here somewhere. I think you'll need them."

I laugh and bend down to get the wet wipes, wiping my hands thoroughly. "Feels like a shame to wipe the taste of you off, but it's probably best that we don't go in Grinny's house smelling like sex."

"Oh God," she wails, flinging her arm against her forehead. "Hand me the wipes."

I kiss her cheek and hand her the wipes, putting the truck in drive again as she cleans up.

"Don't be nervous, Sunshine. My family hoped for this to happen between us when they first met you anyway, couldn't you tell?"

"They won't think I'm a horrible person because things have moved so quickly?"

I pat her cheek and then focus on the road, laughing again. This woman makes me laugh more than I ever have. I'm a fucking cheesy sap and I'm not even mad about it.

"Trust me, the Landmark family cannot say one word on this. Turns out, we're notorious for falling hard and fast. And it's worked out well for my sister and brothers so far. Well... except for Sutton..."

When I look at her again, her expression is wistful.

"What?" I ask.

"You're falling for me?"

I drag in a deep breath and let it out slowly.

"Ruby, if this were a well, I'd be at the very bottom."

We pull in front of Grinny's place and I look at her. There's a huge smile on her face.

She leans over and kisses me, her fingers gripping the pies again. When she pulls away, her eyes shining, she whispers, "I've fallen down in that well with you, and I don't want to ever be pulled up."

I smile against her mouth. "Is this love?"

"I think it is."

I try to deepen the kiss, but she pulls back, breathless.

"I really want to talk about this more, but I don't want to be late to Thanksgiving dinner. I've had two orgasms which did help relax me, thank you very much, but I still feel the need to keep making a good impression with your family," she says, handing the pies to me.

She winces when she sees the bulge in my pants.

"I promise I will *so* make it up to you later," she says.

She bends down to pick up the fruit salad and is out of the truck before I've turned it off.

I do my best to adjust myself and then give up, knowing I'll just have to hope the pies are enough of a distraction, and I guide her around the icy sections as we walk toward the door.

"If you make any better of an impression than you already have, you're going to be Mother Fucking Teresa," I say, as Grinny opens the door wide.

Of course, it's just in time for her to hear my last three words.

Her mouth drops. "Callum Henry Landmark, that is sacrilegious!"

If she only knew.

"Sorry, Grinny," I mutter.

Ruby snorts as she tries to stifle her laughter and it gets worse when I pretend to glare at her. Grinny takes the fruit salad from her and Ruby tries to take one of the pies from me.

"Nuh-uh-uh," I say, stepping out of reach. "You go ahead." I nod for her to go in front of me. "I need to see the view from here."

Her mouth drops and she looks at me wide-eyed over her shoulder. "That is *not* behaving."

I grin. "And it feels fucking fantastic."

"What feels fucking fantastic?" Jamison asks as he steps in behind me carrying two casseroles.

Scarlett shoots us both a look. "Don't let Grinny hear those f-bombs coming forth so early in the day. She needs a little wine in her before she lets them roll off her back a little easier—" She pauses and her head tilts as she studies me, her lips pursed and then her eyes brighten and she leans around me to get a better look at Ruby. "Why, *hello*, you two," she says.

I don't think I've ever seen Scarlett smile so big, and she's a smiler.

"Scarlett," I warn under my breath.

"What?" Sweet, *phony* innocence. "I'm just saying hello!"

"Mm-hmm."

Her laugh is a little deranged as she moves past me to walk next to Ruby down the hall. She puts her arm around Ruby's shoulder and squeezes.

"You're looking particularly gorgeous today, Ruby," she says. She looks back at me. "You too, brother. Such a healthy glow."

She winks at me and I give her a murderous look, which only makes her laugh. She turns back around to Ruby and says something too soft for me to hear. Ruby glances at her and smiles.

"I'd love that," I hear her say.

I don't know when *I* became the nosy bastard in this family, but I want to know what they're saying. When we make it to the kitchen, it's too loud to hear anything but rowdy hellos for the next few minutes. I set the pies down and look around for Owen when I see Sutton.

"He's with his mom," he says. "I'm missing the hell out of him."

"I was certain you had him for Thanksgiving," I say, disappointed to not see my nephew today.

"That was the plan, but a big opportunity has opened up for Tracy. She's going to check out this new job in Arizona. If she takes it, she'll be moving there soon."

"Owen would go with her?" I try to keep the alarm out of my voice because Sutton already seems to be in rough shape.

"No, but we're still talking out the details. She's ready to focus on her career, and she's not saying it, but I'm reading between the lines that her divorce with Jeff hasn't gone smoothly. I don't want Owen to get lost in the shuffle."

"That's fair. Keep me posted, man."

He nods. "Want a beer yet? I brought Laughing Lab for you."

"Sure."

He goes to get it and Scarlett walks to the back door to let Lucia and Delgado in. Ruby loses her mind over them, just as I knew she would.

"I've never seen an all-white chihuahua," she says, as Delgado twirls around her feet.

She lifts him up and kisses his nose. He pants in her face, looking like he's smiling back at her.

"I am in love," she says, sighing happily.

Her cheeks flush and she glances over at me, swallowing hard when she sees my expression.

Lucia nuzzles against my leg and I pet her and then Theo's dog, Fred, when he comes over for his loving. Lucia adores Fred almost as much as Delgado, but she doesn't love having my attention divided, so she stands on her hind legs and puts her front paws on my shoulders. She's a gorgeous, *massive* Siberian Husky, and Scarlett and Jamison rescued both dogs before the two of them got together.

"I see you, pretty girl," I tell her.

Ruby sets Delgado down when he starts squirming and he runs over, jumping up on my leg. I give Lucia one more hug.

"Down, Lucia," I say, and she lowers her paws to sit in front of me. "Good girl." I bend down and pick up Delgado, trying to avoid his speedy tongue. "It's nice to see you too, buddy," I say softly.

"I wish Lucia would be that obedient with me," Jamison says.

"I know. Callum's animal whisperer ways have always been inspiring," Theo says.

"You have a way with animals too," Sofie tells Theo, "but *all* the animals are obsessed with Callum." She looks over at Ruby and grins.

"I am too," Ruby says, sighing.

And then her cheeks flame red and her eyes gape wide.

"Uh, I meant…here, *here* too. Yeah, I've seen it firsthand at his ranch, but wow, yeah, it's…wow." She wrings her hands together and looks mortified.

I walk over to her with Delgado still tucked against my chest and press my lips against hers. I hear the quick intake of her gasp and she's too stunned to fully kiss me back, but I stay right there until I feel some of the tension seep out of her. When I pull away, you could hear a pin drop, it's so quiet, every eye in the house trained on us.

"I'm obsessed with you too," I say quietly, but knowing my family, everyone's ears are straining so hard, they hear every word.

When I step back, she smiles shakily. She takes a deep

breath and grips my hand hard, but she looks more like herself.

Sutton comes over and pounds my back, handing me a beer.

"God*da*—God *does* miracles," Sutton says, catching his curse midstream as Grinny walks over to Ruby and me.

She hugs Ruby and then keeps holding onto her as she leans over and hugs me. Her eyes are watery and she clears her throat and shakes her head, trying to stave off the emotion.

"We're so happy you're here, Ruby," she says. "As you can probably tell, this guy right here means the world to all of us, and he doesn't exactly expose all he's feeling 99.9% of the time, so to see that—" Her voice breaks. "Well, I'm just so happy and thankful, that's all."

I pat Grinny's back, my eyes on Ruby, as I try to decipher how she's handling all this.

"Let's just try not to scare her off today, shall we?" I attempt a light tone and my siblings laugh.

Ruby's eyes straighten and her eyes blaze as she smirks at me. "I don't scare easily, Callum Henry Landmark."

There's a roar of laughter and a lot of *Ooos* around the room, but fuck me, all I want is to bury myself inside her and never come up for air.

"What did we miss?" Pierre calls out and Pappy is with him, both carrying tons of food.

"I'll fill you in," Scarlett says, hurrying over to help them inside.

Ruby smiles at me before turning to hug her uncle, and I can't help but think how much she looks like she belongs right here with me.

CHAPTER TWENTY-THREE

FOUND

RUBY

"I had the best time," I sing on the drive home from Grinny's, hours later. Since we got there mid-afternoon and stayed a long time, it feels later than it really is. "Everyone is so wonderful and the food was amazing...and you get to sleep in tomorrow morning..."

His fingers squeeze mine.

"*We* get to sleep in," he adds. "It was really generous of Hilary and Abby to offer. They claim they want more practice before we go to Utah, but I think the truth is they're getting attached to the girls."

"Who wouldn't?"

His laugh is low and usually just a simple *hmm* sound under his breath—it's rare that he laughs as boisterously as his brothers do—but it never fails to make my heart expand.

"Pack a bag. I'm taking you away for a day or two," he says.

"Really? Where are we going?"

"I arranged it with Blake, that friend I've told you about who owns Tiptop, and his friend Jimbo, who owns several properties in Nesters Park. It's beautiful there and only two and a half hours away. Enough to feel like we're getting away, but not so far that we're doing a ton of driving."

"I'd love to see more of Colorado. When's the last time you took a trip?" I ask.

"I travel to Denver and Colorado Springs occasionally, but I haven't been on a vacation since right after college...a *long* time ago," he says sheepishly.

I poke his gut. "You're not that old, Grandpa."

"Compared to you, I am," he says, lifting a shoulder. "Wait, we went to Vegas for a couple of nights before Theo and Sofie's wedding—that wasn't long ago at all."

"That's still not much! Do you just prefer to be home?"

"Yes. I love to travel too, but it's felt too hard. Having Abby and Hilary willing to help this week has made me realize I could've done something like this long before now."

"I know what you mean. I dreamed of traveling in Utah, but it's hard to make peace with entrusting someone else with your babies...especially when you know they won't do as good of a job. I don't mean Hilary and Abby...people who care like they do are invaluable."

We pull into his driveway and he looks over at me. "You

really want to do this? Would you rather go somewhere else? It doesn't have to be so close."

"How about another time? Tonight I like the idea of us going somewhere close and waking up in a new, beautiful place."

I can see his teeth shining when he smiles in the dark. He squeezes my hand.

"Okay, that we can do."

I go to see Dolly until I'm freezing, and she's too sleepy to visit much longer anyway. Then I stop in the RV to grab a cream sweater dress in case we go somewhere fancy, and a couple of sweaters and jeans I haven't pulled out yet. I thought I'd circulate my wardrobe before now, but I haven't minded paring down on everything. The simplicity has been nice.

At the last second, I pull out my boots that match the sweater dress. They go up to my thighs and I've only worn them one other time—out with Kess when we shopped for my wedding dress. I needed that extra dose of confidence and they did the trick. Around Callum, I feel sexy in leggings and my emu merch, but I'd like to see his face when I walk out in these. I smile and tuck them into a bag, along with the other clothes.

He's walking toward the RV when I step out and he helps me down, taking my things from me. Excitement is buzzing through him.

"What's happening?" I ask.

"Oh, just working on a plan." As usual, his voice is even and understated, but his eyes are twinkling.

"You look like you're choking on excitement," I say, laughing.

He chuckles. "I do, huh?"

"Mm-hmm. It's a really hot look on you."

I put my hand on his back as he opens the truck and sets my things inside. His bag is already in there. When he turns around, I lean on my tiptoes and kiss him. He kisses me back, his mouth catching my moans when I feel his erection against me.

"Are you trying to distract me?" he asks.

"Is it working?"

"It's always working." He takes a step back and kisses my fingers. "Do you need to get anything from the house?"

"Yes."

"Okay, go ahead, and I'll check on everything out here."

"We're doing this?"

"You still want to?" His head tilts and even in the lamp-light, I can make out his smiling eyes.

"Absolutely," I say.

"Then, hell, yes, we're doing this."

He smacks my backside and I yelp, laughing as I walk into the house to get my cosmetic bag and a few other things.

Within half an hour, we're on our way. I'm the DJ, alternating between his playlist and mine, and the time flies by. It's eleven thirty when we pull in front of a winter wonderland villa, all lit up.

"What do you think?" he asks.

"Callum! This is where we're staying?"

"Think you can handle a night or two of this?"

"Uh, yes!" I squeal.

He grins, that excitement from earlier just under the surface.

We grab our things and walk up to the front door. Callum enters a code and then we're inside. It's truly breathtaking— cathedral ceilings in the entryway with stairs winding up, intricate woodwork, and plush, comfortable couches.

"Wow."

"Will this work?"

I cover my mouth, giddy as I keep looking around. "Thank you for this, Callum. It's absolutely stunning."

"The pantry should be loaded and the fridge is stocked with meals. But if we feel like going out, there are a couple of restaurants nearby that Blake and Camilla love."

"I need to meet them soon."

"Yes, you do." He tugs me against him and kisses me but pulls away just as I melt into him. "Wanna see the rest of the place?" he asks.

I nod, and he laughs at how emphatic I am.

There's a hot tub on the deck and a bar area with an elaborate trellis, lights twinkling around the beams. It's beautiful at night, but I can't wait to see what it looks like during the day. Each room is exquisite, but when I see the main bedroom, I'm blown away. The bed is massive and covered with the softest, plushest linens and throw pillows. The ceilings peak in the center and the sky shows through the skylights. A wall of windows faces what I know must be a gorgeous view, and the bathroom is the grandest I've ever seen.

"I love it," I keep saying, with each new area we see.

"I love *you*," he says, his deep voice gruff yet tender.

I turn to look at him, and the raw emotion on his face makes me tremble.

"I love you too," I whisper. "I can't believe how much."

He reaches out and takes my hand. "I'd understand if you're not ready to be saying this yet. I realize it's crazy and you just got out of—"

"What I just got out of was a mistake that I'm so relieved didn't go beyond what it did, and what I'm feeling is unlike anything I've ever felt before. It might be crazy, but if it is, I want to fall back into it and let it carry me away." I lift my hands in the air and my words feel like a proclamation, sealing this moment.

His hands circle my waist and he lifts me, turning me around and around as he kisses me.

A few hours after he's worshipped my body, and I've worshipped his, I'm limp from the workout and orgasm-drugged, but still too excited to sleep. We've talked nonstop and there's still so much more to know about him. He wants to know everything about me, things I'm sure would bore anyone else. And just as we start to fall asleep, he traces his fingers down my body or I kiss his chest or we kiss until our lips are puffy, and it's like coming home each time our bodies sink into each other.

This is love.

And I didn't know I could find happiness like this.

CHAPTER TWENTY-FOUR

MORNING REFLECTIONS

CALLUM

The sun is bright when I wake up the next morning, something that I'm not used to. I glance at the clock next to the bed, and it's later than I usually sleep, but still early.

Ruby's head is on my chest, her leg wrapped around my thigh, and it's the best feeling in the world. We didn't get much sleep last night and haven't since we started sleeping together, but I have no regrets. Worth every ounce of fatigue, one hundred percent.

Once my family got over their shock of me professing my feelings for Ruby yesterday—okay, they never really got over it, they just mixed it up a bit by also teasing me about being the thirst trap lumberjack, whatever the hell that means. While we were eating, Marlow got a text from someone at work who sent a picture of a group of girls standing on the corner of Heritage Lane. When the phone was finally passed to me, I didn't get what everyone was laughing about at first. But when I zoomed in, I saw the sign they were holding had a picture of me, and in block letters, it said, "Get your sexy ax over here, lumberjack!"

While I find it bizarre, something like this would have annoyed me before. I value my privacy and attention is not something I ever go looking for, but when Ruby pulled up her website and saw that she'd sold another two hundred shirts, all I felt was proud of her. She warned me, after another round of apologies, that it could get crazier, but I don't care.

I'd do anything for her.

I love her. She doesn't know that I've never said those words to anyone but my family. I'm fucking thirty-two and it's taken me this long to feel anything close to this.

She sighs in her sleep and I wrap my arms around her tighter as she stirs. She nestles deeper into my neck and I close my eyes and eventually fall back into a blissful sleep.

The smell of bacon wakes me up and when I open my eyes, the bed is empty. Holy hell, it's ten o'clock. *Who am I?* I take a three-minute shower, eager to get downstairs and see what Ruby is up to. When I round the corner, she's in the kitchen, already ready for the day and humming as she flips pancakes. She grins when she sees me.

"Mornin', sleepyhead," she says.

"You're the prettiest thing I've ever seen," I rasp, my voice still not awake.

Her cheeks lift as her smile grows. "Look in the mirror, lumberjack, you're the pretty one," she teases. "You hungry? You showed up right on time."

"I'm hungry." I round the island and stand behind her, my hands on her hips.

When I kiss her neck, she turns and faces me, leaning up to kiss me. I'm ready to feast on her when she breaks the kiss and turns to grab the plate piled high with pancakes.

"Let's get you fed. You must be exhausted with all that exertion you put out last night," she says, smirking.

"Is that what we're calling it? Exertion?"

As she turns to carry the food to the table, I squeeze her ass and she shakes it side to side.

I groan, blood thrumming to my dick. "If you want to eat those pancakes anytime soon, you better get that ass over there and sit down."

She smirks at me over her shoulder. "We're on vacation, we can do whatever we want."

I smack her ass and she squeals, laughing as she moves toward the table.

"Did you see the view yet?" she asks.

"Yep. Haven't taken my eyes off you."

Her eyes are shining so bright it makes my chest ache.

"Well, grab your coffee and then come take a look at the other view." She points at the window next to the table and I curse under my breath. "Right?" she says. "I can't get over it. I mean, your view is incredible too, so you're used to this…"

"But it's different. Both are spectacular."

She nods and sits down, while I pour a cup of coffee.

When I walk over to the table, I kiss her cheek before I sit down.

"Thanks for breakfast and for coming here with me. I can't believe I slept until ten."

"I can't either. I was sure you'd wake up at your normal time."

"I went back to sleep."

"Do you ever pretend like you're on vacation in Landmark Mountain?"

"What do you mean?"

She shrugs. "Like go stay at the lodge, go exploring?"

"I love the lodge, but I guess it doesn't feel like a vacation as much when you know everyone working there. Maybe it'd be fun, I don't know. I used to spend more time there as a kid, but life got busy when I started the ranch. I hike often. Usually alone, sometimes with Theo and Fred. My brothers and I ski regularly. I've missed a couple trips up the mountain since a certain someone has been occupying my mind."

Her cheeks flush. "I don't want to keep you from doing what you normally do." Her tone is way too concerned for the playful way I was trying to get that across.

"Ruby, being with you is what I want to do. Have I not made that clear?"

I slide my foot against hers and up her leg when she grins at me shyly.

"You've maybe made it kind of clear." Her foot slides up my leg and I fist my napkin.

"I'll have to work on that," I say through my teeth when her foot rubs over my dick once and then again very slowly. "Do you like to ski?" My voice is a little higher than usual and her eyes crinkle up as she tries not to laugh.

I'm just trying my damnedest to not make her think I'm

an asshole who can only think about sex twenty-four hours a day. She's making it fucking difficult.

"I love it. At home I never went as often as I wanted, but I do love it."

"Would you like to ski today? Or shop or hike? Or… whatever I haven't thought of…"

"I'm happy whatever we do," she says, her foot doing another detour around my crotch. "I just like being here with you."

"You like seeing what you do to me, don't you?"

"I love it," she whispers.

"I'm taking you out of this house today," I tell her. "I can't bring you all the way here and not show you something besides this." I grab her foot and press it against me.

Her mouth parts and then she pouts. "But it's my favorite."

I choke out a laugh. "You're killing me, Sunshine. You're looking so cute today. Eat up and let's go find some fun."

She rolls her eyes as she smirks. "Whatever." In the next second, her hand hits the table. "The farmer's market! Were you supposed to be there tomorrow?"

I nod, as I finish chewing. "Yeah, but Theo and Sof are taking it, and depending on the timing, they might alternate with Hilary and Abby when we go to Utah."

"You thought of everything. You bring the fun wherever you go, Callum," she says, trying so hard to keep a straight face.

I narrow my eyes, pointing at her. "*You're* the fun one. I'm not really known for bringing the fun to any occasion."

Her head falls back as her laugh fills the villa, and I stare at her in awe.

"And you're sassy on vacation," I add.

"Stick around. You'll find out that's not the only time I am."

"I plan to, Sunshine. I plan to."

CHAPTER TWENTY-FIVE

THESE BOOTS ARE MADE FOR WEDDINGS

RUBY

This has been the best day. We opted to ice skate instead of skiing, although Callum has promised we'll go skiing when-ever I want to back in Landmark Mountain. The shops are so cute around here that it felt wrong to *not* do a little shopping, and it just makes me excited to get back to Heritage Lane and explore there too.

I feel like I've been on hold and floundering a bit, not knowing when I can go check on the emus, and that's still

hanging over me, but this thing with Callum—this enchant-
ment—has taken over every thought. I don't have a name for
what we are. Magic? Nothing seems quite big enough.

I love every single second with him. It's like a constant
yearning even when he's next to me, even when he's
inside me.

I crave him.

My cheeks hurt from smiling and laughing. My hands are
always on him. My skin is on high alert every time he touches
me, which is constantly. His kisses make me weak and exhil-
arated, the topsy-turvy combo making me dazed half the time.

And the best part? *He is deep in this with me.*

He's still laid-back. He's still stoic and grumbles, and I
think he probably imagines he's giving me a full-wattage
smile when he barely shows any teeth. That *hmm* chuckle
comes out more frequently, and it's so *satisfying* when it
sometimes goes deeper. But his eyes drink me up. His hands
have mastered me. And his words...

I've seen the way he is with everyone else. Even the
people he loves most don't get all the words he hands me
freely every second we're together, and it makes me feel like
the luckiest woman alive.

We have a delicious lunch at one of the restaurants Blake
and Camilla suggested, and then spend at least an hour in a
quaint bookstore that happens to have a superior selection of
romance novels and thrillers, my two favorites.

I find Callum in the biography section. He checks out the
books I'm holding.

"Want me to carry them?" he asks.

"I'm good. Your hands need to be free to peruse," I say.

He tips my chin up, his eyes on my mouth. "You're right
about that."

His eyes are heated and my insides twist in his orbit.

"Everything you say sounds provocative," I whisper.

I sound breathless, feel breathless…

"You started it," he whispers back, leaning in my ear. "Saying things like *with free hands to peruse* and *provocative.*"

I shiver and his mouth lifts against my ear.

"Are you wet right now?"

"Mm-hmm."

"Good. I want you to be so needy for me by tonight that you take exactly what you want."

"You're making me wait for it?" I say, louder than I intended.

"*Hmm.*" His chuckle sends a rain of chill bumps across my skin. "Yes, I am."

He straightens, and if his eyes weren't gleaming and focused on my mouth, I might not be able to tell he's also struggling with restraint.

His eyes drift down to my chest and he licks his lips, and my eyes fall down to the bulge in his pants.

I smirk and his jaw clenches as he puckers his lips, playfully defiant. A picture of composure to anyone else who might be looking, *but I see you, Callum Landmark.*

I glance nonchalantly over my shoulder.

"Oh, I haven't seen that area yet." I point to the wall of classics in pretty covers.

And I turn and walk away from him, letting my hips sway a little more than usual.

I hear another growl and barely hold back my smile as I walk to the pretty books.

A few minutes later, I've found a chair to sit in as I order more merchandise to fill the orders from my website. I have some stored in one of the closets in the RV, but not enough. I arrange for it to be shipped to Callum's, hesitating only briefly to wonder if that's a good idea. We haven't really talked about how long I'll stay with him and the timing could be off if I get the chance to go to Utah before the shipments arrive.

It'll work out, I tell myself. *Everything else seems to be going smoothly...this will too.*

I flip through one of my favorite decorating magazines. That was always my splurge, along with books—decorating magazines. I spent so much time poring over them and dreaming of what I wanted to do next. I miss working on Jolene. I need to figure out what to work on next.

While it's on my mind, I do a quick post on my social media sites, some footage of Dolly, some of Thanksgiving, and I thank all the new followers who have found me. I used to post every day, sometimes multiple times, but being busy at the ranch and with Callum has made it glaringly obvious how alone I really was. There's no question that I was also busy there, working nonstop on the businesses, but since I was by myself, I could throw in two or three posts up just showing my life. Callum's been cool about the exposure he's gotten over it, but I'm not sure how he'd feel if that was constant.

Just then I hear a girl's voice.

"Oh my God, are you...are you that guy? Lumberjack guy?"

I grit my teeth and wait for Callum's answer, looking around to see if I can spot him.

I hear him say something but can't make it out.

"You look just like him," the girl says.

Within seconds, Callum rounds the bookshelves and walks toward me. I stand up, gathering the books I want to buy.

"Have you been spotted?" I whisper.

He nods and we hurry to the checkout counter. He keeps his head down and we hustle out of there.

"I'm so sorry about this," I tell him.

He takes my hand and is quiet for a minute as we walk down the street.

"You don't need to be sorry. At all. I just...the thing is..." He makes a face and looks at me sheepishly.

"What?" I'm suddenly terrified of what he's going to say.

He exhales. "I don't want them to think I'm available." He holds up our joined hands and kisses my fingers.

I melt. "That's...understandable. But why do you look guilty when you say that?"

"Because it's childish. It's not like I'm going to be tempted by anyone throwing themselves at me." He shrugs and then frowns at me when I giggle. "I can handle myself."

"I have no doubt."

He frowns again. "It's not just that I'm not available. It's that *you* are the one holding my heart in your hands."

I must gasp because his eyes flicker to mine to assess how I'm taking this. I squeeze his hand.

"I want to shout it to the world that we're together, which is crazy because—you may have noticed—I don't shout anything."

I laugh and my heart feels like it's about to burst wide open.

"But with you, I want to shout it out at the top of my lungs, just how much I love you," he says. "I worry you might think it's too soon. But for me, there are no doubts. I didn't know I could ever feel this way about someone. You blew into my life and I never want you to leave. It might seem quick to everyone looking in, but to me, I think I knew the day I met you, that you are it for me. And I don't expect you to…do anything, that's not what I—" He curses under his breath and stops on the sidewalk, lifting his head to the sky like he's looking for help.

I put my hand on his arm.

"I am so in love with you," I whisper.

His breath hitches and he grips my hand tighter in his.

"I never knew how it felt to be loved like this, Callum."

He's staring at me so intently when bells start ringing behind me. His mouth parts and he gets an expression that I haven't seen yet.

I turn to see what has his attention and whisper, "*Oh*."

We're standing in front of an adorable white chapel covered in twinkle lights. Wedding Chapel is painted on the sign above the door, and the little chalk sign outside says, *Walk right in and get married today!* in scrolly letters. The bells ring for a few more seconds and then it's quiet.

We stare at it for a moment and then turn to look at each other.

"Are you thinking what I'm thinking?" he asks.

A bead of sweat is on his forehead and his hand trembles slightly as he pulls it out of my hand and lifts it to my cheek.

I nod.

"I want to marry you," he says. So soft it's barely audible, but my whole body resonates with the words.

"I want to marry you too," I tell him.

And I really, really do.

I think I'd have no doubts regardless of my circumstances, but because of what I've been through and know how that felt, there is no question in my mind that I want to marry Callum. It's crystal clear.

"You do?" He sets down the bag of books and pulls me against him. "I don't care when we do it. And I'd be happy if you just say you're mine if marriage is not on the table," he says. "But I'd also do it today and not regret it for a second."

"Let's do it today," I say, shocking both of us when I start laughing. "Doesn't it feel like a sign?"

He starts laughing, *really* laughing, and I feel like I could float away on a cloud.

"You're sure?" he asks.

"I can't even express how sure," I tell him.

He laughs again. "I can't believe this."

He kisses me, his hands winding through my hair. It's both grounding and freeing at once, giving him full access to my heart.

Someone whistles at us and we break apart, still holding on tight to each other.

"We'll need a marriage license," he says.

———————

Two hours later, I'm in my white sweater dress and the boots I almost didn't bring. I'm so glad I did—I think Callum almost passes out when he sees me walking down the stairs in them. It's not exactly a wedding dress, but he's already seen me in that. This feels much better.

He brought a suit in case we decided to go to a fancy restaurant, and he's standing at the bottom of the stairs in it. Callum in a suit is *intoxicating*.

It takes me a minute to notice he's holding a ring box open.

"You did this while you were out?" He wasn't gone for more than an hour.

"You look stunning, Ruby." His voice is reverent.

"*You* take my breath away," I say.

I put my hands on his chest and he lifts the ring up, reminding me that it's there.

"We can get something you like better, but I wanted you to have one for today…" His voice trails off.

I glance down and gasp. "*Callum*."

"It's called a Sunburst Halo…seemed like another sign… if you like it," he says. "The jeweler will also size it for you tomorrow if it's not the right size."

He's more nervous than I've ever seen him, and it's so endearing and sexy, I don't know what to do with myself.

I hold up my finger and he slides it on. It fits.

He exhales like he's relieved.

"Are you having any second thoughts?" he asks.

I shake my head. "None."

"Me either."

"How do you feel about kids?" I ask.

"I like them," he says, his lips tipping up when I laugh.

"Me too. So you'd be happy if we were able to have kids together?"

"I'd be fucking beside myself."

I press my lips together, but it's hard to contain how giddy I feel right now.

"Will your family be upset that you're doing this without them?"

He winces. "Yes. But they'll be happy for me too."

"While you were gone, I was thinking about them, wondering if you might wish they were with you. Maybe we do a little something with them later. We could even keep it to ourselves that we got married here and have a wedding with them. That way, we'd still have today for us, and they'd be included too."

"I only need you there, but this a good plan. Otherwise, we'd hear about it for the rest of our lives." He kisses my ring finger and looks up at me while he's still bent near my hand. "And Dolly can be there…"

That gets me. My eyes fill with tears and I press my lips together, trying to hold it in.

"I love you, Callum."

"I love you too, Sunshine."

CHAPTER TWENTY-SIX

PRIMING AND OGLING

CALLUM

It feels surreal when Ruby walks down the aisle of the tiny chapel holding a bouquet of flowers, her eyes never leaving mine.

She looked breathtaking in that wedding dress the first day I saw her, and she looks breathtaking today in her sweater dress that highlights every curve and those fuck-me boots. She'll look breathtaking tonight when I strip her bare and lay her across the sheets with only the moonlight as my guide...

I gulp when she stands in front of me, overwhelmed with how she's taken permanent residence way down deep in my soul.

She places her flowers on a stand nearby and we join hands, facing each other.

The officiant, Mr. McDougal, clears his throat and begins.

"Callum and Ruby, you have picked an excellent day to declare your love in holy matrimony. As Shakespeare famously said, and I'll paraphrase," he adds, smiling wider every time we look at him, "love is an ever-fixed mark that looks on tempests and isn't shaken. As someone who has been married to the same woman for forty-five years, I can tell you there are shaky times, but if you remain steadfast in your love for one another, it will carry you during those times. I'll also paraphrase Buddha's Sermon at Rajagaha—cherish goodwill, be free of hate and envy, and the rule of life that is always best is to be loving-kind. And finally, in the Bible, I Corinthians 16:14, we're instructed to *do everything in love*. So, as you can see, the common denominator here is love. Hold onto it with everything you've got, fight for it, make your love a priority from this day forth."

He glances at me and nods. "Callum, do you have a few words?"

"I do."

Ruby's eyes are shining with tears, but she smiles at my choice of words.

I swallow hard and grip her hands tighter.

"I've never thought of myself as spontaneous, but ever since you showed up, Ruby Sunshine Jones, my heart just says *yes*. Whatever you need, I want to give it to you. Wherever you are, that's where I want to be."

A tear drips down her cheek and I reach up to catch it.

"I want to see you smile. Hear your laugh. Feel your lips against mine."

I wipe another tear and smile at her.

"I'm a goner, pure and simple. I don't care if this is impulsive or too fast or too much or any other things that we might hear from others about our relationship...as long as you're with me...*yes*. I'll honor and cherish you in sickness and in health, for richer or poorer, 'til death do us part."

Her lips tremble and she presses them together, taking a shaky breath before she starts speaking.

"I say yes to you too, Callum Henry Landmark. I've never known anyone like you. I love your kind, gentle heart. The way you nurture those cows and goats and me."

She smiles and sniffles, and Mr. McDougal hands her a handkerchief that she uses to dab her nose.

"You make me want to dream big, to take risks, and not let anything or anyone dull my shine. You treat me like I'm your equal, respecting me, yet with just a look, you make me weak in the knees."

Her cheeks turn pink when she says that last part, and if I didn't want to hear every word so badly, I'd kiss her senseless right now.

"I can't wait to be your wife. I'll honor you and cherish you in sickness and in health, for richer or poorer, 'til death do us part."

When it's quiet for a beat, Mr. McDougal speaks up. "Please present your rings to one another."

I pull both rings out of my pocket, and hand her the one I bought for me.

"You thought of everything," she whispers.

I slide her ring on and she does the same with my ring.

"These rings symbolize the strength of your commitment

to each other and the love you share," Mr. McDougal says. "By the power vested in me by the state of Colorado, I now pronounce you husband and wife. You may kiss the bride."

I don't waste any time. I kiss my bride and I make it a kiss she'll remember. We're both breathless when it's over, and smiling like two maniacs.

Music flows through the speakers out of nowhere, and Mr. McDougal says, "Presenting Mr. and Mrs. Callum Landmark!"

Ruby and I look at each other and laugh because the room is empty. And also because, holy hell, we just got *married*.

As we're walking down the aisle, I say, "I forgot to ask if you want to keep your name. I love your name."

"You think I want to miss out on a name like Landmark? There's no way."

I turn and kiss her again. And again. Mr. McDougal makes sure we make it out of there with our marriage license and the flowers, and we're still kissing when we get to my truck.

"Ruby Sunshine Landmark." I nod, as I open her door. "It does have a special spark, doesn't it?"

"*Mrs.* Ruby Sunshine Landmark." Her head falls back and she laughs, looking fucking radiant, as she adds, "We really did this. We got *married*."

She gets in the truck, and I wave the marriage certificate in the air, while I walk around to the other side.

We have a fancy dinner where we drink wine and eat more than we should, high on life, and when the piano player starts singing, "Can't Help Falling in Love," it feels like another sign. With her hand in mine, we walk over by the piano and dance. As other couples join us, the musician gets inspired, and we dance as long as he plays. My body is so keyed up from having her body lined up with mine, that by the time we get back to the house, I feel like one brush of her hand against me could send me soaring.

She must feel the same way because when the door closes behind us, she turns and puts her hand on me, making a little whimper when she feels how hard I am.

"I don't know if I can wait until we get upstairs to have you inside me. Or another second. Dancing with you...the wine...the wedding..." She moans when I lick my way up her neck. "You have been priming me for hours."

I tug my tie away from my neck and she gets it undone. We're a tangle of clothes and hands and tongues. Her sweater dress isn't the easiest for me to get off of her since I'm still trying to be careful not to hurt her burns, so she takes over.

And she gives me the shock of my life when what's underneath that dress is a white all-lace one piece. She stands in front of me in nothing but lace and boots...

"*Fuck*, Ruby. What is *this*?"

I clutch my chest and my dick bobs around in my briefs with one pulse after another. I'm way too close to exploding. I grip the tip hard and will myself to chill.

She gives me a coy look. "Remember when Scarlett ran home to get something yesterday? It wasn't really food. She brought this back for me. Said she'd just made it and it was a little present for both of us."

Her hand is on her hip and then she turns around slowly, looking at me over her shoulder. The lace highlights her perfect round cheeks, leaving them bare for me to stare at in wonder.

Fuck.

"You never told me she makes things like this," she says.

I scrub my hand over my face. "Not something we share

much with each other." My mouth is watering. "God, Ruby. You. Are. Perfection. I cannot wait."

Her mouth parts. "Well, it's a good thing I'm ready for you."

"Get over here," I growl.

CHAPTER TWENTY-SEVEN

THE VALLEY

RUBY

My body is deliciously sore when I wake up. I open my eyes and Callum's head is propped up on his hand as he looks at me.

"You're watching me sleep?" My voice comes out in a hoarse rasp.

I used my lungs last night. A *lot*.

"If it's creepy, I'm not sure I can stop. You're too beautiful to look away."

"I stared at you for an hour before I got up to make break-fast yesterday. I really wanted to pull the covers off of you and stare at you completely naked, but I thought you might think that was a little *eek*." I hold my hands up and wave them.

"Hmm." His chuckle is deeper this morning from using his lungs too. "My wife has permission to stare at me any way she wants."

"Oh, wait, that's me, I'm the wife," I say, smiling at him before I lift the covers and stare at him in all his glory.

"Hmm."

"I swear that one-syllable chuckle is going to be the death of me."

"One-syllable chuckle?" he repeats.

I mock him and he gives me another one, his cheeks turning pink when I point at him.

"It's my laugh," he says, groaning when he does it again.

"It's so sexy I can't take it."

He bites the side of his cheek to keep from doing it again.

"You can't withhold it from me now!"

"Never," he says, laughing in spite of himself. "I'll never withhold anything from you."

His abs jerk as I run my fingers down his skin. He's thick and long and hard as steel, and I get distracted watching it jolt against his stomach.

"What are you thinking right now?" he asks.

"That I like watching it jolt against your stomach. And how hard you are, how I didn't think you could possibly fit inside me, but you do it *so well*."

"What do you call *it* in your mind?" He grips himself and if I wasn't already hungry for him, that would do it. "So far I've only heard you say *it* or *that thing*."

He chuckles and then rolls his eyes when I bite my lip and smile at the sound.

"That's pretty much what I call it in my head too," I admit. "All the real words were schooled out of me by my mother. It feels wrong to call this a—"

"What?" he prods.

"A willy," I whisper.

A loud laugh bursts out of him, making me jump and he tickles me, both of us cracking up.

He points down. "You cannot call *all of this* a willy," he says, still laughing. "No. Think of something else."

"That's what I grew up hearing. Penis would've never flown."

He wrinkles his nose, grumbling. "I don't need to hear penis either."

"What do you *need* to hear?" I lean in closer, my hand finally touching his hot, velvety skin.

He sucks in a breath when my hand slides up and down the length of him.

"What do *you* call it?" I ask.

He lifts a shoulder. "Dick. But I think I'd like to hear *you* say cock…at least once." He reaches over and slips a finger inside me. "Mm-hmm, I think you like the sound of that too."

My cheeks feel hot. I know it's ridiculous that I'm this way about saying certain words, even when I don't mind hearing them. At *all*.

"If you hate it, you can go back to saying *it* or *that thing*…as long as it's said in a tone of reverence," he says.

I burst out laughing and am moaning in the next second when he slides in another finger.

"Cock," I whisper. I clear my throat and say it again, louder.

He gets even harder in my hand, and his jaw twitches

before he nods and then leans over to lick my nipple and blow on it.

"Yes, I was right," he says, looking up from my chest. "I do like to hear you say that *very much*."

We spend the day in bed and take our time driving back to Landmark Mountain that evening.

"So, we're keeping Operation Elopement a secret until next month?" he asks, as we enter the city limits.

We've just decided that we want something to ourselves. Not that it matters what people think, but we don't want anyone telling us it's too soon either. We want to stay in our little bubble for a bit longer.

We've talked over a lot of options, but I think our favorite is to have a small ceremony at our house—still feels surreal to say that, *our house*—with our families during the week between Christmas and New Year's Day. I'm not sure if my parents will make the trip or not, but I'm sure Uncle Pierre will be there. Maybe even Kess.

"Yes, that seems perfect. I don't think anyone will be surprised that we're keeping it intimate, and they never have to know we're already married, if you think that'll upset anyone."

"I'll let you make that call," he says. "It's our lives. And I think everyone will be fine, for what it's worth."

"I'm not sure my parents will be, but I'm actually okay with that."

He squeezes my hand and when we pull into his driveway, he says, "Welcome home, Mrs. Landmark."

I lean over and kiss him. "I'll never get tired of hearing you say that."

After we've visited the animals and I've had a sweet reunion with my Dolly, we sit in front of the fireplace, trying yet again to have hot chocolate. I look at it longingly and when he notices, he lifts the mug to his lips to see if it's too hot.

"I think it's just right…but please don't spill it on yourself to test that theory," he says.

My phone rings and I glance at it, pausing when I see Kess's number.

"I should take this," I say.

He nods and sets the hot chocolate on the table next to me.

"Hello?"

"Ruby," Kess's voice breaks.

"Kess? What's wrong? What's going on?"

"I'm at the farm and…it's not good, Ruby. One of the…I think it's Thor, but you know how I get him confused with Stan…" She breaks out in sobs and I stare at Callum in alarm.

"What about Thor? Kess, talk to me."

"He's gone."

"What do you mean gone?"

"He's dead."

I put my fist over my mouth and feel my heart crack.

"I was here earlier and saw Junior. He was being a jerk," she says through her tears. "I didn't feel good about leaving…I'm so sorry, Ruby."

"It's not your fault, Kess. It's mine. I should've been there by now."

"No, it's Junior," she says, raising her voice. "I don't trust him, Ruby. I was here yesterday and everything looked fine. But tonight when I got here, they acted like they were starving, and when I confronted Junior, he said he warned you that you needed to get back here."

Tears stream down my face and Callum grips my hand. "I thought I should wait until my RV was ready, so I'd have a place to stay. I should've just gotten there. Why is he doing this?"

"He claims he had nothing to do with Thor, but I've called the sheriff anyway. I'll let you know if he's able to get to the bottom of it."

"Please call me with any updates. No matter how late. I'll rent a car in the morning or see if there's a flight..."

"I'm sorry," she says again. "I've gotta go. The sheriff just pulled up."

As soon as we hang up, I look at Callum helplessly. "Did you hear that?"

He nods, his jaw clenched. "What can I do to help?"

"Just keep holding on to me."

"I'm not going anywhere."

"I have to go home tomorrow...and I need to call Junior."

"Okay, I'm here if you need anything."

I nod gratefully and dial Junior's number. He answers right away.

"Babe, hear me out," Junior says. "I know what happened to that emu now. That section of gate that you kept repairing...he was trying to get out and got cut too badly. I haven't been mistreating your fucking emus. I heard Kess talking shit about me."

"How do you know it was the gate?" I ask, wiping my face as the tears keep falling.

"I saw the blood and feathers on the gate. I'm sorry, babe. I know how much you care about these birds."

My face twists up as I cry harder. He's not sorry. He

doesn't care. I want to rage at him, but I feel helpless being so far away and clueless about what's really going on.

"My RV broke down and needs a part. That's why I haven't gotten there sooner," I tell him.

Callum rubs my back and hands me a tissue, his eyes full of concern.

"So you *are* coming back?" Junior asks.

"As soon as I can. It's just taking a little longer than I'd hoped because the part has been on back order." I dry my face with the tissue. "Please don't let anything happen to another one!"

I sound hysterical, but I don't care. Thor...or even if it's really Stan...both of them are too young for this to be age-related. And Kess thought they looked fine yesterday. Maybe he really was trying to get out of the gate.

"You'll fix the fence?" I ask.

"I'll fix the fence," he says in a soothing voice that makes my nose curl up. "Just get your ass back here, Ruby."

"I already said I was," I snap.

"I've gotta go. The sheriff is here because your cousin is losing her shit. Rein her in, Ruby."

I growl into the phone, but he's already hung up. I toss the phone on the floor next to me and put my face in my hands.

"It's so late, and I'm too tired to drive tonight...and I don't have a car to drive anyway," I sob.

Callum's arms wrap around me. "I'll call Bill to see the status of that part. Maybe it came while he's been off for Thanksgiving. And I'll also call George. He's the main pilot who works for the resort. I'll see if a helicopter is available."

I exhale a shaky breath. "That would be amazing," I manage to get out.

"Do you think you can get some sleep? Maybe take a bath in our tub? I'll keep my hands to myself." He tries to smile but looks so worried about me, I grip his arms so he'll hold me tighter.

"I don't know if I can sleep, but I'll take a bath and then try. I'm so sorry to end such an amazing weekend on such an awful note. I don't want to leave you," I say, the tears falling again.

"I'm going with you. I don't want you anywhere near that fucker."

CHAPTER TWENTY-EIGHT

GOOD NEWS, BAD NEWS

CALLUM

She does eventually sleep. But it's tormented with bad dreams. She wakes up more than once crying and sitting up like she's panicking.

"I should've made sure they were okay," she says over and over.

Meanwhile, I rage all night about that bastard and try to figure out how to get us there...fast.

By morning I still haven't heard from Bill or George, and

Hilary and Abby are in Colorado Springs until this afternoon, which leaves me scrambling for another plan for the ranch. Just as I'm ready to scorch the earth, Bill calls. And as soon as I'm off the phone with Bill, George calls. Ruby comes downstairs while I'm talking to him, dressed but looking drained.

"Would you like to hear the good news or the bad news first?" I ask her when we hang up.

"The good."

I smile and put my hand on her cheek. "How did I know that would be your answer? Okay, the good news is…Bill called and said he's expecting the part for your RV to show up this morning. But…besides shipments not being dependable, the bad news is he won't be able to work on it until this afternoon or tomorrow morning."

"Oh." She sags against me. "That's actually better than I expected."

My fingers slide under her shirt accidentally, but I stay there, caressing her side.

"Plan B, which to me sounds like a better plan…is that George can fly you out at one this afternoon. The flight is around an hour. I have a feeling you're anxious to see about your emus sooner than tomorrow."

She nods, leaning her forehead on my chest. "I'm so relieved. Thank you. "

"I'm still trying to figure out the ranch stuff…Hilary and Abby had to run to see Abby's mother unexpectedly and won't be back until this afternoon. Theo is on call, so he could check on things, but it wouldn't be great."

"You don't need to come, Callum. I can handle Junior. It was fun, the thought of us taking the RV together, but you can't leave your responsibilities behind either. I'd feel worse about everything if I knew you were doing that."

She kisses my chest and lifts her head up to look at me. Her sadness is killing me.

"I can bring your RV as soon as it's ready if that's where you want to stay while you're there. I want to help." I lean my forehead against hers. "I'd just be behind you a few hours." I groan, glaring at the ceiling. "It's not good enough. I'll call Bill again, and if the part does come in, maybe he can either get here sooner or walk me through the repair on the phone. And if the part doesn't show, depending on Hilary's timing, maybe I could even fly with you."

"This is crazy," she says. "My brain hurts."

"You didn't sleep well. I'm glad you don't have to drive today. Best case scenario, I'll bring you the RV and arrive there within an hour of you..." I try to inject some lightness in my tone. Sad Ruby might be the death of me. "Do you want me to bring Dolly? She's fine here, of course, but if it makes you feel better to have her."

"Really, Callum. You shouldn't do all this."

I lift her chin between my fingers, until her eyes meet mine. "Say what you need, Sunshine. Let me worry about you. You're my wife. Remember, I vowed to take care of you in the good times and the bad." I kiss her forehead. "We take care of each other."

There's a flicker of a smile, but it's gone so fast I might've imagined it.

"It would be best to have her there, just in case I have to stay a while," she finally says.

I try not to flinch with those words. Fear crawls into my bloodstream and spreads. I nod, determined to not add to her pain with my insecurities.

"Okay, I'll make sure the trailer's good to go once the RV is ready."

"And George can get you back here whenever you need?"

I nod again, feeling hollowed out.

"Okay, if you're sure. I'd appreciate the backup," she says.

"Happy to help." I lean in to kiss her and it's just as heated as all our kisses have been, but she lets go before I'm ready.

"What did I do to deserve you?" she asks.

"You deserve the whole world, Ruby. Don't forget that."

She packs and goes out to the barn to spend time with Dolly. Delphine meets her halfway and I hear her say, "I'm gonna miss you almost as much as Dolly. You are the world's cutest goat. And I don't believe what everyone says about your naughty behavior. You've been an angel since I got here," she croons.

Irene comes over and moos loudly until Ruby scratches her too.

It puts my mind at ease a little. She's invested here too. She'll be back.

"Take care of my girl while I'm gone, okay?" she says to Irene before reaching Dolly.

Bill calls while I'm standing there.

"Got the part," he says.

I put my hand on my head and tug my hair hard. "Really glad to hear that. Think you can walk me through the repair?"

"I can do you one better. I switched things around and can come work on it in an hour or so."

"You have no idea how much this helps, Bill. Thank you."

"This all you're taking?" I lift her bag.

"Yeah. It doesn't feel as sad that way."

I freeze, waiting for her to say more.

"I don't want to leave. The light bag makes it feel more temporary."

"Knowing you want to stay means everything. Dolly and I should pull in a few hours after you get there. Not as soon as I'd hoped, but…" I pause and forge ahead. "I know you can handle Junior, but I'd feel better if you have Kess with you when you talk to him…or better yet, the sheriff. If it doesn't go well, leave and I'll go back with you."

She leans up on her tiptoes and kisses me. I groan into her mouth and take over, tilting her head to get better access. When I've kissed her senseless, I squeeze her ass and then force my hands to her shoulders, as I plant one more kiss on each cheek.

We walk outside and Scarlett's waiting in her SUV. They're going to hang out together while I get on the road, and Scarlett will make sure she catches her flight with George in plenty of time.

"Are you awake enough to do this drive?" she asks.

"The drive isn't bad…six and a half hours, give or take. And I've got a strange amount of energy pumping through me," I say, grinning.

For the first time today, a true smile comes over her face.

"I still feel the reminders of that energy pumping through me," she says.

I swipe a hand down my face and give her a mock stern look.

"Don't give me another reason to want to press you against this SUV and see how many ways I can get you to moan my name in the daylight."

"You're making me want to shed this coat and drop it in the snow," she says.

"I can hear you guys," Scarlett yells from inside the SUV.

"Close your ears then," I yell back. "Let me know how you're doing," I tell Ruby."

"You too. The second you get sleepy, call me," she says. "I know you rarely have your phone on, but—"

"You didn't think I talked when you met me either, but here we are," I grumble.

"I don't buy your grouching for a second," she whispers. "I love you."

"I love you, Sunshine."

She wraps her arms around my neck and hugs me one more time. And then she opens the door and slides into the seat.

"Thank you," she says, blinking away her tears.

"I'll see you soon," I remind her. "Thanks, Scarlett."

Scarlett smiles and blows me a kiss.

I watch them drive away and Ruby turns and waves. Delphine and Irene flank me on either side and Dolly trots up behind me.

As soon as the car is out of sight, I feel Ruby's absence.

The quiet I used to crave may as well be a clanging church bell, for all the comfort it brings me now. The silence is deafening.

"You missing our girl?" I ask Dolly. "We'll get on the road soon. See if we can make good time."

CHAPTER TWENTY-NINE

REAL TALK

RUBY

Callum standing there watching me leave with Delphine and Irene on either side of him and then Dolly bopping up behind him…it's an idyllic image that will stay ingrained in my mind throughout the day…and I suspect forever.

A flash of yellow catches my eye and I glance at the sticky note stuck to my bag.

Be careful, Sunshine.

I love you.

C

I swallow back tears and try to hold myself together around Scarlett.

"Callum said it's been a rough night. You okay?" she asks.

"I don't even know where to start," I say.

I clear my throat when my voice is all wobbly, and she reaches out and squeezes my hand.

"You don't have to talk about it if you don't feel like it," she says. "And if you do, I'm here."

"Thank you. And thank you for the teddie." I glance over at her and laugh while I'm wiping the tears off my face. "You probably don't want to talk about that either since it's your brother, but thank you."

She laughs, pounding her steering wheel. "I love it." She shakes her head. "No, I can handle it. My brothers are way more uptight talking about that kind of thing than I am. And you're welcome. I thought it might be something you'd like."

She laughs again, and I feel lighter.

We pull into the parking lot of the Landmark Mountain Lodge & Ski Resort, and it's even more beautiful up close. I feel bad that Callum isn't the one showing it to me—he'd wanted to and we just ran out of time. I swallow the lump that's been stuck in my throat since I left him.

Everything feels so uncertain. It's such a drastic nosedive from the elation I'd been feeling before last night. I really don't want to leave Callum. I don't want to leave Landmark Mountain.

We get out of the SUV and walk toward the grand doors.

"I'm sorry George couldn't get free sooner," Scarlett says.

"Oh, I'm just relieved he can take me at all."

"Would you like to look around or do you need to rest? I have a suite open if you need to just chill or sleep, or we can eat in the restaurant...oh, and there's a spa and a great gift shop. One of my best friends works in the gift shop—Holly. I don't think you've met yet."

I'm so tired that I'd love nothing more than to crawl into bed, but I know I'd spiral, and I don't want Scarlett to think I don't appreciate her doing this for me. I've wanted to hang out with her more, so this is my chance.

"I'd love to see the place, maybe get something to eat too. But don't feel like you have to entertain me the whole time. I'll be fine sitting in one of those chairs by the window and reading. It's beautiful in here and the time will pass quickly. Do whatever you need to do."

"Yay," she says, lifting her hands in a little cheer. "I am all yours. It's the perks of working with Jamison—he can cover when I need him to and I rarely take a day off, so ..." She turns when someone calls her name. "I spoke too soon," she says under her breath. "Come meet Albert and Vera."

"Why hello, Ruby."

I turn and Pappy stands there smiling down at me. He's tall and distinguished and so sweet. He got teased a lot at Thanksgiving about all the attention he gets around here, and I can see why. He's the cutest, kindest old man ever.

"Hi, Pappy!"

He holds out his arms and I think he is going to squeeze my hand, but I go for a hug instead. He's wearing a soft cardigan and smells like peppermint. I close my eyes and soak in his goodness.

When I pull back, I'm embarrassed when my eyes fill with tears. Pappy's brow crinkles up and he reaches out and squeezes my arm.

"Are you okay, dear?"

I give him a shaky smile. "I'm not my best today, sorry."

"What's happened?"

"I have to go back to Utah today. One of my emus died last night, and I need to see about the rest."

"Oh, that's awful. What can we do to help?"

"You're helping right now, by being so kind."

He waves his hand. "You're easy to be kind to, tell me something I can really do."

"I don't know. I'm not used to asking for help, I guess. And yet, I feel like that's all I've been doing since I got to Landmark Mountain. I invaded Callum's home, me and my emu. I crashed Thanksgiving." I laugh and roll my eyes. "It's time I did something to repay everyone here who's been so good to me."

"Nonsense. I've seen the way Callum looks at you. He is not complaining one bit." He laughs and it's a full, deep laugh that comes from his fit belly. He leans in conspiratorially. "And if you crashed Thanksgiving, so did I." His eyes widen. "You remember I'm not related to the Landmarks either, right? I'm a hanger-on because of my grandson, Jamison. But that's what's so great about the Landmarks, and pretty much everyone else around here too—it's a welcoming place. If you decide to stick around, you'll find a home away from home."

Someone calls his name and he turns. I look too, and a group of cute elderly ladies sit at a table with a chess game.

"Looks like you've got a game to play," I say, grinning.

He turns around to look at me, his cheeks pink. "I guess I better get over there. I've become the resort's chess coordinator. I think my grandson just wanted to make me feel like I've got something to do, but…" He shakes his head and laughs. "They do really love their chess games around here though." He lowers his voice. "I think they must not have had anyone to compete with before I got here."

"I don't think that's it, Pappy." I lean in and cup my hand around my mouth so only he can hear. "I think they just like your company."

He laughs and pats my arm. "You're so sweet, Ruby. I really hope you hurry back and that your emus are okay. I'm so sorry about the one you lost. Will you let me know if you think of any way I can help?"

"There is one thing."

He nods.

"If I'm gone a long time…can you make sure Callum is okay?"

He takes my hand in his and looks at me so earnestly, I almost cry again.

"You have my word," he promises.

"Thank you, Pappy," I whisper.

He squeezes my shoulder and turns toward the ladies, who all titter in delight when they see him coming.

"Isn't he something?" Scarlett says.

"He's…incredible. I don't blame those ladies for swooning."

"I think he really is oblivious about it too. He thinks they just really love chess."

"He mentioned that." I laugh. "Sorry, I didn't meet Albert and…who was it?"

"Vera. It's okay. They'll be around." She pushes my small carry-on forward and sets it behind the front desk. "I asked

Vera to put your suitcase in my office, if that's okay. She's completely trustworthy."

"Oh, that's great. Thank you."

She loops her arm through mine. "I was thinking...if you liked what I gave you, you know—that white lace number?" She whispers the last few words. "I can show you what we're working on opening soon. Interested?"

"*Very.*"

She grins and we walk through the expansive lobby and loop around. Near the LM Kids section, there's a shop. The lights are off, but Scarlett pushes the code on the door and opens it, turning on the lights.

I gasp. "This is gorgeous!"

She makes an excited face. "I'm so excited about it."

I turn around, looking at the pretty chandeliers and elaborate mirrors against the pale pink walls, and the beautiful vintage chests spaced throughout the room. There are two pink velvet chairs that fit perfectly.

"I love everything about this," I tell her.

She bounces around and opens one of the chests, pulling out a few lacy things.

"I keep wanting to hang things up, but we're not quite there yet. The POS system still has to be set up and the counter for that isn't done. It's going there." She points at the far wall. "And I don't know...do you think we need a painting or two in here?"

"I think that's your artwork right there," I say, pointing to the deep blue teddie she holds up. "That's absolutely gorgeous, Scarlett."

"Aw, thank you. I thought this was just a hobby, and Jamison is the one who has really encouraged me to turn it into more."

"This embroidered detailing. I'm in awe. You *make* all of these?"

"So far, it's just me, yes. We'll see what happens with it." She grins and points at the chest. "Take anything you like."

"No way. I love it so much, and believe me, I felt like a goddess in the one you gave me, but when you get the store up and running…do you have a website?"

"It's almost done, but you can just come in anytime," she pauses when she sees my face. "Wait, you're coming back, aren't you?" She frowns and when I start crying, she takes my hand and drags me to the pink chairs.

"I'm sorry. I'm a mess today."

"Don't apologize. I'm so sad about your emu," she says. She winces when I cry harder. "I hope it's okay that Callum told me."

"Of course. He's so great," I sob.

"He is," she says carefully. She puts her hand on my knee and looks at me desperately. "Is everything okay with you and Callum?"

I feel terrible for making her nervous when she's just trying to show me a good time.

"Things are wonderful. He's perfect. The best man I have e-ever known." I put my head in my hands and sob and then fan my face.

He's my *husband*, but I can't tell her that.

Just when I think I have everything I ever wanted, Junior goes and messes everything up.

"I'm so sorry. I love it here. I love…I love your brother," my voice cracks, and I smile when she lights up.

She leans in, her knees touching mine. "You do? I was hoping with all my heart that you did after seeing him declare himself the other day." She gives me the side-eye and shakes her head slightly as she sputters. "I mean. You just don't know...how *unlike* my brother that was. The fact that he let you stay a single night in his home was telling enough, but God, he is hopelessly in love with you. I heard him talk more at Thanksgiving than I have my entire life." She puts her hands on my knees and squeals. "This is so great. I have been *dying* to pester the two of you, but I've been trying to give you space to get acquainted, and it sounds like you have become *acquainted*."

She covers her mouth and cracks up and then stops suddenly.

"What is wrong with me?" She holds her hands up. "Sorry, I got so excited about you saying you love him that I'm not even getting to what's important right now. You're so devastated about your emu and I'm just skating right over that and making it about my brother."

I've been getting the tears back in check. Her excitement is contagious. But my mouth wobbles when she's so genuine.

"He's everything," I tell her, swallowing hard. "I can't seem to talk about him without crying. I promise I'll get it together here in a sec. At least I hope so. I'm just...I don't want to leave him."

"But he's meeting you there later."

I nod. "He is. But he'll have to come back, and I'm not sure when I'll be able to."

Scarlett looks like I've just slapped her. "*Oh.*"

"Yeah. There's a lot to sort out at home."

"He'll help you figure things out. He will. Don't worry. It'll be all right."

I want to believe she's right, but since last night, I've had the worst feeling.

CHAPTER THIRTY

OPEN FIELDS

CALLUM

The drive isn't bad, but I don't make as good of time as I'd been hoping. It's just not possible with an RV and a trailer attached. Not to mention an emu who, while well-behaved, needs to be watered and exercised and taken on potty breaks.

I do love this emu though. I'd gotten attached to her at my place, but she's always having to share my time with Delphine and Irene and the other pushy ladies around the farm. She's a little out of sorts without Ruby, looking for her every time I let her out of the trailer.

At what I hope is our last stop, I grab my phone and it takes a few minutes to secure Dolly to a leash. I guide her to an open field and can finally check my phone.

Nothing shows up at first and then a bunch of texts come through all at once. I must have been out of cell service for a while.

RUBY

Made it. My first time in a helicopter! It was beautiful. Thank you so much for setting up the rental car. I miss you.

I check the time she left it. Fuck. Almost two hours ago. I try to call her, but she doesn't pick up.

There's a text from Scarlett too, left before Ruby's.

SCARLETT

Your girl is on her flight. I really love her, Callum. You've chosen well. <Heart emoji> Please let us know if we can help in any way. I'm worried about Ruby.

I wonder what Ruby told her. I try Ruby again and leave a message this time.

"We're close. I think thirty miles or so. This is your husband, by the way. My family gives me a hard time about never saying hello. So…hello. I stopped to let Dolly out one more time because it had been a while and there was a good spot. I'm rambling. Did you know you're the only one I've ever rambled with?" I chuckle and feel an ache in my chest. All I can think about is how much she lights up when I laugh. "I love you, Sunshine. I'm trying to get to you as soon as I can. I miss you too. So fucking much."

I hang up and rub my chest.

I pull out Ruby's ring box and open it up, looking at the ring while Dolly takes her sweet time finding a place to do her business. Ruby put her ring in the box this morning before she left. When she saw that I noticed, she said, "I don't think I can keep it a secret with this on my finger."

I understood, but it still unsettled me. More the look on her face than anything.

"And I still need to give Junior's ring back too." She held up his ring and put it in a little pouch that she stuck in her backpack.

Was she giving my ring back to me?

She doesn't have to wear it every minute for me. But I want her to have it with her. Something about seeing her leaving it behind just felt wrong.

I can't even think about the possibility that she was giving it back.

There's a message from Theo that I open last.

THEO

> Hey. Wanted to let you know I was able to stop by the ranch between appointments. Everything looked fine. Delphine seemed a little pissed that I wasn't you, but that's no surprise, right? Hilary got there as I was leaving. We'll take care of things, brother. Don't worry about a thing, okay?

I text him back.

> Thank you. It helps knowing everything's in capable hands.

THEO

> Was that a compliment? Ruby is really good for you. <Wink emoji>

> I was talking about Hilary.

THEO

> Can't even let me bask in your praise for one minute, can you? Fine. I love you anyway. Have fun. And take your time. Maybe a vacation will get your head out of your ass.

> Love you too, man.

I give my brothers shit, but I'm not stingy with telling them I love them. Scarlett has me wrapped around her little finger. I'm pretty sure she knows it too. She certainly has no doubt that I love her. And Grinny. That woman is a saint for raising all of us when she should've been living a peaceful life as a grandma.

But I've never been in love before. Ever.

There's nothing like the exhilaration that comes with this feeling, but maybe because we moved into this so quickly, there's also a lot of uncertainty.

The real world came along and popped the little bubble we were living in, and now it's as if I'm walking on a tightrope with nothing to catch me when I fall.

Dolly finally gets done and I take the garbage bag and scoop it up, dumping it in the trash.

"It's a good thing you're so cute because that is not great," I tell her.

She makes that drumming sound and I make a clicking sound that I've heard Ruby do with her. It seems to calm her as we walk back to her trailer.

"Just a little bit longer, sweet girl," I tell her. "You've been so good. We're almost there."

When she's in place, I secure the door and get in the RV, glancing at my phone one more time.

Still nothing from Ruby.

I get back on the road and it's torture to not speed all the way there, but I've got precious cargo in the back. I'll get there. I told Ruby I trusted her to handle Junior and I meant it.

Now, to get my heart to believe it.

CHAPTER THIRTY-ONE

THE UGLY TRUTH

RUBY

I've never dreaded being at our farm before. In all my twenty-three years here, I have only loved this place. I worked hard to preserve it, and I thought I'd spend the rest of my life here, taking care of the emus and running our family business.

I tried to call my parents before I got here, but they didn't answer, and it's just as well. I don't know what I'd say right now.

When I pull into the driveway, there's a pit in my stomach. I drive slowly past the house and back to the barn, parking in my normal spot and looking around when I step outside. There's no sign of Junior, which makes me relax a little bit.

It's warmer than the weather I left in Colorado, and there's no snow on the ground, which surprises me, but it will make this easier.

Diva and Rue, two of the younger emus, poke their heads out and bob excitedly toward the fence, and it hits me how much I've missed them. I rush toward them and open the gate, careful to not let them out.

"Hello, loves." They duck their heads and let me pet them. Diva bobs her head on my shoulder, and Rue crowds me from the back, trying to get as close as she possibly can.

"Oh, I'm so happy to see you too. Yes, I am."

Others start piling out of the barn, until I'm surrounded. I start crying, hugging them, as I check their feathers, their ears, eyes, beaks, wings, and the feet of a few who let me.

"I've missed you so much," I tell them over and over.

I was heartsick about leaving them all along, but I didn't let myself dwell on it.

It hurt too much.

The shame that I feel for letting them down by not getting back to check on them sooner...that I left them at all...it's unbearable.

I lose track of time going through the old routines I'd do with them. They're low on food and thinner than when I left. There's so little water left out for them it makes me sick. Emus drink 2-5 gallons of water a day, and not only do they need plenty to drink, but they love to play in it. The habitat I created for them is dry and scraggly. A couple of them have bare spots and their behavior is panicky. Not all of them, but enough who weren't that way before, that it's concerning. Their stalls are filthy, so once I've thoroughly looked them over, I get to work on cleaning up the barn.

There's no sign of Thor and I find Stan lying under a tree, so it's clear which one is gone. Stan was more of a loner than the girls, but he's especially melancholy today.

I bend down and talk softly, holding my hand out to him. He startles and gets up, hobbling as he tries to move away quickly.

"What's wrong, Stan? Is your leg hurt?"

He eyes me cautiously and when I hold my hand out, his curiosity would normally bring him right over, but he keeps his distance.

"It's okay, buddy. I'm here now. I'm going to make sure you're okay, all right? We'll take a better look at you when you're more comfortable, okay?"

"You've always talked to these animals like they understand you," Junior says, snorting behind me.

I turn around and he holds his arms out.

"Welcome home, Ruby," he says, his white teeth sparkling in the sunlight. "It's about time you showed up," he adds.

I glare at him. "You wanted this place so bad, but you couldn't take care of them for even this short length of time? What are you doing here, Junior?"

A vein pops out on his head. I always hated when that vein popped out. It meant he was either angry or about to get condescending on me. He steps closer to me and tries to smile through gritted teeth.

"You made a fool out of me in front of our family and friends, but I forgive you. And you had your fun time away, but that's over now. You're back where you belong and it's time we seal the deal, make our marriage official."

My mouth gapes open. "I'm not marrying you, Junior. I thought that was clear when I didn't show up at our wedding." I scoff. "You don't want to marry me anyway. I heard you myself."

That vein pops out more. I don't know how I ever thought he was attractive.

"Here's how it's gonna go: If you want these animals that are so precious to you, you *will* marry me."

My eyes narrow. "*Why?* Why would you do this?"

His eyebrows shoot up and he lifts a shoulder. "Like I said, you made a fool out of me." He looks me over and spits in the dirt next to him, his eyes full of disgust. "You need to make it right."

"This is all about your reputation? That makes no sense. No one cares, Junior. If anyone cares now, they'll be over it in a few months. Move on. You got the land, let me figure out what to do with the emus."

"I'll burn the barn down and everything in it, if you don't marry me."

I gasp, taking a step back.

He moves forward, getting in my face. "And don't think for one second that you can sneak off into the night with these fucking birds. They belong with the land that's mine."

I start shaking. "Why would you do this?" I repeat. "How did I not see who you are?"

He laughs and my stomach churns.

"You were always so preoccupied with your fucking birds, you never did know sense when it was right in front of you." He points his finger and he's so close, it jabs into my nose. "I'll give you two days. I know you like things to be pretty and we sure aren't getting married with you looking like this." He eyes me with disdain.

I don't want to give him the pleasure of seeing me cry, but

I'm so mad and shocked and scared, the tears start falling and don't stop.

His lip curls. "I don't need the fancy wedding—hearing you rattle on about wedding nonsense all those months was torture—but do something with your hair and get a fucking manicure, for Christ's sake. My parents' house, Tuesday at four o'clock. If you're not there on the fucking dot—" He holds his hand up and makes the sound of an explosion.

He starts to walk away, but he turns around and points at me again.

"And if you tell a fucking soul about this, deal's off. These ugly birds are going up in fucking flames, and you'll still be stuck marrying me. Your parents signed papers. It's done."

I wrap my arms around myself, watching as his car peels out. When I'm sure he's gone, I turn back to look around the yard. While Junior's been here, all the emus have gone into the barn. I don't think that's ever happened before. What has he done to them that they'd already know to stay out of his way?

They're not as stupid as he thinks they are.

What am I going to do?

The tears start flooding again.

"Ruby?"

I turn and Callum is there, Dolly next to him. She scuttles over faster than him, but he's right behind her, both of them checking on me.

I pet Dolly and look up at Callum, unsure of where to even begin. I end up putting my head against his chest and sobbing.

CHAPTER THIRTY-TWO

THE BREAKING

CALLUM

"Breathe, Sunshine. I'm here. Breathe, my Ruby."

I've held her and I've given her space and I've wiped her tears and asked her what I can do, but when she starts panicking, I've never felt more at a loss.

"You need to go," she finally says.

"What?"

I can't have heard that right. I wait for her to say something else, but she repeats those same words.

"You need to go, Callum." And then she sticks the knife in. "I can't be married to you."

Her voice crumbles and she bends until her hands are on her knees as she tries to catch her breath. Emus trickle out of the barn and surround her. Some look at me warily, others are so concerned about Ruby that they don't pay me much attention.

It'd be a sweet moment if she wasn't in the process of breaking my heart.

"What happened?"

I want to demand to know why she doesn't want me, why she married me if she could change her mind so fast, but she's clearly distraught.

Get over yourself and figure out how to help her.

Every once in a while, Granddad's voice comes into my head and knocks some sense into me. It's rare, and it's only happened a couple times since he died. He was a no-nonsense, take-charge kind of guy. Loved his family fiercely, but he could also be cutthroat if my brothers and I were acting like idiots. He wasn't perfect, but Grinny was his whole world, and I know he'd be shaking me into action right now.

I move toward her like there's a fire under my feet and put my hand on her back.

"You're cold. Let's get you someplace warm. Is it better in the barn?"

She nods, her eyes vacant when she straightens.

I lead us to the barn and when we're inside, I look around and walk us to a bench, tugging her arm just enough for her to sit. She's exhausted and her eyes and lips are puffy like she's been crying for a long time. Whatever has happened, it's obvious that she's devastated about it.

"Can you talk about it?" I ask.

She swallows, her fingers twisting around each other. But she doesn't say anything. Minutes tick by and it's just her agonized eyes and the now occasional tears that slide down her cheeks.

"Ruby, you're scaring me," I say softly.

I put my hand on her back and she jumps, her eyes meeting mine for the first time since we sat down.

"Tell me what happened."

"We might have to get an annulment," she whispers.

Her eyes look like they hurt when she blinks, and I try to separate myself from the pain of what she's said and just focus on her.

"Why?"

"He's threatening the animals if I don't marry him."

"What? No, he can't do that."

"He's already mistreated them. They all hid in the barn the entire time he was here. One is already dead...because of me." She stares up at the ceiling, rocking slightly.

"Not because of you. If he hurt Thor, it was all him. We'll get law enforcement here, he can't—"

"He said if I told anyone, he'd hurt them and I'd still be stuck marrying him." She looks around. "For all I know, he's got the barn bugged and is listening right now."

I shake my head. "He's not smart enough to have this place bugged."

I glance around the beams, checking for any lights or strange panels that could be hiding a camera.

"I want to believe you're right, but I'm seeing a side of him I never knew existed. He was inattentive and cold at times, but he wasn't cruel. Maybe he's right. Maybe I really was so preoccupied here that I didn't see it."

She turns to face me and I brace myself.

"As much as you love animals, you're maybe the only

one who can understand why I have to do this. I feel awful about what they've already gone through without me here. He doesn't want to be married to me. I don't know why he's insisting we go through with it. He claims I made a fool of him. But whatever the reason, I don't think I'm going to be stuck in a marriage with him for any length of time. I'll make sure I'm not. But I'm not going to ask you to wait for a what-if, Callum."

Her voice cracks again and she turns away from me. I put my hand on her back.

"I would wait as long as it took, Ruby, but you can't marry him. I refuse to accept that option."

"I don't know what else to do. I couldn't bear it if I didn't take him seriously and all these animals died because of me."

"*I'll* die without you," I say.

It's a low blow and I shouldn't have gone there, but I feel like it's the fucking truth.

"We haven't even known each other that long," she whispers.

"Don't you say that, Ruby."

Her eyes are tortured and I put my hands on her face and kiss her. It's sweet and desperate and so full of anguish, it rips my heart apart a little more.

"Don't pretend we didn't know everything that was important," I say, my voice breaking. "We exposed the purest parts of ourselves. Don't make it sound like it was nothing."

"It was everything to me," she whispers.

I grip her face and when she blinks, I let up, knowing I can't force her to be with me.

"It still can be," I say, dropping my hands.

"Thank you for bringing the RV and Dolly all this way. Thank you for all you've done for me, Callum. I can't begin to tell you how much it means to me."

"Do you hear yourself?" My voice rises. "Don't treat me like a fucking stranger! Look at me, Ruby. Really look at me."

"You need to go," she says. "Please."

"I'm not leaving you alone here. You don't seem to get it —I *made vows to you*. I'm not going anywhere."

"I'm going to stay in the RV tonight. Alone," she says.

She stands up and starts picking things up around the barn.

Her eyes are so sad as she turns and looks at me. "I'm not trying to treat you like a stranger. I feel like I'm *dying* inside. I love you. You're the man I want to be with, the one I will always crave. I know that more than I know anything. But I need to handle this. I don't know what will happen for sure, but I'm asking you to give me some space, let me try to figure this out. I'm shaken right now and I can't think, but worrying he'll come back and destroy things or worse, hurt you..." She shakes her head. "I need you to go. This is my mess. Callum, if you love me, you've got to leave."

She reaches into her coat pocket and holds out keys for me to take.

"For the rental," she says.

I stand up, at a complete loss. "What makes you think you're safe from him? If he's capable of all you're saying, you aren't."

"Because all his threats hinge on me marrying him. He won't hurt me...at least not before Tuesday at four."

"What happens then?"

"I'm supposed to marry him."

I curse and it's so loud, she jumps. "This is madness, Ruby."

I put my hands on my hips and try to get my bearings, but everything feels upside down.

"I'll leave, but I'll be close. You get scared for even a second, you call me or blink the lights or scream your head off." I stalk close to her. "Do you hear me?"

She nods. "I hear you."

"When you're in a relationship with someone you love, you're supposed to work together," I tell her. "Two are better than one and all that."

"I'm sorry, Callum," she whispers.

I nod, feeling dazed, as I set the keys to her RV on the bench and walk out of the barn.

Away from my wife.

CHAPTER THIRTY-THREE

KEEPING WATCH

RUBY

When Callum leaves, I'm drained and heartbroken and scattered. I want to call him and ask him to come right back, but I'm too worried about what Junior would do if he saw Callum here. I allow myself to cry for a few minutes and once those are up, I straighten and get to work.

I call Kess and leave a message, letting her know I'm in town and I've checked on the emus. I call the sheriff that Kess talked to, and the situation seems even more hopeless.

He says there was no proof that anything had been done to harm the emu. He saw the place in the gate but didn't see a wound like that on the animal. That maybe the emu had just gotten too cold and died of hypothermia.

When I ask to see Thor, he says that won't be possible. He's already been disposed of.

That's when the tears start flowing again and my nose feels like a faucet.

I have to wonder if Junior paid off the sheriff. Nothing would surprise me at this point.

When I get my bearings, I call the county's office to see when I can look at the paperwork about this property. The lady who answers, Debbie Melton, is polite, but she doesn't waver when she says the office will be closed in five minutes and she can't stay open a second longer until I can get there.

It's ten minutes from here, so I wouldn't make it.

"You're the second person who's asked for this recently," she says.

"Really? Who else asked?"

"I'm not at liberty to say."

Then why did you bring it up in the first place?

"Could you email it to me, please?" I try to remain calm.

"Is your name on the deed?"

I sag against the barn wall. "Yes," I lie. "This is June Jones."

"One second, please."

She comes back on the line a minute later. "Mrs. Jones?"

"Yes?"

"Sorry to put you on hold for so long. What is your email?"

I take a deep breath and rattle off my email.

"Thank you. I'll send this right away. Have a nice night."

"Debbie?"

"Yes?"

"What are your opening hours, just in case I still need to come in?"

"Eight o'clock."

"Thank you."

"You're very welcome."

I toss the phone aside, ready to boil over, and then I'm scrambling for it in the next second, refreshing my email again and again.

Even after I know the office is closed, I'm still sitting there refreshing. I move to pacing around the yard and nothing comes through. My fists squeeze shut and I shake them, every part of me clenched and so livid I don't know what to do with myself.

My phone rings and I jump, nearly dropping it. I answer it without checking to see who it is.

"Ruby?" my mom says. "Are you okay? Your voice sounds funny."

"Did you get my messages?" I scrub a hand over my face.

"It was cutting in and out. Something about one of the emus? Did one of them die?"

"*Yes*, one of them died."

Deep breaths, Ruby.

"That is so sad. It was always so hard to lose one."

"I only remember ever losing one. Thor was healthy when I left. I have a hard time believing he could've gotten in that bad of shape in the short amount of time I've been gone."

"What do you think happened?"

"I think Junior might have done something."

She makes a shocked sound. "You don't really believe that, do you? These things happen and Thor might've appeared healthy, but there might've been more going on than we know. You haven't been there to know for sure, have you, sweetheart?"

"No, I haven't and neither have you and Dad, so I guess we're all to blame, aren't we?"

"That's not what I meant. Where is all this hostility coming from? It's not like you."

"Junior is—" I hesitate, looking around the yard. I told Callum more than I should and honestly, telling my parents might make me feel worse about the whole thing.

"I was actually calling you about Junior. I mean, I was returning your messages too, but…I got one from Junior that was really strange."

"What did he say?"

"He said we need to keep our end of the deal and make sure you marry him. Do you know what he's talking about? I know he's upset about you not marrying him and is exuding extremely *toxic* energy, but I thought it was over. He's acting like he's still hung up on you marrying him."

"He's worse than I ever knew."

"He sure is. He threatened to take away our RV if we didn't get you back to Utah to marry him. He can't really do that, can he?"

My head drops and I close my eyes for a few beats.

"I don't know, Mom. I still haven't seen the paperwork. I don't know what you signed, but I'm trying to get it from the county office."

"It's a good thing you're in Colorado. He doesn't sound very healthy right now. I'm sure it'll blow over in time," she says. "We're about to pull into the park. We're in Washington —can you believe it? It is *gorgeous* here."

"Have fun," I say.

My insides shake with fury. I'm so angry with my mom… with both my parents. I've lost the farm, an emu, and now

Callum. And they're off having the trip of their life, not even slowing down to think about anything or anyone else.

The sun has gone down and the temperature has dropped considerably. I shiver and walk back into the barn, petting each emu as I make sure they're secure for the night. When I reach Dolly, she comes over and stares at me like she knows something's not right.

"How are you more perceptive than my own mother?" I ask.

She leans her beak on my shoulder and I rub her ears.

"Love you, Dolly. We'll be okay. I'll make sure of it."

When the chores are done, I look around, watching and listening for any signs of Junior. There aren't any. But there also aren't any of Callum. I wouldn't blame him if he just turned around and drove back to Landmark Mountain. No one deserves this.

Stepping inside the RV, a fresh wave of grief hits me. It smells like Callum and it makes me miss him all the more.

It physically hurts.

I take a shower and it feels strange to crawl into this bed. My time with Callum was brief and yet it encompassed my whole world. Made everything before seem insignificant. I hardly remember the person who redid this RV and made wedding plans with Junior—it feels like another lifetime.

My phone buzzes and I pick it up, my heart thumping when I see the text from Callum.

CALLUM

> I'm parked behind a few trees, and I can see the back of the barn. I'll walk the perimeter throughout the night and if I see anything concerning, I'll call you and the police.

The next one comes a second later.

CALLUM
I love you, Ruby.

My eyes blur.

I want to thank him. Tell him he shouldn't miss a night of sleep over me. That I want him in here with me more than anything. I also want to tell him to go home and not look back, that I'm not worth this.

But I don't.

I love you.

It's all I can say, but I hope he knows that those words mean everything to me. My heart hasn't gone anywhere.

CHAPTER THIRTY-FOUR

BROTHERHOOD

CALLUM

I'm doing a walk around the property when my phone buzzes
and I see that it's Sutton, so I hurry back to the car so I can be
louder. With every pass, I haven't seen anything that's alarm-
ing, which has been a relief, but I'm still not able to relax.
None of this with Junior is lining up for me.

I answer right before I reach the car.

"There you are," I say.

"I'm sorry, Callum. Are you okay? Scratch that. I could

tell by your messages that you aren't. I had to replace my phone tonight. It's been a crazy day—not as crazy as yours. But I didn't hear your messages until half an hour ago."

"I love her, Sutton. I love her, and I should've known it wasn't going to work when she showed up at my house in a wedding dress, but I fell anyway and now…now she's here in Utah and I'm here and—*FUCK*!" I take a deep breath and slam my fist against the steering wheel. "I don't know what to do. This guy, her ex…he's threatening her. He says she has to marry him and—"

"What? That fucker! She's not marrying him, absolutely not," Sutton yells. "God, you just got my heart rate up with that one. I knew you loved her after Thanksgiving. That was…well, it softened this heartless heart and that's saying something. Listen, Callum. We're going to figure this out."

"He's threatening to hurt the emus if she doesn't marry him," I tell him. "One is already dead. I called the sheriff's department, and they're not doing a fucking thing to protect Ruby."

"What in the ever-loving fuck?" he says.

I hear him rustling in the background.

"I'll call you back. I hope it won't be more than an hour, but I need to make a few calls. I swear I'll call you right back. Okay?"

"Okay."

"Love you," he says and hangs up.

It's forty-five minutes when he calls back, and I've walked around and looped back to the car in that time.

"It's Wyatt," he says when I pick up. "Sutton's here and I'm putting you on speaker. Theo's connected on this call too."

"Hey, Callum." Theo's voice is distant and there's a lot of background noise.

"Hey."

"I've filled them in," Sutton says. "Now, I need you to walk me back a little. I thought you'd said Junior owns that property now...and Ruby found out about it on her wedding day."

"That's right."

"When you called this morning, I emailed the county's office and called again...they haven't been helpful at all, but I was a *little* more forceful today—okay, a lot more forceful—and they emailed the documents over tonight. I didn't see them because of running around to get the phone—it doesn't matter—the point is, he does not own that land."

I freeze and wait for him to say more. When he doesn't, I say the obvious. *"What?"*

"The document her parents signed was something that had been in Mr. Jones' family before. It states that in order to sell the property, it must go to a member of the Jones family. Marrying Ruby is the only possible way Junior could get that land, so she absolutely cannot marry him."

"There's nothing binding her to Junior at all? Nothing binding him to the land? How did her parents get the money for the decked-out RV?"

"If it's something her parents weren't in on, I suspect Junior funded that."

"I'd hate to think they were in on this with Junior."

"As it stands, that property is still in Frank and June Jones' names. Ruby's name *has* been added to another document tied to the property, by a Daniel Jones—her grandfather, I'm assuming? And the land passing on to Ruby is contingent on her marrying, which is twisted as fuck, but you see that sometimes in large properties like this. And it's worth a *lot* of money, so that asswipe isn't letting it go."

"Junior's a real estate agent, so he must've known all

about this." I want to hit something so bad right now, prefer-
ably that motherfucker. "Wait...so everything is already
signed and Junior just needs the marriage to happen, and it's
his. Am I...understanding this right?"

"That's it. Yep." Sutton sighs.

"So, if she were to be married to someone else...would it
belong to her already?"

Wyatt laughs. "His wheels are turning now."

"She'd just need the marriage license signed with
witnesses showing that she's married, and it'd be a done
deal."

I lean back in my seat in shock, and then I start laughing.

"What's going on? Is someone else with you?" Theo asks.

"I think that's him," Wyatt says. "Are you losing it,
brother?"

"Give him a minute," Sutton barks. "He's obviously
upset. Are you crying?" he asks softly.

That just makes me laugh harder.

They continue their assessments of my sanity while I
wipe my eyes and try to stop wheezing from laughing so
hard.

When I blow out a long breath, Wyatt clears his throat.
"Do you feel better?"

"I have something to tell you guys," I say. "Ruby and I
got married...the day after Thanksgiving."

"What the fuck?"

"Are you serious right now?"

"Who even are you?"

They all three go off at once.

Cursing, laughing, yelling at me.

It continues for a while until I yell back, "Okay, enough. I
did it and I'd do it again. It was fucking beautiful, all right?

We'll have a ceremony between Christmas and New Year's so everyone can celebrate with us."

"You were just going to keep it a secret, weren't you?" Wyatt says.

"Hell, yes," I say.

That sends them on another round.

When things finally settle down, Sutton says, "Do you have the marriage license with you?"

"Yes." I glance over at my backpack in the seat next to me.

"Good. And will you be going back to Ruby's in the morning?"

"I'm sitting in my car behind her barn now, hidden behind some trees."

"The fuck?" Theo says.

"I don't trust the ex, okay? Ruby was afraid of what he'd do if he saw me, and I'm not leaving her alone out here."

"Well, we're about an hour in, and I don't want to wake you if you do decide to sleep," Sutton says. "Just let us know when you're coming out of hiding."

"What do you mean you're about an hour in?" I ask.

"We're on our way, brother," Wyatt says. "Think we'd let you face this without us?"

CHAPTER THIRTY-FIVE

FLANNEL BAND

RUBY

I wake up, still exhausted, but shocked that I slept at all. There are no messages on my phone, and I drag myself out of bed and get dressed. My hair still looks decent from yesterday, so I pull the front and sides into a messy bun and leave the back down.

On the plus side, I barely notice my burns hurting at all as I get dressed. They're still showing, but finally starting to fade.

Figures now that Callum isn't here to see me naked.

I try to abolish that thought as soon as it comes into my head. I don't want to cry today, for one thing. And I can't think about Callum without crying, so I don't need to think about him seeing me naked or otherwise.

Thoughts about our wedding and all the nights we spent together have a mind of their own though, and they play in my head on repeat.

I bundle up, saving my work gloves that I'd found out in the barn the day before for last. Right before I slide them on, I get Junior's ring out of my backpack and slip it into my pocket. Seeing it is just another reminder that I have no emotional attachment to this ring or the person who gave it to me, while the one I left at home feels like something precious is missing. When I step outside, I'm glad the day's a touch warmer. The emus are excited when they see me. Stan even comes around and is friendlier. I get their food and water ready, my old habits coming back to me like I've never been gone. After I've cleaned a bit, I step outside and run right into Junior.

He grins, looking me over, his nose curling when he sees my work gloves.

"I don't know how you can stand those things. They're disgusting," he says.

Determined to not let him force me into a spiral, I move to walk past him. He takes a step sideways, blocking my path.

His hands grip my arms and he smirks. We're almost at eye level. I straighten up, shoulders back, knowing he doesn't like it that I'm almost as tall as he is.

"Let go of me," I say, my eyes defiant.

"You got awfully brave in Colorado. I prefer the old Ruby. The one who lived in her own little world and only thought about emus and weddings and decorating crappy

RVs." He laughs. "It's no wonder that thing broke down. It's trash."

"You pretended to be amazed by my *skills* and *determination.*" I roll my eyes when I throw out the words he used. "Was there ever a time in our relationship that you meant what you said?" I shake my head. "You know what? I don't even care. Let go," I say through gritted teeth.

He pokes his lips out and looks up like he's in deep contemplation. And he doesn't let go.

"I meant it when I said you have nice tits...and that your ass is—"

I try to shove his hands away and he grips me harder, his jaw clenching and his eyes flaring with lust and fury.

"Get your hands off of my wife," Callum's voice barrels next to us.

I let out a surprise sound, and Junior and I both turn to look at Callum.

He looks like an avenging god, his chest rising and falling as he towers over Junior.

"What the fuck did you—" is all Junior gets out and part of that is muffled when Callum shoves him away from me and punches him in the face.

Junior goes down and Callum barely looks winded.

Why was I ever afraid of what Junior could do to Callum?

"Did he hurt you?" Callum asks me.

I shake my head. Junior scuttles back and tries to wipe the blood away, and when he stumbles to his feet, he keeps his distance from Callum.

"I'm calling the police," he yells, pulling out his phone.

His hands are shaking and the sight of that makes me nervous. I have no idea what he's capable of anymore.

"I've already called them and you need to get off our property," Callum says, his voice a deadly calm. "*Now.*"

I lift my eyebrows, turning to look at Callum. I'm not sure what he's doing, but *his wife, our property*...I'm not sure this is going to help the situation. He looks me over like he's seeing for himself that Junior didn't hurt me. When we turn to look at Junior again, he's inching closer.

"This is not your property," Junior says, spitting blood on the dirt.

"It's sure as hell not yours." The voice comes from behind us.

I turn and Sutton is holding up a piece of paper, and Theo and Wyatt are on either side of him. I've never thought the brothers look very much alike—maybe Scarlett and Sutton do, and Theo a little bit too—but seeing the four of them standing in flannel shirts, messy hair, and scruff on their faces...I see it now. They're like a sexy band of lumberjack brothers.

Callum glances at me again. "You okay, Sunshine?"

I nod. "I think so. Want to tell me what's going on?"

Junior grabs my arm and yanks me against him, his arm across my neck as he backs up with me. Callum follows us, but he waits, looking at the tension on my neck.

"You're not going with them," Junior spits out. "I've worked too hard for this—"

"I'll have you arrested so fast, it'll make your head spin," Sutton calls.

A siren sounds in the background.

"Oh, listen to that, there's backup now," Sutton says.

Junior loosens his hold on me, and as soon as I duck out of the way, Callum punches him again.

"That's the last time you'll touch her," Callum says, standing over Junior's sprawled body. "Are we clear?"

Two officers hurry over and it seems like they've already

had an interaction with Sutton, or maybe all four of them, because they're nervous and almost reverent.

"He's over there," Sutton points at Junior, who's just standing up, and the officers walk over to him. When they get closer, Junior gets antsy.

"He hit me." He points at Callum. "He should be arrested."

"You grabbed my wife!" Callum yells. "And you were about to hit her."

"Why the fuck do you keep calling her your wife, you piece of shit?" Junior yells.

"Because we're *married*, motherfucker." Callum's voice is a low growl.

Junior's attention shifts to me, everything about him tense, and I nod. It's like the life drains out of him. He curses under his breath and then looks around like a caged animal.

"Junior Fitzgibbons, you are under arrest for blackmail and aggravated animal cruelty. You have the right to remain silent..." His hands are handcuffed while he squirms.

"This makes no sense," Junior says, but it's weak.

"Can they do this?" I ask Callum.

His jaw tightens as he nods.

"The land is yours, Ruby, should you decide to follow through on the paperwork with your parents. Technically, now that you're married, it's yours and mine. But don't worry, I'm not coming after your land. And if you decide to never tell your parents about our wedding and annul our marriage, the land will still belong to your parents."

I look at him in confusion, trying to understand what he's saying. And is he just telling me the facts, or is he distancing himself?

"Sutton got the paperwork last night. I'm not sure your parents ever knew what they were signing, but once we saw the contracts and knew it was contingent on you getting married, it all became clear."

My gut twists like I've been hit. "I'm—I don't know what to say."

I don't feel very steady at the moment. I want Callum's arms around me, but he hasn't touched me except to make sure I'm okay.

"I don't believe my parents would ever knowingly conspire against me. I really don't. But Junior knows how gullible they are and this was all a game to him. He manipulated all of us."

I glare at Junior as he's led past me, shaking with rage.

"You are lower than low," I say when he's within earshot. "Wait."

The sheriff pauses and I dig into my pocket. When I pull the ring out and hold it up, Junior's nose flares. I walk over and put it in his shirt pocket and then tap it twice to make sure he doesn't miss that it's all his.

"It'd serve you right if I sold this ring and kept it for myself, but something tells me you're gonna need this more than I do." I step back.

Junior doesn't look at me. His nose and mouth are puffy and bloody, and the arrogance is gone as they lead him away. He's shoved into the police car and looks small as he's driven away.

CHAPTER THIRTY-SIX

OPEN BOOKS AND DETACHMENTS

CALLUM

We're sitting around the dining room table in Ruby's house. Once she realized Junior had never moved in, she was more comfortable going inside. Most of her parents' things are in storage, and when she first stepped in the door, she looked shaken, but she has more color in her cheeks now.

Theo and Wyatt pick up coffee and breakfast sandwiches for us, and Sutton explains the details of the contract and the paperwork her parents signed better than I ever could've.

After I apologized to her for telling my brothers we'd gotten married after we'd agreed to wait, I've just sat here and listened.

Ruby's eyes keep meeting mine, furtive glances that I'm not used to seeing from her. Or maybe it's all in my head.

I'm wondering about a lot of things right now—was it all in my head?

Did I dream up her love for me?

She's home where she belongs, with nothing hanging over her head now.

I should be happy for her, and I am.

But where does this leave me?

I'm a selfish prick for even going there.

But I'm worn out from staying awake all night and relieved beyond words to be done with Junior...and I feel oddly detached from the woman who has been an open book to me before now.

"Callum?" Ruby says.

Everyone's looking at me, and there's a small frown between Ruby's brows.

"Oh, sorry," I say. "What did I miss?"

"I asked if I could talk to you?" She motions behind her.

I get up and she jumps out of her chair too, leading the way down the hall. When she opens the door to her room, she's taken aback.

"I wasn't expecting my things to be here," she says.

I look around her room. It's large and tastefully decorated, with a bathroom connected. It's beautiful and so her. Yet, I've never felt the difference in our ages more than I do right now. I've never felt it at all besides my initial alarm when she first showed up at my house and I realized I couldn't be around her without wanting her.

She's young and her life is here. She's never even lived on her own, for fuck's sake.

I see a picture of her and Junior and turn it face down.

"What are you thinking, Callum?" she asks.

"That it must feel good to be back where you belong."

Hurt flickers over her face and I want to wrap my arms around her, but I don't.

"Why are you being so distant?" She moves in front of me. "It's like the longer we're here, the more you're shutting me out."

"I'm right here."

She shoots me a look and rubs her hands over her arms.

"You're not acting like the man I married just a few days ago." Her arms cross over her chest.

I tilt my head. "Maybe I'm acting like the man you were quick to leave."

She gasps and I swipe my hand down my face.

"I'm sorry. I shouldn't have said that."

"You must've meant it."

"I wouldn't blame you for wanting out of this thing with me, Ruby. You said it yourself—we haven't known each other long. This is your home—"

Her eyes fill with tears. "You told me not to say that. I felt backed into a corner. I didn't know what to do."

"You told me to leave and I can't just assume you still want me after your situation has changed."

"I love you," she says, her face crumbling.

I can't take it anymore. I hold onto her hip with one hand and my other touches her face.

"I believe you love me, and I love you so fucking much, but I don't want to hold you back from anything, Ruby. Including me. If you want me, I'm here. If you need to think about it, I'll wait. If you want me to go, I'll leave today and our marriage can be dissolved without argument."

She leans her forehead on my shoulder and sobs. I wrap my arms around her, feeling like my heart is being stomped on.

"It's okay, Ruby."

"It's not okay," she rasps. She looks up at me, eyes blazing, and swipes her face. "You have one foot out the door already and I'm not letting you go."

Hope blooms in my chest.

And then her finger is poking that same spot in my chest. "We are married. I wasn't telling you to leave me *forever* last night. I'll admit, I didn't know what I might have to do. I was worried for your safety because Junior was obviously unhinged…worried about the rest of the emus." Her hands fling up. "I told you I loved you last night. You think I just throw those words around?"

I start to smile and her eyes narrow.

"If I hear you say one more word about dissolving our marriage, I'm going to lose it." She takes a step back and puts her hands on her hips. "I handled it wrong yesterday, okay? He was killing my animals, Callum. I was so scared and all I wanted was you, but I didn't know what he would do. I should've trusted that you'd take care of me. I knew that when I saw you level Junior without even trying. "

Her lips twitch then and I take a step closer, my hands going back to her hips.

"I shouldn't have turned you away," she says softly. "I'm really sorry I did. We've got some things to figure out," she says, sighing, "but I want you to be part of the conversation. Not walling up and turning into the silent, broody man that everyone thinks you are." Her finger is back on my chest. "Not with me." Poke, poke, poke.

"So, you're saying you still want to be my wife?" I ask gruffly.

"Yes, you big oaf, I do," she grumbles.

I laugh. "I'm your big oaf then, Sunshine."

I lower slightly so she'll meet my eyes.

"Okay?" I ask.

"Yes," she says, still somewhat sullen.

I lift my eyebrows. "Are we having our first fight?"

"Oh yeah, we definitely are."

I grin and put my hands on her ass. "When can we get to the making up part?"

"Sometime when your brothers aren't waiting for us in the next room," she says.

When she finally smiles, I feel like I can breathe again. I bury my face in her neck.

"I love you," I whisper against her skin.

When I lift my head, her lips are on mine, and it's like coming home.

It was only yesterday, but it feels like a lifetime since I've kissed her. I want to strip her down and sink into her, show her that I am hers and she is mine, but there's plenty of time for that.

Now that I know where she stands, I'm never letting her go.

CHAPTER THIRTY-SEVEN

AVENGERS

RUBY

"The sight of you guys standing right behind Callum, all in your flannel, ready to *avenge the wrong done to me*," I say, lifting my cup with those last words and then leaning into Callum and cracking up. "Ahhh, it was so good. I wish you could've seen them, Kess."

It's mid-afternoon and we've hung out with the emus, walked around the land, and had more than enough pizza and alcohol. A huge weight has lifted off of me, and everything looks so much brighter than it did when I woke up this morning. I'm slap-happy and it's not just from the drinks.

Kess has been here an hour and she still hasn't recovered from how good-looking the Landmark brothers are. She also hasn't recovered from the fact that I'm married to Callum, but she's happy for me. She'll make the trip to Landmark next month and I can't wait for her to fall in love with the town. She keeps catching my eye when the guys aren't looking and makes a face like, *Are they even real?*

I know. It's a lot to take in at once. I feel that way just looking at my very own Landmark. He turns like he knows I'm thinking about him.

"What's that look?" he asks.

Since our discussion in my room, his hands have been on me. Right now, my legs are tangled with his under the table and his arm is draped on the back of my chair, his hand tracing shapes along my back. I love it.

"Just that you're mine and I'm really glad about it," I say.

He shifts and whispers in my ear, "I *am* yours."

"So, have any decisions been made yet, or is it still up for discussion?" Sutton says, and everyone gets quiet and looks at us.

"Decisions about what exactly?" Callum asks.

Sutton looks at him like *come on now.*

There's a long, quiet pause, and Callum looks at me.

"There's a lot to consider, and we haven't gotten into all of it yet," he says. "But, I'll be wherever Ruby is."

"Awww," Kess cries, as my already-mush heart melts even more.

There's a lot of back-slapping and the guys start teasing Callum about being whipped.

He lifts a shoulder. "Yep."

I lean into him, wrapping my arm around his waist.

"I don't know what to do with all this property, but I want to be in Landmark Mountain," I say it to him first and he swallows hard, his eyes full of emotion.

"Yeah?" he asks.

"I really, really do. I love my home and I was crushed when I thought it was taken from us, but what I've found in Landmark Mountain is everything I want. You, your family—"

The guys carry on around us, rowdy and playful.

"I know that's right!" Theo yells.

"Landmarks for the win," Wyatt says.

I bury my head in Callum's shoulder and laugh. My cheeks are flaming when I lean back to look at everyone again.

"Kess is leaving soon for school, my parents are traveling the country…and even if obnoxious, you guys are the family I want to be surrounded by."

They looked moved at first and then realize the rest of what I said and their expressions morph one by one. It's hilarious.

"Hey now," Sutton says.

"You think this is obnoxious, wait till you see us at Christmas," Wyatt says, laughing.

"I'm glad you're staying in Landmark Mountain," Theo says. "You're nice to have around and you make this guy really happy." He leans over and squeezes Callum's shoulder. "Looks like you'll need a bigger barn. I owe you one after all you did on ours."

I shake my head. "Oh, I didn't expect—" I turn to face Callum.

He tilts his head and lifts his shoulder. "Why not?"

"You'd really put up with twenty-*five* emus?"

"You're like a package deal with the emus," he says,

grinning.

"*Callum*." My voice cracks and I'm crying again.

"We've got room for them while we're getting something new built at your place," Theo says. "Between the barn at my place and Sof's old place—Hilary's place," he corrects himself. "I'm warning you now though, Hilary and Abby will probably want to keep a few if they get attached...and they will." He laughs.

"I can't believe this. Really?" I look at Callum again and he brushes my hair back.

"The more the merrier," he says.

"He only says that about animals," Wyatt teases.

Callum points at him. "Check."

Everyone laughs.

"Ahh, this is the best. I am—I just can't believe this. This is—I'm overwhelmed." I shake my head and sniffle, laughing at what a mess I am. "I'll start looking into options for getting them there."

"Oh, no one told you?" Theo smirks. "I borrowed a 53' foot semitrailer from a farmer we know and parked it at the truck stop near here. The guys picked me up there when Callum said there hadn't been any suspicious activity during the night. Didn't know what we were dealing with when I left and wanted to be prepared in case we were sneaking emus out in the wee hours." He laughs and I stare at him in shock before my shoulders shake with laughter too.

"This is madness," I say. "Had I known this kind of goodness was in Landmark Mountain, I would've made sure to visit Uncle Pierre sooner."

"Have you told him you're married yet?" Wyatt asks.

"No. Only the people at this table know," I say. "What do you think?" I turn to Callum. "Should we still keep it quiet?"

"My vote is to tell the whole world, but I'll be good with whatever you decide," he says.

The guys elbow each other, eyes twinkling in mischief when they look at Callum.

"This is gonna be so fucking fun," Sutton says. "Seeing you this way...God, it's still *shocking*."

Callum grumbles. "Whatever. Don't forget I can wipe the floor with you just like I did Junior."

"Mm-hmm. You're too lovesick to even think about hitting us," Wyatt says, cracking up.

"Don't test me," Callum mutters.

But his lips twitch and the room echoes with the sound of their laughter.

I don't think this place has ever seen so much joy.

CHAPTER THIRTY-EIGHT

PREY TELL

CALLUM

After Kess leaves, my brothers hang out a little longer, going over barn ideas and ways to keep the emus warm enough until we can get something new built for them. They tolerate snow for short periods, so we'll need something large and warm for those snowy, extra-cold days. I hope it's a good move for them. If not, Ruby's open to figuring out a new plan for them, but Dolly's done great in Colorado so far. We talk until we're all yawning, the night before catching up with us.

They reserve a couple rooms at a hotel not too far away, and Ruby keeps apologizing for not having enough beds for everyone here.

"Don't worry about us. We're fine," Wyatt assures her. "I could sleep on the floor right now, honestly, but a bed will be better. We'll get out of your hair, let you guys raise the roof."

I bop him over the head and he just laughs. Ruby fans her face and tries to cool her cheeks.

"And before we separate for the night, let's let them tell everyone back home," Sutton says, pointing at his brothers.

Wyatt lifts his hands. "I haven't said a word. But Marlow and Dakota are going to be thrilled." He grins.

"Same here. Sofie's already crazy about you."

"I feel bad that I didn't tell Scarlett when we were together yesterday," Ruby says.

"She might give you a hard time for a minute, but she'll be too excited to make it a thing," Sutton says.

Theo nods. "If she'd known we were driving here in the middle of the night, she would've been on our doorstep, demanding we make room for her too."

"I love her," Ruby says softly. "All of them. I can't wait to get to know all of them better."

They take turns hugging her and then me.

"Can you tell we have a hard time with goodbyes?" I say under my breath.

"We'll see you in the morning," Theo says, moving toward the door. "You know...I wish you could take your time on the way home—this is supposed to be your honeymoon." He lifts his hands up, grinning. "I don't have a lot of experience with emus, but I'm certainly willing to try."

Ruby shakes her head. "I trust you so much more than Junior and the people who were supposedly helping out here, but no, there's no way I'd do that to you. Besides," she says, grinning up at me, "we've been away for a few days now, and I'm missing home. *And* we have a party to plan."

I tug her toward me, bending down to kiss her.

"*And* that's our cue," Sutton says. "Night, you two."

We stand in the doorway, watching them drive away. I rub my hands over her arms when she shivers, and I shut the door behind us. We walk into the kitchen and put the trash in a garbage bag to take with us the next day.

When we're done cleaning up, she leans her elbows back against the counter, her long legs stretched out in front of her.

"My room or Jolene?" she asks.

I grin and mimic her stance across from her. "Wherever you're most comfortable with me doing wicked things to you."

"Wicked?" She licks her lips.

Her eyes brighten and she laughs.

"I never imagined I'd have a man who looks like *you* standing in my kitchen. You are something else, Callum Landmark." She walks toward me, and I'm so gone.

"Your eyes are predatory," she whispers when she reaches me.

Her lips touch my neck and she kisses her way up to my lips.

"You looked like a panther about to pounce when you walked over here," I say against her mouth. "Who's the predator here?"

"Can I be tonight?"

I'm not sure I get a coherent sound out, but she's on her knees, undoing my jeans before I've taken a full breath.

"How did I know you'd be hard for me already?" she says, licking up the length of me and then circling over my head.

I grip the back of the counter with one hand and reach out for her hair with the other.

"Always," I grit out. "You look at me and I'm hard. Smile at me…breathe near me…"

She laughs and the hum around me makes me groan. One hand doesn't fit around the base of me, so she adds a second, fisting around me as she teases me with her tongue. Agonized sounds come out of me and it spurs her on. She gazes up at me with those perfect puffy lips as she takes as much of me in her mouth as she can. Her cheeks hollow as she sucks, her hair falling forward as she slides up and down me, her hands working where I don't fit and the sight is more than I can take.

"Sunshine," I rasp, pulling her hair back in my fist. "You feel so good, Ruby. So fucking good."

I squeeze my eyes shut, but I don't want to miss anything, so as soon as I've gotten some control back, I look again. Her rhythm picks up and I shift, putting my leg between her legs. She rubs against me as she works me faster, and when she takes me even deeper, swallowing around me as she tries to take in more, my head falls back as my vision blurs and goes white.

"I'm com—" I try to warn her, but she knows.

She doesn't let go, her eyes on me as she swallows and swallows, and still some drips out of the sides of her mouth.

I'm hoarse as I cry out, twinges continuing long after I start coming down.

"God, Ruby," I say when she lifts up, her lips sliding off of me with a pop.

I help her stand the rest of the way and with my thumb, I wipe her mouth.

"Was that wicked enough for you?" Her voice is coy and I jerk against her stomach.

Her head falls back as she laughs and I bite her neck and lick away the sting.

"It was perfect, but I'd like so much more," I tell her, pulling my pants up.

She takes my hand and leads me to her room.

"We've already christened Jolene. Let's give this room some action it's never seen…not from me anyway."

I lean her against the wall and kiss her. "You haven't snuck any boys in here for a quickie?"

"Ha, no. These walls are way too thin for that."

"Good thing we sent my brothers to the hotel," I say as I take off her clothes. Her panties are the last to go. "On the bed, Mrs. Landmark. I've got some things I want to try on you."

She giggles and hurries to the bed, stretching out. She leans up on her elbows. "The burns are so much better. You don't need to be so careful anymore."

"You'll let me know if that changes?"

She nods, her eyes swallowing me whole. They settle between my legs on my dick and I smirk, pausing before I climb on top of her.

"What are you thinking right now?" I ask.

"I'm thinking you have the prettiest cock I've ever seen."

I chuckle and she sighs happily.

"I can see we're gonna have to work on your adjectives now, Sunshine."

"The wickedest cock?" she says.

"Much better."

CHAPTER THIRTY-NINE

A NEW DAY

RUBY

We force ourselves to get a little sleep since we have the long drive back, but not much. I crawl out of bed early, quiet so Callum can sleep a little longer, and go out to feed the emus. It feels so good to be with all of them. I get emotional all over again thinking about what Callum and his brothers are willing to do to make this happen.

The sun is bright when I'm done, a beautiful crisp morning. I go into Jolene to take my shower since all my things are out here, laughing when I see myself in the full-length mirror on the bathroom door. My chin and mouth are pink and raw from kissing Callum so much, and so are my inner thighs. There are pink splotches in all the places Callum sucked or nibbled, and my nipples are still standing at attention from all the love they got last night.

When I told him my burns were better, he took that as permission to finally have his way with my breasts. He's been so careful with me, and it's not like he's completely ignored that part of my body, but I've assumed he is strictly a butt man. After last night, I don't think that's the case at all. He's definitely into both.

I step under the water and wash quickly, wanting to be ready before the guys get here, and Callum steps in behind me just as I'm about to get out. The shower is not spacious, especially not with a giant like him.

"There you are," he says.

His hands slide over my hips and up to my breasts where they squeeze, his body lining up against my back. His erection fits against my lower back and when he bends just a little bit, he slides between my cheeks.

My head falls back against his chest.

"Mornin', Sunshine," he says.

"Good morning," I say weakly.

"You worn out?"

"I'm surprisingly awake, and so are you." I grin when I look at him over my shoulder.

He skims my nipples between his fingers and grins. "It was a good night. Great motivation to get up." He does the slide thing again and I whimper.

"Mm-hmm." I sigh. "You're up all right."

"You did all the work already?"

"Pretty much."

"Sorry about that." He kisses my shoulder.

"I wanted you to sleep. You're overdue a full night."

He moves my hair to the side and kisses my neck.

"Your brothers will be here soon," I warn.

"Sutton said they're stopping to grab coffee and breakfast for us. We've got a little time...unless you'd rather do something else?"

I close my eyes when his fingers move between my legs.

"No, I'm really, really good with this," I whisper.

We're in the shower longer than intended. It got all kinds of crazy when I bent over as far as I could and he impaled me from behind. I don't think Jolene will ever be the same. And neither will I. Turns out, I really love that position. I came *three* times...which just didn't seem possible after the night we had.

We're scrambling to get our clothes on and back to the house before the guys arrive, but it's too late, I hear a commotion outside.

"Shoot, shoot, shoot," I say, running around the RV.

I hear him chuckle at me. "Have you ever thought the word *shit* in your life?"

"Not really," I admit.

"Sunshine, through and through. You'd still be if you let it all fly out though. I'm here for it if that ever happens."

I laugh and throw on my jacket. "Let's go before they tease us to death."

He frowns. "You're not sick, are you?"

"No, I'm just hoarse from screaming all night...and just now."

He grins, looking very pleased with himself, and I throw his gloves at him.

"Come on," I say as I open the door.

The brothers are all standing there, facing the RV, when we step outside, each wearing their own smirk. Theo at least has the decency to pretend like he's studying the barn.

"Shit," I croak out loud, and Callum belly laughs.

"Good morning," Wyatt sings. "We went to the house first and then came out here to see if you were in the barn…and the rest is history."

"Thin walls," I say, my cheeks so hot.

"Indeed," Sutton says.

He's holding back a laugh as he hands me a coffee from the carrier.

"Guys," Callum warns.

Wyatt lifts the bag of food and starts passing out the breakfast sandwiches. I open my wrapper and start eating right away, glad for something to hide behind.

"We've all been there," Theo says.

They all laugh at him, Callum included.

"*What?*" Theo says, laughing now too.

"We've all been there," Wyatt says in Theo's sweet voice.

"Well, it's true," Theo insists. "Granddad and Grinny have both heard me and Sofie having sex."

"No," I cry.

"On separate occasions," he adds.

I shake my head. I'd die. This is bad enough.

"What?" Sutton asks. "Why have I never heard about this?"

"Because Sofie was mortified and I knew you guys would never let it go." He rolls his eyes. "She's gonna kill me. I was just trying to make Ruby more comfortable."

"Thanks, Theo," I say.

"No problem."

It's comfortable within minutes. I've never had brothers to give me a hard time, and it might take some getting used to, but I think I'm going to love it.

After we finish eating, we fill the floor of the semi with hay and start rounding up the emus. There aren't any major complications, it just takes time. Most of them have never been out of this yard. I do have reservations about uprooting them, but I'll watch closely and if there are any problems, I'll look into selling them to someone in a warmer location.

I don't want it to come to that though.

When we finally get on the road, Callum's driving Jolene and I'm in the passenger seat next to him, Dolly and her friends Lorde and Aretha are in the trailer behind us. Sutton and Wyatt are in Sutton's SUV, and Theo is hauling the semi. Quite the crew for a road trip.

I felt so helpless when I got here. It's still hard for me to believe that it all worked out. I turn back to look at my house one last time.

Callum reaches out and takes my hand. "Are you sad to leave?"

I shake my head. "I'm excited for what's ahead. I couldn't have done this without you, Callum. Without all of you."

"Get used to having us because once a Landmark loves you, it's forever."

I lean my head against the seat and turn to look at him. "I'm counting on that."

CHAPTER FORTY

FALALALALA

CALLUM

Our first morning back, we wake up to a crash and I hurry down the stairs with a baseball bat while Ruby huddles behind me with her phone, ready to call 911.

Nothing seems amiss in the living room, but I follow the sounds, getting more certain the closer I get that it's Delphine up to her old tricks.

Sure enough, she's in the pantry, knocking things off the shelves.

"Delphine," I say loudly and she startles, turning around with her innocent eyes and pitiful bleats. "Don't you give me those eyes, this is very naughty."

I hold up the empty peanut butter jar and wave it.

"Was it worth it?" I ask, hearing Ruby's giggles behind me. "What did you wreck to get in here this time?"

I have to make a few repairs, but fortunately no one else escaped.

Ruby makes a video about it, and I get texts and phone calls about it for days. Word's traveled around town that we have an influencer in our midst, and when I go to the grocery store or to Clip-Clop for supplies, I'm teased by Cecil or Clip-Clop Clive calling me *Thirst Trap* and *Too Hot to Drop Lumberjack*. How the hell do they even know where to find these things? I mean, I'm an avid viewer of everything Ruby puts out now, but I wouldn't have had a clue about it if she hadn't shown me.

Anyway, the video with Delphine and me goes viral, and the CBS Morning Show has called to set up an interview. They're coming out next week.

You can't make this shit up.

It's hectic, getting the emus situated. We have four here with us, and the rest are spread out for now. So far, they seem to be adjusting well, and we've been working on insulating sections of the three different barns they're staying in until the ground thaws and we can build a new one for all of them at our place. Ruby goes back and forth between Theo and Sofie's and Hilary and Abby's each day, and they've all been great about helping where they can too.

We're having the family over tonight for dinner and telling them about the wedding. We've already put the word out about having a party here after Christmas, and if my brothers didn't already know, we would've just kept it a secret until then, but it's too much to ask that of them. My brothers love surprises, but they aren't always great about pulling them off. We pulled off a surprise party for Grinny because of massive guilt over missing the actual day, and Wyatt's engagement party was another exception—I don't think he could've pulled that one off without me.

After getting my morning chores done, I head to the house to see what Ruby's up to. There were a pile of shipments for her when we got back from Utah, and they've been arriving daily. Every kind of size. She's been quiet about what they are, and as I pick up a slew of new packages to take inside, my curiosity is piqued.

She got back from Theo's an hour ago and I haven't seen her much. When I step inside, Christmas music is playing and she's stringing lights in the fresh greenery she's hung on the fireplace. I put my hands on her waist and kiss her neck and she looks back at me, her sweet smile never failing to fill me up.

"I like that," I tell her.

"I hope it's okay. I've usually decorated everything in sight by now. I'm trying to show restraint."

"This is your house, Sunshine. Do whatever you want to do."

"Really?" she asks. "You're sure you're okay with that?"

"Of course. I want you to feel like this is your home. You can redecorate everything if you want."

"If it wasn't perfect already, I would be all over that." She laughs. "Do you have a tree?" She turns around in my arms, excitement bouncing off of her.

"No...but we can get one. I can chop one down for you if you'd like."

"I'd *love* that." She grabs her phone, her eyes sparkling. "Can I record you chopping it?"

"Does that mean it'll be over the internet by nightfall?" I narrow my eyes at her.

"Yes," she says, laughing again.

"Fine," I mumble, but I've got my hands up her sweater and couldn't care less what she does as long as she does it with me.

"I'll make it up to you, I promise," she says. "Come on, let's go find a tree."

"Now?" Now I really am grumbling.

"Yes! I can get it all decorated before I put the lasagna in the oven. I've already made the pies. I want everything to be perfect for your family. All we need is some Christmas spirit."

I lean in and kiss her. "I can't even be annoyed with you for a second, you know. It's very *off brand* for me." I parrot one of her phrases.

"I know," she says, ducking out of the way and yelping as I smack her ass. She giggles and puts her coat on. "If we hurry, we can have sex under the pretty tree before things get too hectic."

"Hustle, hustle, woman." I clap and she cracks up.

Once she's sufficiently bundled up, we head out and I lead her to a few trees I think she might like.

"Ooo, that one," she says, pointing to the tallest one.

I toss my jacket to the side and get to work, looking up at her when she says, "Hey, my lumberjack."

I smirk when I see that she's recording. "Hey, Sunshine."

"Do you have any Christmas wishes?" she asks.

"I'm looking at her."

She bites her lip and lowers the phone.

"I'm so glad I married you," she whispers.

I chuckle. "You just wanted a lumberjack to chop down a tree for Christmas…I see how it is."

"No, I just want you to hurry so I can get you under that tree," she teases.

———————

Sutton calls an hour before the dinner. "I'm trying my best to get there on time. I've got a last-minute interview with a nanny possibility. You're not gonna believe who she's related to."

"Who?"

"Weston fucking Shaw."

My eyes widen. "No shit? The Mustangs football player?"

"Yep. I know. I've been working with one of his teammates and when I mentioned I needed to cut our time short for a nanny interview, he mentioned that this girl is looking. This first meeting will just be a short Zoom to see if we should pursue a meeting later, and then I'll be over."

"Okay. So far I'm all for you hiring her," I tease.

"Yeah." He laughs. "We'll see if she's actually got any skills."

By the time the family arrives, our halls are thoroughly decked, and then some. Everywhere I turn, there are lights and something pretty and festive. Apparently all those packages she was receiving were sponsors that follow her, and I have to say, it's pretty fun seeing all the things she gets. And her posts about all of it makes it obvious why she's been so successful.

Dinner is delicious, and it's over the pies, which are a hit as always, that we tell them our news.

It's met with equal parts ecstatic joy and outrage.

First, there are cheers and hugs and kisses all around.

And then it begins.

"But, wait...you already had the wedding...you're already married?" Grinny clarifies.

"Yes," I say.

"And you knew that day we talked in the shop and didn't say?" Scarlett cries.

Ruby makes a face. "I feel so bad about that. I really wanted to tell you, but we'd agreed to wait—"

"And they knew it before we did?" Sofie says, pointing to the guys. "They're *horrible* secret keepers."

"Hey," Theo protests.

"I'm feeling a little left out that I didn't know about it," Jamison says. It's hard to tell if he's joking or serious. "For the record, I would've been happy to go help whip the ex's ass."

"You had that international meeting the next morning," Sutton says. "I nearly called you but didn't want that pressure on you."

They clink glasses.

"It's all good, man," Jamison says. "Cheers, you guys."

"Wait, does this mean you're my Aunt Ruby now?" Dakota cries, clapping her hands.

"Yes, I am," Ruby says, hugging Dakota.

Owen goes over to hug her too. "I'm happy Uncle Callum's not alone anymore," he tells her. He looks back at Sutton. "Now, my dad is the only one who needs someone...and Grinny...and Pappy!"

Sutton looks gut-punched. "I've got you in my life, buddy, and our family. I don't need a girlfriend...or-or a wife," he sputters, taking a long sip of his wine and looking more than a little unsettled.

"Same here!" Pappy says, cheeks flushing. "But thanks for caring about me, Owen. That means a lot."

"And don't you worry about me either, my sweet boy,"

Grinny insists, also flustered. "All I need is to see my family happy. That's more than enough for me."

"We're happy. Really happy," I say, looking at each person one by one.

My eyes reach Ruby last and her eyes well with emotion.

I can't believe this is my life.

And Owen is right. Now that I know happiness like this, I want everyone I love to have it too.

EPILOGUE
SURPRISES

RUBY

It's been a whirlwind around here. The emus are adjusting really well, I'm filling orders nonstop from my online sales, and every day I wake up in Callum's arms and pinch myself that this is my life.

Junior's real estate license has been revoked and Kess says he's left Utah. She heard he went to Montana and I hope he stays there.

Christmas was a dream. I've never had a more perfect day. Callum got up earlier than usual, and when I came downstairs, he'd already fed the emus at the other barns and the ones we have too, the cows were milked, the morning free to open presents. There was a fire in the fireplace, and we slowly worked our way through the presents.

I gave him a few new flannels and a sweater, and he loved the emu T-shirt that says, *me and emu for life* inside a heart on an emu's chest that looks just like Dolly. And he loves the illustration of him with Delphine, Irene, and Dolly for his branding.

"Someone important is missing here though," he said, tapping my nose before kissing me.

He gave me a new blanket that is the softest thing I've ever felt, and new slippers, and a bracelet that I haven't taken off. My favorite gift is an oval flat-top silver ring engraved with *C & R*. I haven't taken it off either.

And I think his favorite gift from me is the small wedding album I made him from the pictures I ordered online from our little wedding chapel. We didn't have many taken, but the ones captured were beautiful, and I filled in the rest with snapshots of our trip.

We made love in front of the fire and after a nap, we went to Grinny's to celebrate with the family.

I even reached my parents finally, on Christmas day, and while it was a fine conversation, the hitch came when I asked them to please come tonight. They hemmed and hawed, saying they were exhausted and not sure if they could make it, and I tried to be understanding, but they're within four hours. I didn't tell them why until the very end of the conversation.

"I married Callum Landmark, and I'd like you to be here to celebrate our wedding. I've been trying to call you for weeks. Don't even get me started on the fact that Junior does *not* own the house. I don't know if the two of you were in on it with him or if you were oblivious, but either way, I'm asking you to be here. I'm tired of feeling like the parent and I need you guys to step up for this. I love Callum and I want you to be part of my life."

When I finished, there was a long pause before the barrage of questions.

They insisted they had no idea what was in the contracts...it wasn't in the paperwork Junior showed them, and I believe them. We'll figure out the rest with time.

I'm just glad they'll be here tonight.

I've tried to keep a few surprises for our "wedding" party. Scarlett arranged the catering, and I ordered flower arrangements from Feather Whims, an exquisite floral shop in town. And I can't wait for Callum to see the dress I'm wearing. He's expecting me to wear the sweater dress I wore for our wedding, but I got a new dress, and it's even more beautiful than the one he first saw me in. It has a lower neckline and the lace is soft and delicate. It's form-fitted except for the sleeves and the bottom of the dress, which flare out. It doesn't show my bare back, which I know he appreciated about the other dress, but I don't think he'll miss that touch. And if he does, he'll get over it when he sees what I have on underneath.

I left a gift for him to open at Sutton's, where he's getting ready, and he calls when he opens them.

"I love the cuff links," he says. "Didn't think I'd be a cuff link kind of guy, but these are perfect." He laughs. "Delphine will be pleased."

His cuff links are silver goat faces, and when I found them I knew he had to have them.

"Are you sure I have to wait to see you?" he asks. "I'm missing you."

"I miss you too, but yes. This is our pretend time apart before the wedding."

"Feels real to me," he grumbles.

"Yeah," I sigh. "I don't love this part, but I didn't know another way to have some surprises up my sleeve."

"Wait a minute. You never said anything about—"

"It's nothing big."

"What if I want to be the one surprising you?"

"You surprise me with how awesome you are every day."

He growls.

"Shush." I laugh. "It's just an hour now. I'll see you soon."

"Not soon enough."

I hang up smiling and finish getting ready.

When I walk downstairs, just a few minutes before everyone is due to arrive, there's a knock on the door. I look around the room, happy with how everything looks. Before I open the door, I peek out and it's the girls. There's a long pause when I open the door, as they stare at me in surprise.

"Oh, you look beautiful," Marlow says.

"Like a princess!" Dakota adds.

Scarlett and Sofie both look like they might cry.

"So beautiful," Scarlett says.

Sofie hugs me first. "I said I wasn't going to cry, but I already feel the tears coming."

"You all look so beautiful too," I tell them.

"It's not every day we're invited to a wedding party. It's like a hipper version of a reception," Scarlett says. "I'm all about it." She looks at the living room. "Whoa. It looks even more beautiful than when I was last here!"

Marlow glances behind her. "Do you think you could come outside for a minute?" she asks. "There was something going on with the porch light?"

I frown and move toward the door. "Really? Okay, I'll take a look."

I open the door and Callum is at the end of the walkway in front of a horse and a carriage lit up with lights. I gasp.

"So you had this surprise planned when you were giving me grief about my surprises?" I call out.

"Got to keep you on your feet, Sunshine." He walks forward with a fluffy white wrap. "And you're still the one surprising me." He takes my hand and twirls me around. "This is my favorite one yet."

"I thought it might be."

He puts the wrap around me. "Take a little ride with me?"

"I'd love to."

I glance back at the girls, but they've disappeared. We get in the carriage and he leads us to an area behind the barn. It's where we found the Christmas tree, and now the ones that were left are all lit up, and there's a pretty arch in the middle. Surrounded by the lights and trees, all bundled up, are our families. And so are Dolly, Delphine, and Irene. They each have floral wreaths around their necks that are lit up.

"What have you done?" I ask, my voice full of tears.

"I would've had the whole barnful out here, but it would've gotten chaotic," he says, laughing. "Had to be selective."

He helps me down and I hug my parents.

"Thank you for coming," I tell them, ready for new beginnings. There will be time for deeper discussions later.

I walk with Callum to the arch. He faces me and then turns toward the family.

"We'll keep this brief since it's cold out here, but I wanted to say in front of our families, our animals, and under this beautiful, wide open sky, how much I love this woman next to me. Ruby Sunshine Jones took my breath away the first night I met her and she's been injecting life into me every day since. I'm honored to have you as my wife, honored to love you until the day I die, and honored that you want to be a Landmark here by my side."

He lifts my hand to his and kisses it, and everyone cheers.

When they quiet down, I say, "You are the best thing to happen to me, Callum Landmark. All of you are. I feel like my life has just begun, and each day with you, Callum, I can't even believe the happiness." I turn and put my hands on his cheeks, leaning in and kissing him hard.

The cheers erupt again and when Callum and I break apart, an array of fireworks go off above us.

"My surprises have nothing on yours," I tell him.

"I'm a simple man. I just need you."

"Well, that's easy. I'm all yours."

He kisses me again and leads me back to the carriage, driving us home.

"You've created an even *more* magical winter wonderland inside, haven't you?"

I laugh, glancing over at him. "What makes you think that?"

"Besides the amount of lights taking over our house since the time I left? It could be the way you're all lit up, Ruby Sunshine."

"That's all you, Callum Henry, *all you*."

He sighs, leaning in to kiss me once more before we go inside. "I'm so glad you're mine."

. . .

Would you like more of Callum and Ruby?
   https://bit.ly/FallingBonusScene

Sutton's love story is next and I can't wait for you to read it!
   https://geni.us/StayLM

FIND OUT WHAT'S NEXT

Linktree @willowaster
Newsletter http://willowaster.com/newsletter

———————

All your fun Landmark Mountain merch can be found here: https://willow-aster-store.creator-spring.com/

ACKNOWLEDGMENTS

I'm so thankful to all who have contributed to making this book what it is and to those who helped ME while I wrote this book!

I LOVE YOU ALL DEARLY!

Nate, Greyley & Kira, Indigo, and Kess, thanks for being my family and being the best people ever. And to my favorite artists, Greyley, Kira, and Kess, thank you for making the Landmark Mountain swag/merch so beautiful. Special thanks to Kess for this book's artwork!

Laura Pavlov, I'm pinching myself that we're getting to do this life together. Thank you for cheering me on so well. Catherine Cowles, my kindred empath/list maker/true crime podcast lover, so happy we found each other. A.L. Jackson, we've both been doing this a long time and I'm so glad we're finally getting to know each other the way I've wanted to all along. To all three of you, thank you for your love AND for the sprints during the most critical time of this book.

Nina Grinstead, thank you for ALL you do, for your input with this series, and for making the process more fun.

Christine Estevez, thank you for all your help and ideas and hearing me try to endlessly plot. So grateful.

Natalie Burtner, thank you for taking over the part of my brain that wasn't functioning anymore! Just in time. <3

Meagan Reynoso, your comments and input give me life.

Thank you with all my heart to Kim, Christine, Sarah,

Valentine, Amy, Ratula, and the entire VPR team- I'm so grateful for each one of you!

Emily Wittig, thanks for making both the couple and landscape covers so special!

Regina Wamba, thank you for the stellar photographs!

To my family who loves me whether I write or not, and same with my friends. I love each and every one of you so much! Tarryn, Tosha, Christine, Claire, Courtney, Savita, and Terrijo…I know you have my back and I'm so grateful for it. And Kalie, thank you for reading every single one of my books!

Thanks to everyone who reads and reviews/shares my books! I couldn't do this without your support and I don't take it for granted. THANK YOU!

ALSO BY WILLOW ASTER

Standalones

True Love Story

Fade to Red

In the Fields (also available on all retailer sites)

Maybe Maby (also available on all retailer sites)

Lilith (also available on all retailer sites)

Miles Apart (also available on all retailer sites)

Falling in Eden

Standalones with Interconnected Characters

Summertime

Autumn Nights

Landmark Mountain Series

Unforgettable

Someday

Irresistible

Falling

Stay

Kingdoms of Sin Series

Downfall

Exposed

Ruin

Pride

FOLLOW ME

JOIN MY MASTER LIST…
https://bit.ly/3CMKz5y

Website willowaster.com
Facebook @willowasterauthor
Instagram @willowaster
Amazon @willowaster
Bookbub @willow-aster
TikTok @willowaster1
Goodreads @willow_aster
Asters group @Astersgroup
Pinterest@willowaster

Landmark Mountain merch:
https://willow-aster-store.creator-spring.com/

Made in the USA
Monee, IL
29 June 2024

60929927R10184